DOUBLE TAKE

DEAD ENDS
BOOK 1

BECK LEWIS

1

They're all over each in the hotel lift.

One of Greg's hands is under Josie's blouse on the small of her back. The other is trying to work its way into her pants as he presses himself hard against her. Her hands are in his hair, cupping his head, pulling him down to kiss her again.

The lift pings, the door opens and they drunkenly stumble out onto the fourth floor. Greg has a room here. He's staying here since the split with his wife - Greg definitely said she was no longer on the scene.

As they cling to each other in the corridor, there's the buzz of a phone.

"Shit," says Greg and fumbles under his twisted shirt to get to his trouser pocket.

"Leave it," says Josie.

"It might be Rachel," he says.

She pulls back a second. "Your ex? It's one in the morning, Greg."

He shoots her a look. It's cold and irritated but also a little bit scared.

Josie suddenly sees the complete truth written on his face. Rachel is not his ex at all. Greg Scabbard and his wife are very much a current and on-going thing.

And maybe Josie knew that all along. Maybe Josie only chose to believe his 'my wife doesn't understand me' story because they were swept up in the moment, drunk and horny.

"You aren't separated," she says.

"Oh, grow up," he snaps.

And now, looking at him – his drunk, slightly unfocussed eyes, his thinning dark hair tousled and untidy – all sexual attraction to DI Greg Scabbard drains from her.

"Jesus Christ." She feels sick.

He pulls out his phone and looks at it.

"It's work," he says as though that's somehow okay. "DI Scabbard."

Someone talks on the phone but Josie can't hear. Josie is still reeling from the momentously stupid decision she was about to make.

"A shooting?" says Scabbard. "Where?"

Thirty-three years old and a detective constable for five years, Josie expected to be something more than she is now. Her planned rise through the ranks has turned into a slog - a struggle to stay afloat. A floundering mess. It was a bad idea to try to ingratiate herself with the team by joining them on this drinking session celebrating someone else's case success. It's occurring to her now, with increasing, pounding certainty, that screwing the boss was never going to be a good idea.

The alcohol is evaporating from her system as she fumes.

She's already halfway from drunk to hungover already. Her mouth is dry.

"So, you need someone to do a statement," said Scabbard. "And uniform? Right. I'll get someone." He ends the call and looks at Josie. "What?"

"What?" she says in hissed fury. "You told me you were divorced!"

"It's complicated," he says.

"Your marriage is not a Facebook status, Greg!"

He sniffs, straightens and then waves an arm to the corridor behind him.

"We gonna do this then or what?"

She gives him the look of disgust he deserves. "I'm going."

He nods slowly like she's made the wrong choice.

"There's been a shooting near Frog Island," he says.

"I heard."

"You need to go take the initial statements. Chief Inspector Moghul is Post Incident Manager."

"What?" she says, not understanding, even though she really does understand.

He straightens. "You need to go and take a statement from this witness. There's been a shooting. A man is dead."

"You can't be serious. I'm still drunk."

"It's Mansfield House station. You can walk."

"You're not being serious, Greg."

His expression hardens. "Kaminski, I'm your DI."

"Sir." She wants to grind her teeth at his tone, but she also wants to puke. "I—"

"Are you going to be weird because we nearly fucked?"

There is no good answer to that question, although Josie generally reserves the right to be weird any time she fucking likes.

"Are you going to stand there staring at me all night?" says Scabbard.

She breathes in deeply. Wonders what the hell is happening.

"I'm way too smashed to interview anyone," she says and adds an afterthought, "Sir."

"Call for someone. Call Walker."

It takes her a second to place the name. "Walker? He's one of the Duncans."

"He just needs to sit there and write things down if you're too pissed to see."

He's making her do this. He's actually making her do this.

"Be good to get to know your new colleague better," says Scabbard.

"What?"

"Moving some desks around tomorrow."

In the suite of offices that Leicester CID have at Mansfield House there are specific teams, knots, clusters. In the lightless corner of the largest open plan office sit the Dead End Duncans. The rest of the office are protected from contamination by a wall of filing cabinets that have nothing in them. Officially the two detectives in there, DS Rob Joseph and DC 'Walker' Smith are on Operation Chainlink, a rural crime prevention scheme. The truth is they've just been placed there to keep them out of the way.

Being told to join them is a new low, possibly lower than letting the DI fuck her in a city centre hotel.

"Come on, guv," she says. "You know I'm better than that."

Scabbard eyes her up and down, works his jaw and raises his eyebrows. "You've got a cute arse. I'll give you that much."

2

Josie walks to Mansfield House. Leicester city centre is almost quiet at two in the morning.

The familiar landmarks are all still there, but in shades of grey under the street lighting. Josie's still not sure how she feels about Leicester. She regularly sees people bumping into friends on the street, which would never have happened in London. And yet, the place is still large enough to swallow her up. She came here to stand out.

Music pumps from a club on Sandacre Street. Disjointed groups of young people drift around. Heading for home or for the next party venue? It's hard to say.

At Mansfield House police station she gets through reception without making eye contact with anyone and then goes to the lockers, swaps her top for a spare, sprays herself with deodorant until it stings her nose and eyes, then goes to find the witness.

The station is normally quieter at night, but there's a buzz in the city policing team office. She reports to the duty DI, Neelam Gill.

DI Gill takes in Josie's dishevelled look. There's no doubt that Gill can read her like a book.

"What was the incident?" Josie should probably know this, but she doesn't. Scabbard was snoring when she came out of the bathroom. She wasn't sorry to miss out on more of his sparkling repartee.

"Man reported with a handgun. Immediate threat to life. Firearms officers challenged and then shot a man on site. They're giving their accounts, awaiting a police complaints investigation. Your witness, Esther Butler, is in a secure interview room."

The police shot a man. Any violent death brings an immediate response. But when the police kill someone, it brings a unique energy.

"Anyone else hurt?" she says.

"Not that we're aware of," says Gill. "Anyone joining you?"

"I've sent a message to DC Smith."

"Walker?" says Gill, clearly thinking it's an unexpected choice.

Josie nods and collects a laptop to type up the witness statement.

Her witness, Gill had said. While the big boys are dealing with the fallout from the incident, she's doing mop-up on the small stuff.

The secure interview rooms are on the lower ground floor. Josie goes down and catches her reflection in the mirror glass of a fire door. No improvement there.

An interview room door is open.

A uniformed constable sits just inside. At the table, her hands wrapped around a cup of station coffee is a woman. She's probably in her thirties, white with what Josie reckons is dyed blonde hair. She's wearing a blouse, waistcoat and jacket like she's a bank cashier or hotel concierge.

"Esther Butler?" says Josie.

The woman looks up.

"I'm DC Josie Kaminski. I'm here to take your statement. You want to tell me what happened?"

"Sure." Esther face is tired and haunted. "I was at work. The Meridian Casino."

That explains the waistcoat. Josie starts to jot some notes, but it makes her head swim, so she stops. "What role?"

"Floor manager."

"Carry on."

"I was at the entrance with Baz when I saw this guy across the street."

"Okay. What made you first notice him?"

3

"Him. Over there." I nudge Baz, who's doing security on the casino door.

"What about him?" Baz looks at the guy over the road but doesn't see it.

"He's got a gun."

Baz turns to stare at me. "You saw it?"

"No. He's keeping it hidden, but it's there in the band of his trousers."

"He's wearing a jacket."

"There's a bulge, a weight," I say. I want to say that it's there in his swagger, too, but Baz won't know what I'm talking about.

"He's got something in his belt? Could be anything." Baz has a very fleshy face. When he frowns it's a slow-moving thing.

"Yeah? Like what?"

Baz thinks on this. "Phone. A hat."

"A hat?" What's he on about? "I think it's a gun."

Baz gives me a wide grin. That grin tells me that he's not

convinced. He doesn't come out and say anything, because he's not a complete idiot. "Maybe you should call the police?"

That's his solution. Get someone else to make the call. I give a small shake of my head and step away. Baz is security here at the Meridian Casino. Nice enough guy, but sooner or later I'll be doing his performance appraisal – he forgets that I have a foot in both camps. I'm out here, at the sharp end of the floor manager's job, but I need to do the company stuff too: the admin and paperwork that the manager, Savage, never seems inclined to do. I'll have time to think about the formal wording I'll use on Baz's appraisal form, but let's just say that he lacks the ability to sniff out a wrong-un unless they're throwing punches or vomiting on his shoes.

You develop a knack for reading people, and the guy over the road has set something off in my early warning system.

On the face of it, he looks like a lot of the other punters we see around here after midnight. People inside the casino don't realise it's after midnight, of course. The environment is deliberately outside of regular time and space. There are no windows or clocks. The lairy carpet, chrome fitments and wall mirrors give the light the same brassy tone whatever the time. We have a lot of people come in here to lose themselves for a few hours. Where else can you sit, cocooned at your own console with snacks and a drink? For some, it's social, but for many more, it's a chance to be surrounded by people while sitting alone.

He's in his late twenties, the guy over the road. Wearing jogging bottoms with a bodywarmer over a base layer. Maybe he thinks it's the look of an off-duty Hollywood A-lister, like a low-rent Ryan Reynolds. But he actually looks as if he might have come from a workshop or a warehouse job. He's talking to a woman. She's wearing a leopard-print coat and a velvet baseball cap over long brown hair.

Low-rent Ryan has an energy about him. Agitated or excited. I don't think it's drugs. At least, not coke. Coke makes you cocky – this is tension. Anticipation. Like a dog pulling at the leash.

The woman has a lot to say to him. She's not happy. I can't hear what the two of them are saying, but the body language is clear. He's pissed her off, and she's angry-afraid. Boyfriend and girlfriend? A first date?

The gun or whatever it is at his belt keeps drawing his attention. And drawing mine too. His hand dips to the bottom of his bodywarmer to feel it through the material, as if he needs to check it's still there.

How certain am I that it's a gun? It's statistically unlikely here in Leicester. But if it's not a gun, it's something else that is giving him way too much confidence and has made the woman nervous and annoyed.

I should talk to her, see if she thinks she's in trouble. I step into the road.

"Excuse me?" I say loudly. If I can get her on her own, just for a moment, I can do this.

But she's away, walking briskly. I'm not sure she's running because I called out to her, but she's off. She's had enough. And then a second later low-rent Ryan's right behind her.

"Excuse me? Wait!" If I can stall him for a moment, that will give her a chance to get away. She's in trouble if he goes after her, I'm certain of that.

He doesn't seem to hear me. The road isn't busy, but there's noise from the dual carriageway behind the casino. Ignoring me or not hearing me, it doesn't matter. He's walking off after the woman in leopard print.

I step into the road.

"Boss?" says Baz.

I look back.

If he can't see anything wrong with the people who just left, he can at least figure out that I'm not happy about it. "Should we call the police?" he says.

One thing is immediately clear to me after talking to Baz. If he, who was standing right there, couldn't see something odd about the man, then what chance have I got of convincing the police that something's the matter?

"It's fine Baz. I'll take a quick look."

"What do you mean?"

I set off across the street after the man.

"Wait," Baz calls. "You can't do that." His meaty face is compressed into folds of concern.

"Fucks sake." I shake my head.

If I had the time, I'd explain that he had an opportunity to act, but he let it pass. The fact that he only bursts into life to try and stop *me* doing something is – what? Laughable or annoying? It's both.

The notion of Baz trying to stop me spurs me on. I hurry to see which way they went and I follow.

4

The streets in the city centre are quiet, so it's easy to spot where they've both gone. Heading down towards the Vaughn Way dual carriageway. She's in front, but I can't tell if she knows that he's following. She must know, surely?

As much as I wanted them to talk to me when we were back there on my turf, things are different now. I don't want them to know I'm here. I follow silently, hanging back. The woman skips across the dual carriageway as the lights change. The guy in the bodywarmer follows as the pedestrian lights turns red.

The traffic moves on before I can cross.

"Shit."

I watch them. I can see them heading down a pedestrianised bit past the Novotel and towards Frog Island. I pull out my phone. I put in the number for the emergency services but don't dial. It's there if I need it.

I don't wait for the lights to change but find a gap in the traffic and run over.

Probably about now, Baz is telling someone at work that stubborn Esther Butler has gone running off like a nutter.

The area north of the dual carriageway, Frog Island, is full of old textile factories. Lots of redevelopment going on. There was a plan for fancy apartments, filled with young professionals. Not seeing it yet. It has a reputation for being that place you don't want to walk through at night.

Down here, caught between redevelopments, you're hemmed in by those hoardings that builders put up. I feel like a rat in a maze. No windows that someone might glance out of. Nobody around at night. Not for any good reason, anyway. Why on earth has the woman come this way?

I can't see her now, but I can still see the guy.

Ahead of me, walking away, low-rent Ryan's dipped his hand inside his bodywarmer where the gun is.

Fuck.

Now I really do need to call the police. I press myself against an apartment advertising board. I stab the call button on my phone. The operator asks me which service.

"Police. There's a man with a gun."

Ahead, there's a fenced off-area and a gap where the fence panel's been pulled away. It's a building site. The man approaches the gap as though wondering if the woman has gone in there.

He looks round. His face turns my way. I'm not well hidden, but his eyes don't seem to latch onto me.

And then I see it. I bloody see it. He flicks his bodywarmer back and pulls the pistol from his belt. I see light glint off its dark surface. I see the mass of it, the shape it makes of his hand.

And then he goes in.

That renovation site has brick walls on the sides and,

above that, angular girders that mark the upper walls of the old building.

If the woman's gone in there then there's no way out for her.

The operator's asking for a location.

"Right. Yes." I swallow and look around. "Just off Great Central Street. They've gone inside a building site. By the old train station. I can't see them now, but he followed her in there."

The operator's a woman. She's talking to me, telling me to get myself to a safe place, but I don't know where that might be. It's not as if I can leave. Now I've committed to this, I'm part of it. I need to stay here and do what I can.

It turns out that all I can do is stand there and try to stop my knees from knocking together. It's an actual thing – I had no idea that my stupid legs would behave this way through fear, adrenaline or whatever it might be. They become so wobbly, I have to move.

I move forward.

A terrible curiosity has gripped me.

I just need to know. It's mad and it's stupid and I wonder what the hell I've got myself into, just because I got mad at Baz trying to tell me what I can and can't do.

Oh, Kieran's going to love this when he finds out. My husband will have words to say about all of this.

My head jerks up. Was that a siren? I pause, listening hard. Yes!

I haven't seen or heard anything from inside the fenced-off area, but surely they must hear the sirens too?

And I'm standing in the middle of this empty road, exposed, halfway to the building site. I am an idiot. I am, as my grandma used to say, "A girl who won't be telt."

The man, low-rent Ryan, appears at the gap in the fence. He sees me. He totally sees me.

He's got a stunned look on his face. He's got a 'caught raiding the biscuit tin' look on his face. It's a child's expression.

He's seen me and he's surely holding that gun.

The girl who won't be telt. Stubborn, contrary. Dead.

5

There's a knock at the interview room door. Josie looks up from her laptop notes and sees Detective Constable Smith – Walker – come in.

Everyone calls him Walker. She's certain it's not his real first name but she doesn't know what that is or why everyone calls him Walker. She'd hoped that she'd never need to know. He's in his fifties and is very much the kind of officer who knows he's stuck in his current role until he retires.

"Good evening, Josie," he says and then checks himself. "Or good morning, I suppose."

He smiles at Esther and carefully pulls out a seat to sit next to Josie.

He's dressed in a grey suit with a tie and looks far more alert and awake than anyone should be at this time of night. That's one of the things she finds weird about Walker. He's stuck in the corner with DS Joseph, the two Dead End Duncans, a little unserious crimes unit, given the detective work that no one else has time for, yet he dresses like an inspector or one of the other higher ranks. That distinguished face, the management level suit – he should either be mingling with the upper ranks or learn to dress according to his lowly station.

There's a story there. Josie's sure of it. She has no interest in learning about it.

Josie realises she must look like an absolute shambles of a human being next to Walker. She's regretting the excess of deodorant she sprayed herself with. Between that, the sweat and the stale alcohol, she probably smells like a teenager's bedroom.

"I was just getting Ms Butler's statement," she says, trying to be professional.

"Sorry I'm late," he says. "Seems you've had something of a traumatic experience tonight, Esther."

"I don't know if traumatic is the right word."

"Facing down a man with a gun. That's what I heard?"

There's a hesitation on Esther's face. "I ... I don't know if he properly saw me," she says.

"You said you saw him in the building site area on Great Central Street," says Josie.

"That's right."

"Then what happened?"

6

The man – low-rent Ryan Reynolds – is looking straight at me when the first of the police vehicles turn into the road.

A van and a patrol car.

In the sudden blue and white light that frames me, I look back at the gap in the fence but he's ducked back inside.

There's a clatter of feet. Officers in black are running towards me. I can't tell if they're men or women. They're dressed in chunky clothing and wear clumsy-looking helmets with cameras. I see the swing of guns in their hands. We don't see police with guns in English cities. Not like this.

And I think to myself that I did this. I made this happen.

They see me, of course they do. I try to look harmless. My hands jerk up, all on their own, as if they grab hold of the idea that I don't want to be shot before my brain does. Then I realise that I can hear the operator telling me to identify myself to the officers. I totally forgot I was on the phone.

"Esther Butler," I croak.

One of them strides across to me. "Name?" he demands. I can't see his face but he has a Scottish accent.

"Esther Butler," I repeat, a little louder.

"You made the call," he says. "Where is the gunman now?"

I point at the area behind the fence. "In there. The woman got away. It's just him, I think."

He speaks into his radio then turns to me. "I need you in the back of the van out of harm's way."

"I'll take her, Nick," says another.

"No, wait," I say, "I didn't do any—"

Someone grabs my arm and pulls me non-too-gently in the direction of the van.

The rough treatment makes my hackles rise, but I don't resist. As one officer pulls me along in a forced jog, the other officers move towards the gap in the fence.

"In you get," says the officer on my arm. The voice is a little more friendly now.

"But—"

"Do it now. It's like Ferguson said, we need you out of harm's way. You'll be safe here."

I barely understand. Safe? The man is gone. He disappeared from sight. It's all over now isn't it?

Then I hear a shout, a whole bunch of shouts in quick succession. And then a single gunshot. It's halfway between a crack and a pop, like a distant firework.

7

"I was sat inside the van when I heard the shots," I say.

The two detectives across the interview table are watching me, waiting.

The older one, Walker, looks like so many other middle-aged men, the kind who don't hide the grey and the lines in their cheeks and forehead but dress it up in expensive shirts, with tans from foreign holidays and buckets of unearned confidence like they're George Clooney. He seems nice enough, but there's a million solicitors, accountants and sales managers out there strutting the same stuff.

The younger woman, Kaminski. She's something different. I can't tell if that tangled hair is a choice or a genuine mess. I can't tell whether she's made a bad job of cleaning the make-up from her eyes or the bags around them are really that grey. I've seen faces like that before: usually as they're staggering out of a kebab shop at midnight, or about to start a fight in a pub car park.

"Shots," she says.

I blink. It's late and I'm tired and the adrenaline is wearing off.

"Shots," says Kaminski. "How many shots?"

I think. "Just one, I think."

"Think?"

"Just one."

Kaminski looks at her mess of notes on the table. "You were at the door to the casino when you first saw the man and the woman. Why were you at the door?"

"Why wouldn't I be at the door?"

"I mean, you're the floor manager. I don't know the Meridian. Is it a big casino?"

"Three floors," I say. "Gaming machines and some tables on the ground floor. A lot of Mahjong."

She seems surprised at that.

"We have a significant Chinese clientele," I say, picturing the mothers and grandmothers who come in to play, chat and take advantage of our free teas and coffees. "First floor is roulette, blackjack, poker, sports betting. Restaurant bars on both floors. I cover it all when it's my shift. I was at the door to speak to Baz and get a breath of fresh air."

"Baz?" says Walker.

"Baz Obi."

"So. Baz. He was outside with you. He saw the man and woman too?"

"He did."

"Who noticed them first?"

I shrug at the question. "I mentioned them first. I can't tell you when Baz saw them."

"Did he see the gun?"

The cup of coffee I'm holding between my hands has lost any sense of warmth. There's a shiny patch on the surface, like a little oil spill. I try to think straight and make sure I give them the right answer.

"I didn't see the gun at first. I got an ... impression that he had a gun on him."

"Impression?" says Kaminski. There's almost a sneer on her face.

"I could tell," I say, feeling my temper rising. "The way he stood, the bulge beneath his body warmer. The way he placed his hands. His attitude."

"So Baz didn't see it either?" the woman persists.

I shake my head. "He's a bit of a lump. He's a big guy. He knows how to treat the customers with respect and he can step in when someone gets out of line, but he's not got... He doesn't have much in the way of initiative."

Walker chuckles. "I've met him. I can vouch for that. He's a good guy though."

"I didn't say he was good," I say, finding myself smiling a fraction.

"So, he didn't think anything was suspicious," says Kaminski.

"He did not."

"And the woman. You said they were arguing. You said she might have been afraid."

It's only a hour or so ago but I have to cast my mind back.

"I think they knew each other. They were talking a lot for them to be total strangers. They were arguing like boyfriend and girlfriend, like she'd had enough his shit for one night. But there was an edge there, I thought."

"Did he seem threatening?" says Walker.

"Yeah. He did. I was across the road. I didn't hear the words, but they were arguing or sniping at each other. Like maybe one wanted to do something..." I run it through my head. "Like maybe he wanted to go on somewhere for another drink but she'd had enough."

"Did he seem drunk? Did either of them?"

"No," I decide slowly. "They might have been drinking. But there wasn't any—" I shook my arms "—loss of control. Loose actions. I'm good at spotting drunks. I thought he might have done a couple of lines of coke, mind."

Kaminski raises her eyebrow.

"He was buzzing," I say. "He was up. He was raring."

"Did she look like she was in danger?"

I don't like her questions. She seems to think I'm some sort of psychic, like I just magically intuited the gun was there or could somehow read their minds. I saw what I saw. I drew reasonable conclusions.

"She was alone with an angry man who I thought had a gun," I say.

"But she didn't look to you? Make eye contact? Make a silent plea for help?"

"I don't think she even knew we were there. They weren't looking at us."

Walker was making his own notes. "Now, I'm playing catch up here, Esther, so apologies if I'm asking questions about things you've already covered. You didn't see the gun at first but got a strong impression he was carrying something. When did you actually first see the gun?"

I have to mentally walk myself through the event.

"Sort of near the Novotel. There's a cut-through to where the old train station is. He was ahead of me. I saw him take it out."

"And where was the woman at this time?"

"It was dark. It's not well-lit there. She was either ahead or round the corner." I shake my head.

"And what was he doing with the gun?"

"Holding it?" I don't know what answer he wants.

"But he'd not seen you. He wasn't looking at the woman?"

I shrug and shake my head.

"And at what point did you decide to call nine-nine-nine?" says Kaminski.

I don't know if she's actually being bitchy or if she's simply got a bitch voice to go with that bitch resting face. Maybe she's just bone tired. We're all tired. I should be home by now.

"By the way, I need to make some phone calls," I say. "My husband. Work."

"Absolutely," says Walker. "We'll take a break in a minute. Maybe get you a better coffee."

"But the call to emergency services," says Kaminski. "Why did you wait to call?"

"I thought he had a gun," I say. "I didn't know but I thought it; and then when I saw it I ... realised then I should have called earlier but I wasn't sure. I didn't want to waste police time."

"Even if you merely suspect, you should have called at once."

I hold my expression, maybe even attempt a smile. I don't know what else I'm supposed to do when someone gives me advice that would only be useful if I had a time machine. What the hell do people expect to achieve with "You should've" sentences?

"You could have stayed at the casino and made the call from there," Kaminski says, trying to drive the point home. "What was the point of following them? Were you concerned or were you just curious?"

Okay. I've had enough. I can feel anger rising through my tired brain.

"I did what I did," I say. "I was concerned for her safety. I show some actual fucking interest in another human being. It's called empathy! Compassion! I did what I thought was right. Don't even try to come at me with your half-arsed accusations."

Walker's hands are raised to plead for calm, almost coming directly between me and the detective bitch-face.

"Okay, okay. Maybe it's time for a coffee break, huh?"

"Bitch," I mutter under my breath.

"Coffees all round," says Walker. "A short break. I know you need to go home, Esther. You being here is of great help to us."

He's laying it on thick. They're not playing good cop, bad cop. She's being shit cop and he's cleaning up after. The nice words he's pouring out – I even think he means them.

He turns to Kaminski. "Let's get Esther a drink."

I put down the tepid coffee I'm still holding.

"I've got some frothy latte sachet things somewhere," he says to me. "It's still Nescafe but they're not bad. Want one?"

I tilt my head then nod.

He moves his hand. He's literally directing Kaminski to leave the room.

"You know something, Esther," he says. "You made the right call tonight. You possibly saved a woman from serious harm. Maybe more people. You did a good thing."

He gives me a warm look. Genuine concern. Like those rare teachers back at school – the good ones – who actually see you as a human being.

I nod, managing to accept the compliment.

He pauses at the door. "And the man and woman? I didn't ask."

"What?" I say.

"You'd not seen them at the casino or in the local area before."

I shake my head slowly.

"Not around the place? You never met them before?"

"Never seen them before in my life," I say.

8

Walker can see Kaminski bursting to say something. She waits until they're on the stairs.

"What's this fucking business?" she says, waving her arm like a ticket barrier in front of them.

"Sorry?" says Walker.

"Trying to herd me like I'm a sheep," she snaps.

He takes a deliberate pause before answering. "You seemed to be goading her, Josie. She's a witness, not a suspect."

"I was asking reasonable questions."

He could tell her that it's a matter of tone of voice, that she sounded confrontational with everything she said. But that kind of comment wouldn't go down well. Walker decides not to respond.

"Let's get us all a drink and get her final statement drawn up."

His knee twinges as they climb the stairs. It's a hangover from playing too much five-a-side as a younger man. It's usually not a problem, but he must have been sleeping funny on it when the call came through to attend the station.

Walker suspects Kaminski has not been to bed. Scabbard and half of CID went out to celebrate the Rosenthal case. Walker was among those implicitly not invited, but he saw Kaminski grabbing her jacket to go to the pub like the rest of them. Yep, the jacket she is currently wearing. He suspects she might even still be drunk, but she's hiding it well.

Kaminski is a young detective but old enough to think she's thrown off the immaturity of youth. A dangerous age. A good age for putting your foot in it; maybe even getting fired.

They pause at the ground floor, stepping in opposite directions.

"Kitchens," she says, pointing one way.

"Fancy sachets," he says, pointing another.

She sighs and follows him.

They make it to the first floor but not the sachets. DI Neelam Gill spots them and waves them into the main office. Gill is in her thirties but, unlike Kaminski, has tipped over the youth threshold into proper functioning adult. It's a grey zone but it's a real thing.

"Morning, Walker," she says.

"Morning, ma'am."

"You two still doing the witness statement from the woman who called it in?"

"Esther Butler," says Walker. "We're taking a break and then finalising her statement."

Gill goes to a side office and silently directs them to come in with her. She takes a seat and gestures to the chairs opposite.

Gill fusses with a computer and a wall screen until she

manages to bring up a map of the city centre. Sections are outlined in red.

"Great Central Street. Vaughn Way. The Meridian Casino," she says. "What's the woman's account in terms of movements?"

Kaminski moves to the display. "She says she saw the man and the woman outside the casino. She followed them across Vaughn Way and down through this pedestrian walkway to Grand Central Street and saw him go into a building site. Is that this bit here?" She circles a large section of building that's outlined in red.

"And has she talked about when she saw the gun?"

"She said it was concealed until she was following him down here." Kaminski runs her finger along the pedestrianised cut-through.

"And she saw him holding it at the entrance to the building site," Walker adds. "Just before the Authorised Firearms Officers turned up."

Gill nods but it's slow, sad even. She sighs.

"Okay. AFOs came from this direction here. Based on Esther Butler's account and a credible threat to life, they entered the building site at this point here, the only viable entrance." She outlines the site again. "This is the derelict remains of the back end of the station, currently being rebuilt and refurbed. Brick walls – eighteen, twenty feet high. All of that wrapped in security fences. It's open to the sky. It's just —" she steeples her fingers "—roof supports."

"Uh-huh," Walker's waiting for the important bit.

"No way out. Just a big empty space within," says Gill. "A box. AFOs entered one at a time. They saw the man and challenged him. It's near pitch black in there. I'm not going to question..." She pauses, mushes her lips. "Split second decision. AFO Constable Ferguson perceived a threat and a shot was fired. The suspect was pronounced dead by paramedics at the scene."

"This all matches Ms Butler's account," says Josie.

"No. It doesn't," says Gill. She goes and closes the door, shutting out the noise from the main office.

Detective inspectors, even mature ones, aren't above a little flair for the dramatic but Walker is suddenly intrigued about what Gill needs to say behind closed doors. Whatever it is, it doesn't seem good.

9

By the time the detectives come back, I've sent several WhatsApp messages – to Natalie Raynor, the Meridian floor manager who's due to come in at six a.m., to Savage, the overall manager, and to Kieran. I'd already messaged Kieran when I first came into the police station but now my husband's woken up and responded with:

You want me to come collect you?

I don't know when I'll be done, I reply.

I'm hoping it's soon. It's near enough three o'clock in the morning now. I've told the police everything. I don't know if they need me to sign anything.

The detectives come back in. Walker is carrying two mugs of coffee. He puts one down in front of me. It does indeed look frothy and more appealing than the brown water I was given earlier.

Kaminski produces several sheets of printed paper and puts them in front of me.

I read the opening sentence.

This statement (consisting of 5 pages each signed by me) is true to the best of my knowledge and belief and I make it knowing that, if it is tendered in evidence, I shall be liable to prosecution if I have wilfully stated anything in it which I know to be false or do not believe to be true.

"I've typed it up based on what I understood you to have said," she says. "Can you read it and mark stuff I've got wrong. It's fine if I've misunderstood you. Even the tiniest thing. It should be your statement."

I nod and start to read. I sip the coffee as I go through. It's hardly barista quality, but it's on a par with the free coffee we lay on for punters at the casino.

"You've said here that I thought he'd taken cocaine," I say.

"Yes?" says Kaminski.

"I'm just saying he was buzzing, ramped up. You know? He had that look. I don't know if he'd actually done coke."

"Okay. We'll strike that."

There are a couple more details. The timing of them crossing the road. How far ahead the woman was after they'd crossed. But it's mostly right.

Kaminski takes the sheets from me and scribbles on them in pen. "I'll change those."

"But it's otherwise correct?" says Walker who's been leaning back in his chair and sipping his coffee like he's relaxing at a beachfront café.

"Yes,"

He shifts his jaw and takes a deep breath like he's tired or happy.

"And the bits about the gun." He pulls the paper to him. "'*As he went into the building site, I saw him take the gun from his belt. It was a pistol.*' That's factually correct?"

I remember the glint of light off the gun, his hand making a fist around the grip.

"Yes."

"What kind of gun was it?"

"A pistol."

"What kind?"

"What kind?" I laugh. Does he think I'm a gun nut? I grab a piece of paper and draw an L-shape. "A pistol. Square. It wasn't a, er – it wasn't a revolver. It was dark."

"But you saw it? In that moment?"

"Yeah. I thought he was going to shoot me at one point. I was kind of focussed on it."

"And it was definitely a gun you saw?"

"I mean, it could have been fake." It suddenly occurs to me that the police might have shot a man carrying a stupid fake gun. You read about such things happening. "It looked real."

"Ignoring whether it might have been a replica, was it a gun in his hand?"

Nice foamy instant coffee or not, this Walker guy is badgering me now and I don't take kindly to it.

"It was a gun, officer. I saw the gun in his hand. A hundred percent certainty."

The detectives share a look. I've no idea what it means.

Kaminski makes notes for a few minutes while Walker, tense now, sips his coffee. Kaminski goes out and comes back with fresh printed sheets.

"Please read it all again," she says. "I've only made the changes you've indicated. If there's anything still wrong, let us know."

I read through. It's a tedious process and I'm tired now, like whole body tired. I read it and it's all correct.

"You want me to sign it?" I say. I pick up a pen.

Walker lightly raises a hand to stop me.

"Esther. I want to tell you what our officers discovered at the scene."

"What?"

"You know that a shot was fired. The man you reported to the police was shot. He was pronounced dead at the scene by paramedics."

I nod. I've already surmised this. It's not a nice thought, but I've put it in its own special mental compartment. The police shot him. The man had a gun. I might have made the call but it's not on me, this thing.

"The inside of that building site is part of the old train station. It's nearly all high brick walls and then there's the security fence. There's really no other way out."

Kaminski shifts in her seat. "There was no woman in there with him."

I blink.

"You said that the woman went in there."

"I didn't see her go in there," I say.

Walker takes the witness statement back from me.

"'*I saw the man go into the building site to follow the woman*'," he reads.

"I assumed that was what he was doing. I didn't see her. I don't know where she went."

"We've not actually found the woman anywhere," says Walker. "Our officers haven't picked her up. We're still searching the area."

"No, okay," I say, not sure what to make of these facts. It doesn't change a thing.

"And we've searched the area," he continues. "The interior of this derelict building. We're searching it again and the streets nearby. The building site is mostly cleared inside. Very open."

I'm not following. Do they think the woman is hiding behind some bricks or an advertising hoarding or something?

"We can't find the gun," says Walker.

"We can't find any gun," says Kaminski.

"But he had it," I say.

"And we're still searching," says Walker. "We have cordoned off all the nearby streets and we will search right through the day, if we need to."

"But he was in that building. Those walls are high," says Kaminski and she tries to mime throwing an object up high.

"It would seem reasonable that if there was a gun then we'd have found it by now," says Walker.

That word. *If.* It hits me like a punch in the gut.

They can't find the man's gun and they're now saying I invented it, imagined it.

"But the police shot him..." I say, my voice robbed of almost all power.

"Authorised Firearms Officers are highly trained individuals," says Walker. "But they have to make split second decisions, often when other human lives are at risk."

The police shot a man. They're saying that the police shot an unarmed man. They're saying that the police shot an unarmed man because I told them about the gun and the woman he was following.

They can't find the woman.

They can't find the gun.

The police shot a man because of what I told them.

10

I feel sick. I feel like I might throw up the coffee in my stomach. I won't but I feel it.

I stare at the paper witness statement in front of me.

"Given this information," Walker says gently, "do you want to reconsider your statement?"

I don't follow him. My head is filled with white noise. My body wants to puke. I'm still processing what they've told me. "Huh?"

"Given that we can't find a gun anywhere, or the woman, do you want to reconsider your statement? A statement is a legal document that can be read out in court as evidence."

I mentally claw my way back into the room. "You think I'm lying," I say.

"No, not lying, Esther. It was dark. It was an unsettling situation. Sometimes what we see and what we think we see are two different things. We're not saying you are lying. But maybe you want to reconsider your statement."

"A hundred percent certainty, you said," says Kaminski.

I look at her. I'm possibly imagining it but the bitch officer seems to be enjoying herself now.

"You said it was a gun. A hundred percent certain," she says.

"It was..." I say.

I try to remember more clearly. The gap in the fence going into the building site. The man – the now dead man – reaching into his belt. The gleam of light on something. The shape of his fingers around something. In my mind's eye I can see the shape of the thing, black on black but defined by the gleam of light and the shape of his hand.

"We will be getting CCTV from local buildings and from the main road," says Kaminski.

"I saw it," I say.

"What did you see?"

"A gun. A gun in his hand. I know it was. I just know."

"Like the way you knew he had a gun under his jacket even when you couldn't see it?" said Kaminski.

I flung my fingers at the papers. "This is what happened!"

"And we are not going to tell you to change your statement one way or another," says Walker. "These are your words. This is your account. But it is a legal document and it is illegal to lie in a statement."

"Knowingly making a false statement to the police is a criminal offence which can carry a custodial sentence of several years," says Kaminski.

"I saw what I saw!"

"But maybe you need time to think about what you really saw," Walker suggests.

The glint of light on metal. The shape of his hand. I know what I saw. I know what I felt.

"You want me to lie?" I say.

"Absolutely not," he says.

"I saw what I saw," I repeat, quieter now.

I look again at the lines at the top of the first sheet.

I shall be liable to prosecution if I have wilfully stated anything in it which I know to be false or do not believe to be true.

"You'll find that gun because I know what I saw," I say and pick up the pen.

11

Kieran's waiting for me in the police station reception area.

He stands as he sees me come through, but I'm not ready to speak to him yet. The detectives, Kaminski and Walker, are still with me.

"Is there anything I need to do?" I ask them. "Sign out?"

"We're all good," says Walker. "You've been very helpful."

Kaminski gives a grunt. She looks as tired as I feel.

"Okay," I say and go to Kieran.

He's wearing a polo shirt with none of the buttons done up like he's got out of bed and grabbed the first thing to hand. He gives me a one-handed hug and I lean into his shoulder.

"You didn't need to come," I say.

"I was worried."

He's managed to find a space in the tiny car park out front. My car's in another car park. I half think to tell him that I need to pick it up but, no, I'll just collect it tomorrow.

I get into the passenger seat of his BMW. The BMW he's paying too much for every month but which he says is a vital business expense. The seats are comfortable though, and I feel I could go to sleep right there.

As we circle round onto the dual carriageway, I can't help but look over to the right, down towards Frog Island. Police lights flash silently off the buildings. I don't see the police cordons but I can picture the lines of tape, the area in which they're searching for the man's gun.

They will find it.

They must find it.

"You want to tell me what happened?" says Kieran.

I don't want to tell him. I really don't.

But I do. If I don't share this then I'll just explode.

I give him the bare bones of the story and I don't even get to the bit where the police can't find the gun when he says, "Is that part of your job?"

"Huh?" I grunt, even though I know exactly what he means.

"Chasing after people who are carrying guns?"

"I wasn't chasing him," I say. "I just followed him."

"What's the difference?"

"Speed," I say and know it sounds stupid.

He reaches over and squeezes my thigh. "I worry about you, bunnykin."

This is him showing affection. I think he actually does care, or I think he tries to.

"You don't need to worry about me. I wasn't in any danger," I lie.

"You go rushing in," he says. "You need to stop and think."

"I *was* thinking. A woman was in danger."

He nods reluctantly. "Always thinking of others before yourself. You're a good person."

"I'm shattered," I say. "Sorry to get you up."

"Not a problem. I was discussing the GymOne account with Trey until late."

I grunt. I'm too tired to talk now. I'm ready to go into shut down.

His satnav says it's a three mile drive home from here. Ten minutes. Kieran sees the satnav time estimate as a personal challenge – something to be beaten. He accelerates, five, ten miles an hour above the speed limit.

He doesn't ask for the rest of my story.

I don't tell him that the police can't find the gun or the woman.

12

When he wakes in the morning, Walker acknowledges that three hours sleep is not enough but knows he will cope.

He's alone in the bed. Helen is already up and out. Most days she goes to the pool and does twenty lengths before heading straight to the Botanic Gardens. He didn't even notice her go. He moves around the house as though it is his entirely. Their daughter Amber is away at university, studying Film Production at Portsmouth. Their son Oscar is in his room. Walker and Helen see him so infrequently, he might as well be living away as well.

He drives through the city, watching the frenzy of rush hour. Leicester is no different to any other city with its traffic congestion. In fact, every driver he can see wants to get from A to B as efficiently as possible. Walker recognises the petty futility of it all. Each driver assumes their needs are unique and special, when they most certainly are not. He settles back in his seat with a practised patience.

Walker is back in work by eight o'clock.

He goes straight up the offices being used for the shooting incident.

DI Gill is still there. She looks as if she's been running on caffeine all night and doesn't seem any worse for it.

"Ay up, ma'am. How's it going?" he asks.

"No gun," she says simply.

"More area to search?"

"We've covered the ground back and forth. We're searching in areas we've searched too many times and even looked in places where it's just not possible for the gun to be. There is no gun. Your witness was either lying or has failed to mention something."

"Like what?"

"Like a detour past the Grand Union Canal where he threw it in."

Walker thinks on this. "Esther Butler strikes me as a competent, level-headed adult."

"There's no gun," says Gill and there's almost a note of madness in her voice. Maybe a night of caffeine has taken its toll. "But we're drawing CCTV from the area. Not as helpful as we'd like. We've fingerprinted the dead man."

"No ID on him."

"No. Only his phone. We'll do an appeal for witnesses. The AFOs have been allowed home. AFO Nick Ferguson is going to have to speak to IOPC this morning."

That would be tough. Walker knows Ferguson. He's ex-military, like several of the AFOs, and he was fast-tracked into that unit. He'll be putting up a brave front but he's just shot an unarmed man and now has to face the Independent Office of Police Conduct, an organisation that can only justify its existence by judging and condemning hardworking police officers.

"You know," says Walker, "sometimes I can't find my wallet at home and I search for it everywhere. Kitchen, lounge, this table, that counter. Everywhere. And then I find it right where I first thought it was. Staring me in a face. There's hope."

Gill purses her lips. "I suspect you think that anecdote is meant to be comforting."

He gives her a shrug and a smile.

"More of an insight into the geriatric mind," she says but at least she's smiling.

Walker goes to the main CID office. It's a large open office. There's a wall of filing cabinets that separates the area set aside for Operation Chainlink from everyone else. Most of the detectives see it as a quarantine zone. Walker sees it as the cosy nook it is. It only bothers him a little that he and Rob Joseph are labelled Dead End Duncan. It bothers him less than it does Rob.

DS Rob Joseph is already at his desk. Maps, pinned papers, and images of stolen or high-risk agricultural machinery cover the vertical surfaces.

Rob tends to dress smart, often with a thin square tie that somehow makes Walker think of a keyboardist in an eighties synth band. Rob wasn't even alive in the eighties. Rob is a younger officer, not handsome, but lean and distinctive enough that he can pass for handsome in poor lighting. Today his shirt sleeves are rolled up and a bandage dressing covers his left forearm.

Walker squints, tries to remember and says, "Like a rose and thorn thing?"

"Tribal thorn patterns," Rob nods.

"Does that hurt? With the laser?"

Rob grins. "Yeah, it hurts. Irritates more than hurts. The skin blisters too."

Walker winces. In the year or more that he's known Rob, the man's been going through a steady series of tattoo removals on various parts of his body. Walker has talked to him about it but Rob's motives aren't entirely clear. They're not ugly. They don't make him a worse detective. They're not the reason he's here with the Dead End Duncans.

"A busy night last night, I hear," says Rob.

"AFOs shot an unarmed man."

"Shit."

"Mmm. I was helping DC Kaminski with a witness statement."

"Yeah, I had an email from Scabbard about that somewhere..."

"Is she in?"

Rob stands and looks over the top of the cabinets. Walker turns. Josie Kaminski is in DI Scabbard's glass-walled office at the far end. She's standing and there's definitely a heated conversation going on there.

Walker is automatically on her side, whatever it is. He and Rob are here on Operation Chainlink because Scabbard wanted to punish them. They exist as a cautionary tale to all the other officers in Leicester CID.

"She's quite fiery, isn't she?" Walker says.

"Office rumour is she fucked Scabbard last night," says Rob.

"None of our business," says Walker earnestly.

"Couldn't agree with you more, mate."

The office door is flung open and Kaminski storms out. DS Dean Beaches, who has an office right by Scabbard's, says something Walker can't hear.

"You want to say that again, cunt?" Kaminski barks at him.

Dean Beaches' Adam's apple bobs in something like fear and he apparently doesn't want to say it again, but he puts on a leering grin once Kaminski has gone past.

She strides, a face like thunder, down the length of the office. Rob and Walker follow her until she's at the little opening between filing cabinets that is the entrance to their place of internal exile.

"Apparently I'm working here now," she says in the most bitter of tones.

Rob smiles. "Welcome to Operation Chainlink." He turns to Walker. "Coffees all round?"

"Coffees all round," agrees Walker genially. "Posh little sachet?"

"We do posh sachets," Rob says to Kaminski. "We're saving up for a coffee machine."

She's fuming too much to respond. Walker goes to make coffees and hopes that she'll calm down eventually.

13

I wake to a message on my phone from Gabe Savage, the casino general manager.

Heard what happened. Hope you're okay. Take the day off. I've got your shift covered.

I don't need my shift covering and I tell him so in a reply message.

I go downstairs, threading my way past the bulky boxes of RBuzz that seem to have taken up permanent residence there, as well as in the third bedroom and the dining room. Kieran and his mate, Trey, have a contract to be the UK's sole distributors for 'Righteous Buzz', a Korean energy drink that tastes like nothing humans have ever drunk before and comes in shades of orange, green and purple that are so fluorescent I can't believe they're legal.

From what Kieran tells me, they're always *this close* to getting a distribution deal with this vending machine company or that gym chain. Meanwhile, he's bombing up and down the country to meetings and getting deeper into credit card debt, always certain that they're one handshake away from making all the money back.

And I have to live in a house that's an obstacle course of RBuzz boxes.

Kieran's already gone out for the day to yet another pitch meeting. I could check our shared calendar on my phone. Nottingham. Northampton. Cambridge. It doesn't matter.

I put the kettle on for a cup of tea. I feel tired, washed out, unhappy. A little masochistic part of me knows exactly what to do when I feel like that. I text Jeety and ask if she's up for a run once she's dropped the kids off at school. Yeah, that's right, body – think you're tired now, huh? Wait till you've done 5k. Ha!

I meet Jeety at the corner by the Aberdale pub. She's got her long black hair tied back in a ponytail. She wears brightly coloured lycra and a compression top to run in. We're the same age – we went to school together. Back then she was Navjit Kaur. She adopted the nickname 'Jeety' somewhere in college and switched out her surname when she married a white guy called Joel Etheridge. I don't know how a busy mum of two under-twelves with a graphic design job on the side manages to look so damned trim and healthy, but she does. She puts it down to wine and bitchiness. I doubt that's true, but I do know that I always have to put in effort to maintain pace with her on our runs.

We go down the relatively quiet Asquith Boulevard and then over into Knighton Park where we can do laps until we've had enough. On the way, I tell her everything about last night. Everything.

"Fuck me, Esther," she says when I've finished.

"I know."

We overtake an old man with his dog which gives her further time to process.

"And now the police really can't find the gun?"

"Nope."

"But they were searching in the dark."

"Yeah – you kinda hope they had torches," I say.

My lungs are gently burning as we run. I'm at that perfect point where my legs know they're working out, my lungs are cooking, and my heart rate is a constant high. It's that sweet spot where I know I could maybe just run like this forever, do that 10k or half marathon Jeety and I keep saying we'll sign up for. Once you've reached a certain level of fitness, running is all just psychology, the willingness to keep going. And I'm a stubborn cow at times.

"Were the man and woman together?" says Jeety. "I mean, like an item?"

"I dunno," I say. "When they were together, across the road, I thought they were like a couple or on a date, but then..."

"Maybe he gave the gun to her," she says. "Before they split up."

I think about that but it just doesn't work. I don't know where she went. Maybe the police will find her and get her version of the story, but if she wasn't inside that building site when I saw the gun in his hand, then it can't add up.

"That's not what happened," I say.

She pants. It's good to hear that she's also out of breath.

"Maybe..." she says.

"What?"

"Well, maybe, are you sure he had the gun on him?"

"Fuck off," I say with some passion, causing a woman on a bench to look at us.

"I'm just saying..."

"And I'm just saying fuck off. You sound like the police."

"Sorry, mate." She says it like she means it. She's my best friend and always has my back.

In my mind is the flash of light glinting off the thing in the man's hand, the shape of his hand round it. That man is dead now. That fact sits like a stone in my stomach.

"If you say it happened, it happened," says Jeety.

"Right."

"I'm serious. You're the most level-headed bitch I know. Decisive. Perceptive. Take no prisoners."

"Thanks."

"Seriously, when the zombie apocalypse comes, me and the kids are coming round to your house for protection."

"What about Joel?" I say. Joel's her husband.

Her flushed pink cheeks twitch. "Meh. In all my zombie apocalypse fantasies, he gets eaten in the first five minutes."

I give a grunt of laughter at that.

"You know if you did come to mine," I say, "there'd be nothing to drink but RBuzz."

"You see? You've already got supplies in."

"Have you tasted that stuff? It's fucking awful."

"It's not that bad," she says.

We press on for another lap. Just the act of running, of being with Jeety, is siphoning the anger and stress from my system.

14

"Here we go," says Rob. "The great outdoors."

Josie Kaminski looks at the green fields, coarse hedges and the wide open sky and pulls a face like she's been dipped in sewage.

DS Rob Joseph has taken his new detective constable on a drive with him to see Operation Chainlink in action. The look Josie Kaminski gave Rob when he suggested this was priceless. It was like she still thought her whole relegation to the CID naughty corner was some sort of horrific joke and she was waiting for DI Scabbard to leap out, yell "Surprise!" and welcome her back into the fold.

Rob and Walker are a happy little team and they don't require any fresh additions. Operation Chainlink is primarily a rural and community policing issue. It doesn't demand the services of two full-time CID officers, let alone three. The weirdness of being part of a team based in the centre of Leicester working primarily in the countryside is all part of the Duncan experience.

But, if Josie has been sent down to the dungeon, then Rob feels it's his duty to show the new inmate around.

He talks while he drives.

"So, Operation Chainlink deals with a wide range of rural crime. Agricultural machinery and equipment theft, livestock theft, poaching, hare coursing, fly-tipping. We work with uniform across the force and in surrounding forces to stop the gangs and bring individuals to court."

"Gangs?" says Josie.

"Absolutely. This is organised crime. This isn't lone yokels pinching Farmer Giles' tractor or syphoning his diesel. It's an organised enterprise built on the knowledge that our response times in rural areas is much lower. That's why the area around Anstey is one our hot spots. Rural but with easy access to the A46 and M1. They swoop in, nick what they like, and vanish again."

Operation Chainlink has last pick of the unmarked pool cars. The Skoda is a few years old but Rob can make it power up Sharply Hill as they leave the city behind.

He points ahead.

"We've had some big ticket thefts in the area, so we're doing spot checks at farms considered likely targets. Big ticket stuff includes GPS antennae, display screens, and a couple of RTK base stations."

"RT-what?" she says.

"RTK. Super high tech. Provides guidance to tractors, down to the centimetre, for automatic steering and planting. Tractors out here practically drive themselves."

"Wow," she says, unimpressed.

"Stolen units can go for fifteen thousand or more. It's big business."

She nods.

"You'll get to enjoy the work," he says.

"Sir, if I can be honest, I don't want to get to enjoy it."

He clicks his tongue. "Well, then you're going to be a miserable little monkey, aren't you?"

She shoots him a look.

He shrugs. "I get it. Your career is not currently going the way you wanted."

"Fucking understatement," she mutters.

"Yeah, well, join the club."

He could tell her his own story of woe. He could tell her about how he successfully pulverised his relationship with his parents and wider family for the sake of the girl of his dreams. He could tell her about how the girl of his dreams turned into a nightmare and walked out on him six months back. He could tell her that he's messed his private life up so completely he spends good money to see a therapist once a week to try and put the pieces back together. Any of the pieces.

He's not going to tell her. She's being a mardy sod and he's not going to bare any of his soul if his words are going to fall on deaf ears.

He tries a different tack. "You went for that role in organised crime last year."

"Yeah." She frowns. "You did too."

"Yup. Guess they didn't want either of us."

She just about manages a laugh.

"Looking for any other roles?" he says.

"I'm actually..." She glances at him like she's not sure. "I'm actually looking at New Zealand."

"Bloody hell. I've thought about transferring to another force but that's... Can you transfer to New Zealand?"

"You can apply," she says. "I'm just starting the process."

He watches white clouds cross the blue sky as he thinks about that.

"Well bloody good luck to you, mate," he says. "Kiwis and hobbits and that shit. Nice."

"Thanks. Don't tell anyone."

"Lips are sealed." He takes a turning on the right up towards the first farm on their list for today. "But while you're here let's try to get you up to speed with stolen farm equipment, huh? This might not be late night city centre shootings, but it can be good work."

She says nothing. At least she doesn't argue.

15

I go into work and go straight up to the second floor.

"I told you to stay at home," Savage calls out from his open office door.

You can never tell when Savage is going to be in. He doesn't just keep odd hours, he keeps wilfully odd hours. Like he's always there at the casino when you least expect him.

I push his open office door wide and step inside.

Gabe Savage is a local Leicester boy, but his parents must have had some Mediterranean genes in the background which came out in force when baby Gabe arrived. He's a guy with a permanent tan, permanent five o'clock shadow, and thick dark hair. He also uses his hands too much when he talks, but I don't think I can blame that on genes.

"What would I do if I stayed at home?" I say.

He presses his lips together and gives a little head shake. "Are you okay?"

I give the question proper consideration. "Yeah. I'm fine."

"I heard what happened."

"I'm sorry I went off."

"What? And abandoned your post?" He cracks a grin. "You were moved by your conscience and a duty to protect others. A woman was in trouble. And you..." He waves a hand expressively at me. "You are very public-spirited. I just need to know you're okay?"

"I'm fine, Gabe."

He nods. Due diligence is done.

Gabe doesn't mollycoddle his people and I respect that.

I like Gabe a lot. Too much, to be honest. In a country where nearly all casinos have been bought up by global chains, the Meridian has managed to remain steadfastly independent, and that has meant it's had to be ... flexible. I've never met the owners – I don't even know who they are – but I know without needing evidence they are the kind of people that regular folk don't want to get too close to. Gambling may have worked hard to improve its image over the years, but it's still a grubby business.

Gabe might make approving sounds when he speaks of me being driven by my conscience, but for him and his bosses, a moral conscience is something that is valued only up to a specific point.

"I hear the police want to come in," he says. "Maybe look at our CCTV."

"Sorry," I say.

He shakes his head. "Do we have anything to hide?" It sounds like a rhetorical question, but maybe it's not.

"We have nothing to hide," I say.

He spreads his hands wide, deeply satisfied.

That's my cue to leave. I start my rounds. It might be mid-afternoon, but there are plenty of punters in.

A group of regulars – Chinese grandmothers the lot of them – are playing Mahjong on the ground floor. There's a lot of chatting, a lot of arguing. A man – I don't know if it's a husband or a son – sits to the side of them and fetches cups of tea when they tell him.

On the first floor there are two roulette wheels in operation. The croupiers watch the customers. The inspectors watch the croupier and the customers. Camelia, the roulette pit boss, watches everyone. She's good at her job and takes crap from no one. She's a younger version of me in that regard. Her Romanian accent and mannerisms give her a certain sharp edge too. I never need to worry about Camelia's section when she's on.

Bank notes go into the drop box in front of the croupier, pushed in by a Perspex T-bar. When the box is collected to go to the strongroom, I go downstairs too. Our strongroom is on the ground floor towards the rear. It really doesn't get used much these days. Like everywhere else we're mostly cashless. There are two sets of keys to the strongroom and Mica, on security detail, has access to one set.

I watch him go in. The cash box is logged and secured in the tiny first space in the strongroom. It will be counted up later. The room beyond we don't use anymore, apart from some things Gabe occasionally stores in there.

I leave Mica to it. I've got paperwork to do. Time sheets, staff records.

Orla Hawkes, who works on the bar, waves me over. I hope it's not to tell me the automatic pizza oven has stopped working again.

It's not. She's got her phone out. "It's your man," she says.

"My man?"

I come round the side of the bar and look. It's a video from some web streaming service. I see the people in police uniform and the crest of the Leicestershire Police, the slogan '*Our Duty: Protecting Our Communities*' underneath.

It's a press conference.

A woman in a senior officer's uniform is at a podium. The title 'Chief Superintendent Becky Ayres' runs underneath.

"*Good afternoon,*" she says to the unseen audience before her. "*I'd like to begin by acknowledging that the events of last night in the Frog Island area of Leicester have been deeply distressing, not just for those directly involved, but for the wider community as well. We are here today to provide a clear and honest update on what we know so far.*

"*Late last night, our control room received a nine-nine-nine call from a member of the public reporting a man behaving suspiciously in the city centre, and potentially in possession of a firearm. The caller observed the man in the company of a woman and expressed concerns for her safety.*

Based on the credible threat to life and the nature of the information received, Authorised Firearms Officers were deployed and responded swiftly to the location. Officers arrived in the Frog Island area within minutes and located the individual inside a building site. During the operation to secure the area and challenge the suspect, a single shot was fired by one of our officers. Tragically, the man was pronounced dead at the scene by paramedics shortly thereafter.

The reported firearm has not yet been recovered from the scene. We continue to search the area extensively, including adjacent buildings and public spaces, and I want to be clear, this remains a live and active investigation."

"They didn't find his gun?" says Orla.

I don't say anything. There's nothing to say.

"But he did have a gun? Right?"

"He had a gun, Orla," I say and wave her to be quiet so I can hear the rest.

16

There's mud on Josie's shoes. They've only visited two farms and barely got out at either, but there's mud on her shoes and she's spent the journey back to Mansfield House nick wondering if Operation Chainlink comes with free wellies.

She pauses as they head back through the open plan CID office. A press conference is playing on the largest wall screen.

It's coming live from the media suite.

Chief Superintendent Ayres, head of Local Policing for the force, is leading the briefing. Next to her is Chief Inspector Moghul, who's got the unenviable job of dealing with IOPC and the fallout from the police shooting a member of the public.

But there, just on edge of the frame, is DI Scabbard, alongside DI Gill. Josie doesn't understand what he's doing there.

"*A full referral has been made to the Independent Office for Police Conduct, which is now assessing the incident,*" the chief super is saying. "*We are cooperating fully with that process. We are also conducting our own parallel investigation into the circumstances that led to this outcome.*"

Walker appears beside Josie. "They've IDed the man from his fingerprints but not released the information to the public."

She gives him a questioning look.

"Seamus Wollacott. Previous for drugs and weapons offences. Given an initial twelve month sentence for brandishing a blade in public. More recently, served two years for cocaine possession with the intent to supply. He'd been out less than six months before..." Walker waves at the screen.

"Wollacott. As in the Braunstone Wollacotts?"

Walker nods. Josie knows the family. Every copper who's patrolled in Leicester knows of the Wollacotts. Not exactly the heights of criminal enterprise, but being brought up before a magistrate seems to be a rite of passage for every member of the family. The dead man is a known criminal.

"A piece of work then," she says.

"Still no gun though."

As Ayres wraps up and refuses to take any questions, Scabbard shifts in the background on screen.

"Ma boy's looking good," says DS Dean Beaches.

Josie makes the mistake of looking his way.

Beaches, slouched in his wheelie chair, tapping his teeth with a biro, waggles his eyebrows at Josie. "I can see why you wanted to bang him."

Josie is strongly tempted to go over, pick up his stapler and threaten to staple Beaches cock to the wall. Or she might just do it without the warning.

But Walker steps forward. "Actually our Dean here knows a thing about looking good on TV."

"Fuck off, Walker. No one's talking to you."

Walker jerks a thumb at Beaches. "Appeared on the Weakest Link. You know: BBC quiz show."

"All in the past."

"Twenty twelve," says Walker. "A moment in the spotlight. Hey, Sarge – name a country beginning with the letter J."

"Fuck off," he says and pretends to go back to his work.

"What answer did he give?" says Josie.

Walker smiles. "Germany."

Josie snorts.

"Fuck. Off," says Beaches.

Josie gives Walker what she hopes is a grateful look. "I'm going out for some fresh air."

Walker nods and she heads out.

She needs to walk to put her head in order. A full day of her new reality with the Duncans in Operation Chainlink sits heavy on her, along with the events of last night.

She doesn't really know where she's going until she's already heading there. It's a ten minute walk from Mansfield House to the Meridian Casino, and only a further five minutes to the scene where Seamus Wollacott was shot.

It's not Josie's case, she just took Esther Butler's witness statement, But Josie just has to see the scene for herself. Put it in context, along with all the other crap she's had to put into context in the last twenty-four hours.

Is it because she's not prepared to give in to the idea that this is her life now? Sidelined in the corner, one of the embarrassing ones. It might be true, but she doesn't have to accept it.

Josie approaches the scene, which is still taped off. Of course it is.

This isn't an area where people would normally stroll past. There are very few open businesses – everything's in the middle of being knocked down or built up. There are a surprising number of people here, though. She wants to hate these nosy bastards, but she has to acknowledge that a detective is the nosiest person of all. These idiots aren't even being paid for it. Some linger, definitely watching, others walk past as if this area is now a must-see for anyone who's out and about on their lunchbreak.

Josie approaches the taped-off area. If she goes inside, her presence here will be logged. She does it anyway.

The body has been removed, but Josie just wants a feel for the place. She heads inside and looks at the large rectangle of real estate that the fence is protecting. She gets it now. Gets why Esther described it the way she did. It's a box. The fence is high and very solid. It even has a lid. Whether the metal girders that stretch over the roof area are being added or removed, Josie has no idea. Only one way in and out. She looks around. There's no way she's going to spot a gun that everyone else has overlooked, but that won't stop her looking. There are places here that might conceal a weapon, but not many.

Once she's taken a small tour of the building site, Josie exits the crime scene and crosses the road, heading back towards civilisation. As she walks up the thin alleyway by the Novotel, she wonders what made Esther come down here in the dark. It's claustrophobic in broad daylight – it would be ten times worse at night.

Who steps away from their job, and the security of their

workplace, to follow a suspicious man into an alleyway? Josie can't help thinking that it's not a normal response.

17

There's nobody on the door of the Meridian Casino as Josie approaches. Door security is just for the night time and it's not yet six. There's a reception desk where she shows her warrant card.

"Is Esther Butler in?"

The woman on the desk gives a nod and picks up an internal phone.

Moments later, Esther appears and gives Josie a long appraising look.

Her face is tight. Composed, but it looks as though it's taking some effort.

She beckons Josie over. "You'd better come through."

Esther leads them across the downstairs gaming floor and through into a small office space. Josie can't be sure if it's a meeting room, because the room is cluttered with assorted detritus. A box of paper towels, a shelf of ice buckets, a tool box. There's a table in the middle with chairs. Esther waves a hand for Josie to sit down but doesn't sit herself.

"What the hell was that I just saw on the TV?" Esther demands.

Josie gives her a quizzical look. "The press conference?"

"Damn sodding right. You lot are making out that I've invented the whole gun thing."

"Now, I'm not sure that—"

"How do you think that makes me look?"

Josie opens her mouth to speak, but Esther's not done.

"How do you think that makes me *feel*?"

Josie nods slowly. She can do empathy if she concentrates, even with the remnants of her hangover. She makes deliberate eye contact with Esther. "Those press conference statements that they make. They have to give themselves wiggle room."

It would be easy to expand on that idea. Lean into the corporate blather that they spew, but this is not the time for Josie to air her personal bugbears.

"There's wiggle room and then there's making me look like a fucking idiot, Detective...?"

"Kaminski. Josie Kaminski."

"I know! I remember. I have a good memory."

"I understand this might not be ideal," says Josie with a nod. She can tell by Esther's contemptuous expression that empty platitudes are not working. She needs to switch things up. "Tell me, how long have you worked here?"

Esther's surprised, even wrong-footed by the question. "Years."

"That long?"

"The casino's a funny environment. Doesn't suit everyone, but it suits me."

Josie would love to feel like that about her job. As if she fits. She feels strongly that being a detective is a perfect fit for her. It's other people who seem to have a problem with the idea.

She tries to remind herself why she came here. "I just came from the site of the shooting. Have you been over there at all?"

Esther shakes her head. "Why would I do that?"

Josie has no good answer, or at least nothing that isn't some variation on the idea that Esther might want to revise her story after seeing things in the cold light of day.

She doesn't look like she's the kind of woman who backs down from a situation.

The phone on Esther's belt buzzes. She answers. The phone is loud enough for Josie to hear.

"Visitor for you," says the receptionist.

"What? More police?" says Esther.

"No, it's someone else. Says she just wants a quote."

Esther doesn't quite jolt but she's instantly on guard. "Is it a journalist? Tell me you haven't let a journalist in here?"

18

I wait for Georgette on reception to tell me that she really hasn't let a journalist come wandering in. The silence on the phone tells me that a journalist is now roaming the casino. I need to nip this in the bud.

"On my way."

I glare at the detective, Josie Kaminski. Last night in the interview she looked as rough as a badger's arse. Today, she seems to have tidied herself up a bit. A bit.

"Did you have any actual questions to ask, information to give?" I ask.

"Just checking in," she says and passes me a business card. "But if anything new occurs to you..."

Anything new? The press conference implied there was no gun. Now this woman wants me to play along with that narrative?

I drop the card on the table, escort her as quickly as possibly back to reception and then, glaring daggers at Georgette on reception, ask her where the journalist is.

I find the woman snapping photos of the roulette table.

She's impossibly young. I wonder if she's even old enough to be in here.

Journalists. Anyone with a phone and an internet connection thinks they can be a journalist these days.

"Excuse me," I say. "Can you stop that? I can't let you photograph customers."

"No worries." She beams at me. "Super conscious of privacy issues, yeah?"

I recognise the distraction of an empty question. "Can we go back to that photo you just took? I want to see you delete it, please."

She makes a show of deleting it with no protest, which makes me think that she probably has more.

"Hey, listen..." she says.

I can't tell if she has a slight Aussie accent, or whether she just has that habit of making everything sound like a question.

I give her an attentive, listening face, but I am not yet ready to give this woman the time of day.

"I was wondering if I could just ask you a few questions. You were there when that guy got shot, yeah?"

"Who do you even work for?"

"Self-employed." She pulls out a business card. I don't reach for it, but I can see that it says Kayleigh Chandler and that she's a freelance journalist.

"And where do your stories appear, Kayleigh?"

"All over. General interest stories. Local, national, international. You want my portfolio?"

"No." I'm not even sure why I asked.

A phone and a business card and she thinks she's Lois Lane.

"I don't want to talk to you," I say.

"Esther." She uses my name like one of those people who believe it's charming. Maybe it is charming, but I'm not in the mood. "People are curious about you. Your face is very much all over this thing. Don't you want to tell your side of the story?"

"No."

"Letting the world know your story is very valuable."

"I said no."

She smiles broadly as if I haven't just refused. "No worries at all. Just remember me as a friendly face when you do want to share, yeah?"

The business card's there again. I take it against my better judgement and slip it into a pocket. I show her out.

Is this more stuff I need to deal with now? My face being all over this thing? Kieran, who says there is no such thing as bad publicity, would wet himself if I told him a journalist had come sniffing round.

19

I get home around seven. I can tell that my body is overwhelmed with fatigue at this point, but I have a buzzing core of angry energy that's not letting me give into it.

Kieran's shifting boxes around when I let myself in. I can't even tell if they're new ones. It's like those crazy cat ladies who don't know how many cats they have. There's a point where the boxes in this house are uncountable and we passed it some time ago.

"You got a mention on the TV," he says.

"Not by name?"

"Well no. But everyone knows it's you. You're famous."

I don't want to be famous. Not like this. "Who's everyone?"

Kieran shrugs.

I get a tiny flicker of suspicion about what he means. "Did you post about this online?"

He licks his lips. "It's been shared so many times, Babe!

This could be really big for us. Raise the profile of RBuzz, you know?"

His face reflects real excitement. He genuinely thinks that me being the centre of attention for getting someone shot is going to sell energy drinks.

My anger levels are already so high that I don't know how to process this new affront. What he's done is wrong on so many levels.

"Did you actually listen to what the police said?"

It's not the right question, but it's the one that's at the top of the deck. The one that my mind has been turning over for the past few hours.

The reported firearm has not yet been recovered from the scene. We continue to search the area extensively, including adjacent buildings and public spaces...

"Yeah," says Kieran. "They said they're investigating."

I shake my head. "You need to listen again. They're stepping right back from the idea that he had a gun at all. They're making out that I invented it."

"Nah, Babe. They didn't say that. Not exactly."

I catch his tone and narrow my eyes. He thinks the same thing.

I turn away.

"I'm putting the kettle on."

I make a cup of tea and take it upstairs, so I don't have to look at Kieran. I lie on the bed and try to clear my mind.

I wake up and it's totally dark. I check the time and it's just after one in the morning. I'm fully clothed, lying on top of the duvet, while Kieran snores beneath the covers. Everything is twisted around my waist, as if I have turned over countless times.

I give up trying to get comfy and I get out of bed. My mind's so busy that I can't imagine sleeping.

Instead of getting undressed and trying to sleep, I drift around the house like a ghost. Outside, the sky is clear, and I can see stars. It's both comforting and terrifying, as if the pressure of the universe is all on me.

The world knows who I am, because Kieran's told them.

The police don't believe that the guy had a gun, they think I invented it.

Most pressing of all, out there, under that same sky, there's one less person in the world because I told the police he had a weapon.

20

A new day and I'm back on shift at the casino. The mood-boosting effect of this morning's run has worn off and I'm afraid that the exhaustion of the past couple of days is about to catch up with me.

I've barely made my first cuppa when I get the call that a police officer's here to see me. That bloody Josie Kaminiski. Does she think she's got some sort of recurring role in my life?

But the copper at reception is one I've not met before. He hands me his warrant card.

His face is one of those weaselly ones, all sharp features, but not in a clever way. The worst thing you can do with one of those faces is grow a bum-fluff moustache, so obviously he has.

"Detective Sergeant Beaches. Mind if I ask you a few questions?"

"Sure. What happened to Kaminski?"

He pulls a face. "Kaminski?"

"Woman detective. You can't have many Kaminskis."

His expression is very peculiar, like none of this computes. Then he pushes that expression aside and puts on his lying face. It's not a good lying face.

"Oh, Kaminski. Sure. No, she won't be working the case. She was just filling in before."

"Uh-huh."

I lead him through to the meeting room.

He sits down, spreading himself comfortably, arms on the table, legs stretching out. I watch him, wondering why he feels the need to make himself bigger than he really is.

"I'd like to show you a picture if that's all right, Esther," he says.

I nod and he puts a photo on the table in front of me. It's a man in his late twenties or early thirties. He has intense eyes and a lean face. It takes me a moment or two to realise it's Low-rent Ryan, the man they shot. I never saw his face this clearly, but it's him, I'm sure.

"Oh." It's all I can muster.

"You recognise him?" asks Beaches.

"He's the man I saw." I point over towards the front of the casino, as if we can both see through the walls.

I turn back to the photo with interest. He's alive in this picture, so they know who he is.

"Do you know him?" Beaches asks.

"No. Never seen him before."

"Are you sure?"

"I don't know him. I'm good with faces. Not seen him before."

"His name is Seamus Wollacott," he says.

He's watching me intently as he says it. The more intently he watches me the more his eyes look like little shiny buttons. He's expecting a reaction from me.

"As I say, I don't know him."

Beaches nods and picks up the photo. "Thank you. Just had to ask."

He stands. He runs thumb and forefinger over his moustache and then round the side of his mouth so they meet together under his bottom lip.

"We'd like to talk to everyone who was here that night," he says.

I shake my head. "What do you mean?"

"Everyone." He tries a smile. "You had staff on duty here. You had regular customers in, I'm guessing. We'd like to talk to them."

"Well, that's not happening."

It was bad enough having a pubescent journalist wandering around the gaming tables. I'm not having the fuzz harassing our customers with their "*Where were you on the night in question*?" accusations.

"I'm sure you would like to have some people corroborate your version of events," he says.

The weaselly bastard. He might as well have called me a liar to my face.

"I would need to check with management about talking to the staff."

"I thought you were management, Esther."

"*Upper* management. There's no way in heaven and earth that we're going to share our customers' details with you."

He tuts. "Shame. Well, you get onto your bosses and the sooner we can talk to your colleagues the sooner we can get this story straight."

21

Gabe isn't in his office. I send him a message. *The police want to talk to all staff who were on duty last night.*

He sends back a thumbs up, nothing more. And then an hour later he's in, sweeping past me with a "My office in five minutes" instruction before going straight to the lift.

I go up. He's at his desk. He's parked at it like he doesn't intend to stay.

"Shut the door, Esther."

I do as I'm told.

He flexes his big fingers. "I love you, Esther. You know that."

I nod enough.

"We are all a big family here. We love each other."

I've heard the speech before but I'm not going to stop it by pointing that out.

"We are a family and we look out for each other. When Baz overstepped the mark with that lairy punter, we rallied round him, didn't we?"

When Gabe speaks of rallying around Baz he means we told barefaced lies to the police and then the court, so that Baz was spared a conviction for Actual Bodily Harm.

"Didn't we?" says Gabe.

"We look out for each other," I say dutifully.

"We value loyalty. We help smooth out the bumps in each other's journeys through life."

"Yes, Gabe."

"And you went above and beyond the night before last. You saw a woman in trouble and you set out to help her."

I don't respond. There's a 'but' coming.

"But we don't let the police poke their noses into our business."

"You know you and I agree on this, Gabe," I say. "I told him—"

"Told who?"

"The copper."

"Name?"

"Beaches. DS Beaches."

Gabe writes it down like it's the start of a to-do list. "What did you tell him?"

"I said that he's not going to talk to the staff. He wanted to question the punters too."

"No fucking way they're doing that."

"That's what I told him," I say.

"That's just taking a fucking liberty," he says. "The bloody cheek."

"Right. As I say. You and me are on the same page."

Gabe seethes, his teeth bared. "Not fucking happening," he mutters. "This is a respectable leisure venue. Leave it with me."

I hesitate. "Leave it how?"

"Well, they're not coming in here to question them for one thing. We'll arrange for some of the boys and girls to go over to the station and give statements."

"Not everyone though?"

"Hell, no. Esther. Some of our employees – God love 'em – they've not got the brains they were born with. A couple of them, you put them in a room with a copper and they'll talk themselves into a prison sentence in the first five minutes."

I know what he means. Some people do not rub along well with the police. Besides, casino work isn't your regular nine-to-five Tesco supermarket type job. It's a whole range of special skillsets. It's a fluid job market. People come, people go. And sometimes they've come from a long way away. Leicester is the most culturally diverse city in the country and that goes doubly so for the casinos. No matter what they say, the police have their prejudices and casino people tick a lot of their boxes.

"We handpick some staff to speak to the police then," I say.

"I'll sort it with the police. You pick the people and give them the script."

"There's no script," I say tersely. "Only the truth. If they've got nothing to say then we're not putting words in their mouths."

He tilts his head and spreads his hands. So be it.

If I didn't know better, my own boss is starting to doubt my version of events.

22

Rob stands with Walker in their corner, the two of them leaning close together so that they can speak in low tones.

Fifteen minutes ago, Dean Beaches came back in and went straight into Scabbard's office.

Ten minutes ago, Scabbard came out and yelled for Josie to come in.

Kaminski's in there now, her face a mask of barely-suppressed rage and contempt while Scabbard is delivering an extended monologue that the two men outside cannot hear.

"How did you get on with Kaminski yesterday?" Walker asks conversationally.

Rob sits back down. "I think it's fair to say that she's moved through denial into anger."

Walker grimaces.

Both of them understand that it's a shock to the system being relegated to the Duncans, even Walker who was a founding member.

"Hey. Any transition is a good thing," says Rob. "Getting stuck is what we want to avoid."

There's a low divider at the back of their desks. Rob has a variety of pictures and memos stuck on there with little magnets.

Walker nods to one of them, which is a picture, showing the five stages of grief.

Denial, anger, bargaining, depression, acceptance

Each word sits within a circle.

Since his breakup with Veronica, Rob's become familiar with the language of therapy.

He leans over and moves a little magnet from the first circle to the second. "Anger. There we go."

"We're calling this progress, are we?" asks Walker, with a wave over to Scabbard's office.

"If our girl's getting stuck anywhere in the grief cycle, I suspect it might be anger," Rob admits. "Seems like her natural habitat. Any idea what all that's about?"

"I reckon she's been poking her nose into the shooting case. Saw her name on the logs for the crime scene. Guv will've seen it too," said Walker.

Rob raises his eyebrows. "Yeah. That'll do it." He pauses. "Apart from the fact that it's more interesting than stolen combine harvesters, what's yanking her chain? Any idea?"

Walker sits at his desk and pulls up the record of the interview they were in. "Esther Butler, the witness. Kaminski was pretty hard on her, but the account that she gave doesn't match the evidence. Says she saw a gun, but there's no sign of it anywhere."

Rob's wearing his new glasses. He thinks they make him look thoughtful. Intellectual almost. He pushes them up his nose in thought. "Unreliable witnesses – tale as old as time, aren't they?"

"They are. It's true."

Walker pulls a slight face. He has that polite older guy thing where he doesn't want to directly disagree. Rob wants to learn how to do this, so he's watching carefully. Rob would have cut across the conversation with a blunt statement by now.

"Kaminski's full of angry bluster," says Walker. "I almost called it youthful energy."

"Everyone's young compared to you." Rob smiles to show it's a joke.

"I do think she has a good instinct though," says Walker.

"Spidey sense," says Rob, his fingers wiggling.

Walker continues, a finger stabbing the words on the screen. "Esther Butler seems very switched-on. An observer of people. And she was very certain about this." He looks up at the ceiling for a moment. "Are you aware of the studies that have proven how expertise improves perception?"

"Say what?" Rob sits up. If there's one thing that gets his goat, it's when people switch on that fucking intellectual thing, try to make him look dumb.

Walker knows this. He makes a conciliatory gesture. "I'll send you a link. You can read all the detail. The gist of it is that trained people are better at spotting anomalies, subtle threats. Something fishy goes down, your regular person either does a double take or doesn't even notice. But trained people – Police officers, airport security..."

"Casino floor managers." Rob gets the point. He is mildly excited to read the research. He's self-aware enough to recognise that he's actually mildly excited to be the sort of person who reads research papers.

"Yeah." Walker points a finger over at Kaminski. "And at some level, our new recruit reckons there's something not right in all this."

23

Josie knows that she's lost control of her face, but she doesn't care. Scabbard deserves her bitchiest expression.

"But how do you think it looks, Josie, huh?" he says. "I send one of my team in to speak to the key bloody witness only to be told that you were there earlier, asking the same questions?"

"I was in the area. I thought I'd check in with her."

It seemed like a weak defence when she first said it. This is the third time now, and he's not buying it.

"It makes us look unprofessional. That's what it does."

"I was the officer who first interviewed Esther Butler when she came in."

"I don't fucking care. I don't give a flying pig's arse. You have no role in this." He reaches out and lifts up a sheet of paper. "And then I see your name on the log sheets for the actual bloody crime scene. What the hell?"

"In the area," she says.

"Jesus."

"I mean, it's really interesting. Esther's story is so consistent when it comes to the gun, and yet they've not found it which—"

He slams his palm down on the desk.

"None! Of! Your! Bloody! Business! You're on Operation Chainlink and no amount of sulking is going to change that."

Josie wonders who gave the rural crime operation that name. It even manages to sound like a punishment. Like a fence for the weird prison that's the team she's now in. Duncan jail.

"We've got a lot of eyes on this," Scabbard fumes. "We have to be squeaky clean. Any idea of the shitstorm that's going to rain down on this department if we have a rogue DC going where she fucking pleases?"

"A detective doing detective work, you mean?" Josie knows she should keep her big mouth shut. It's so hard sometimes. She looks away.

"Out!" yells Scabbard. "I've had it up to here with you. I'll talk to DS Joseph about putting you on a reflective practice review."

Josie grinds her teeth in fury and leaves the office.

She plonks herself at the desk across from Walker and Rob, screwing her eyes up so she doesn't need to engage with them. She's not ready for human interaction until she can bring herself back down from her current orbit of red hot anger and frustration.

It's not so much that she's fucked up and been punished for it, although that's shitty. It's more that she's fallen even further into the crevasse of hopelessness that she'd always assumed was not for her.

"Cup of tea?"

Walker puts a steaming mug on her desk and steps back round with drinks for him and Rob.

"You know that study you're sending over?" Rob says to Walker. "Send it to Kaminski too. I reckon she's gonna find it interesting."

She opens her eyes and glares at the two of them, daring them to offer the slightest hint of mockery. She's ready to pull someone's head off.

She sees nothing there but mild concern and perhaps some curiosity. Is this what the Duncans are? The soft squad?

24

I've worked casino shifts for a long time. I have a high tolerance for adjusting my hours. I sometimes think of it like shock absorbers. Some people feel every bump if their routine changes. People like me, we coast over it. Today though, I feel fragile and exhausted. I don't dare add up the amount of sleep I've had since I went chasing after the guy with the gun, because it's not enough to function.

By the time morning rolls around, I'm dressed and fed and I know I look like a person, but inside I feel hollowed-out. I make the mistake of opening the laptop. I look to see if there's any news from the police, but no, it's still just that crappy press conference. Then I look at Kieran's post. He's included a picture of me drinking fucking RBuzz. What a star. The text talks about me like I'm an avenging angel powered by an energy drink. All I see in that picture is someone who's been persuaded to chug down that syrupy muck against her better judgement.

Facebook shares are in triple figures. I can't even see

where they've all gone. Into private groups probably, which makes me feel queasy.

Like an idiot, I look at some of the comments on Kieran's post. Some are supportive, and talk about how brave I was to go and help. Many of these people have seen the press conference and have picked up on that sliver of doubt. I get called a Karen at work quite often. I take it in my stride when it's some lairy fool who's had too much to drink and needs dealing with. It's something else when some keyboard warrior's passing judgement on me from afar.

Has Kieran put any of these people in their place?

Has he fuck.

I see his comments, but they're all about him and his energy drinks.

He comes into the kitchen. He's chirpy, like a person who's had a good night's sleep.

"Morning, morning!" he says. "It's proper blown up, hasn't it? Absolute gold." He nods to the picture of me on the screen.

I want to articulate the enormity of how much this is not gold. Not for me.

"People don't believe me."

"What people?" he says, grabbing the Weetabix from the cupboard.

"*These* people." I wave at the screen. "The police. You."

"Well, first of all, those are not real people are they? Online is online." He waves a dismissive hand at the laptop.

"Course they're fucking real," I growl.

"They're not here. They don't matter."

I don't bother pointing out that they matter to him. If they buy his energy drink, they matter.

"The police are just working the case. Innocent until proven guilty, eh?"

He's chewing Weetabix while looking as if he just solved a complex puzzle for me and I should be grateful.

"And you? What about you?" I ask.

"Me?" he makes a magnanimous gesture. "Keeping an open mind, aren't I?"

He doesn't even know what he just said. He's saying that he's waiting for proof. What he just said is that he doesn't believe me.

25

Walker sends a WhatsApp to Oscar. The messages have been going backwards and forwards all morning. Oscar has said he would do the dishwasher every day. It's also that time of week when Walker sends his son his pocket money – if it's still called pocket money when your son is twenty years old. Walker giving Oscar the money is not dependent on him doing the dishwasher. That's not part of the deal. Back and forth the messages go, Walker trying to suggest that if Oscar wants paying then he needs to do the dishwasher, without actually saying so.

It's a dainty dance and currently Oscar has either not picked up the hints or is just ignoring them.

Dean Beaches pokes his head round the filing cabinet wall into the land of the Duncans.

"Where's Miss Marple and Pretty Woman?"

Walker looks round at the otherwise empty space and then at Beaches.

"In that analogy, which one is Miss Marple and which—?"

Beaches glares at him, pale eyebrows raised.

"They're out. Doing farm checks around Newton Linford."

Beaches, irritated, bares his teeth in an unattractive expression. "You'll have to do."

"I live to serve," Walker says with a smile.

"We've got more than a dozen people coming in from the casino to give statements about their activities on the night of the shooting. We need people to do the donkey work of initial statements so that *we* can then select those for further interview."

Beaches relishes the words 'donkey work' and leans on the 'we' too much.

"Happy to help," says Walker.

"I wasn't asking."

Walker smiles. He finds that, in life, it's best to treat arseholes with kindness and smiles, not least because it annoys the living hell out of them.

"We've got all of them in reception," says Beaches as they walk down the stairs.

"They just ... sent them over?"

"We asked. They delivered," says Beaches. "The manager, that Esther Butler, was being a prick about it all, so Scabbard chatted to her boss and now we're doing the interviews; plus we're also going to use their lobby area for part of the crime scene recreation they're filming at the end of the week."

"That's good," says Walker honestly.

He looks at the list of people to be interviewed. Scabbard's got other officers on the task too. Greg Scabbard and Neelam Gill have maybe a dozen officers attached to the investigation between them. They're spread thin over crime scene, forensics, questioning family and following up leads. It's no surprise that Scabbard has had to reach into the back of his kitchen drawer to do some of the work.

Walker doesn't mind. Variety is the spice of life and all that.

He looks at the list of people to be interviewed then looks round reception. "Baz!"

The big guy looks up, rolls of neck fat shifting.

"Shall we get you into an interview room and you can tell me everything?" says Walker.

Baz Obi stands. The whole row of joined seats wobbles.

26

At home, Kieran's cheerful. Annoyingly cheerful.

He keeps checking his phone. He's convinced that there's a massive order for his energy drinks coming his way because of the viral content he's created. He's probably wrong, but I can use that optimism.

"You know, it might be an idea to get your stock in order," I say to him.

"All up here," he says tapping the side of his head.

"You know the expiry date of every box?" I ask. "Be a terrible thing to ship something that's not fit for purpose if you get your big break."

His face falls.

"If you wanted to be prepared, you'd organise everything so you can access stuff in date order."

He nods. "Be worth a couple of hours. You're right."

It's a leadership skill that they don't teach on any management training. Matching someone's personality and mood with a task that needs to be done.

With a few more nudges to get the boxes piled up in areas

where they'll be out from under my feet, I leave him happily lumbering round the house, shifting boxes.

I meet Jeety for a run. She's dressed in those eye-popping colours that she loves. It's like she saw a safety video: *Be safe, be seen*. Instead of a fluorescent armband, she's made it her whole personality.

It's drizzling slightly, but both of us like to run when it's like that.

"We're out," she declares, her face to the sky. "Bring it on, weather."

"I need the boost," I growl, as we head out.

"Yeah. You've got it all going on," she says. "Want to talk about it?"

I think on this. "Can I just vent? I need to vent."

"Sure. Get it all out."

My feet hitting the pavement helps with that release. "They had a press conference."

"I saw."

"Made it sound as if I invented the gun. And the woman."

Jeety shakes her head, makes eye contact, but leaves me to continue.

"Then I get home and find that Kieran's put up some social media bullshit telling the world that it was me who made the call. He thinks it's going to sell his energy drinks."

I concentrate on my feet for a while. I watch the pavement as my feet hit.

Jeety looks as if she owns the whole pavement. Her stride is confident; her feet connect firmly each time she lands on her neon-coloured Nikes.

Me though, I get the feeling that I might pass right through the paving slabs. Am I spaced out through lack of sleep? Probably. Still though, I have the weirdest feeling that

I'm taking up less room than I did yesterday. I'm clearly not. I'm still the same size. I just don't feel the same size. It's like my place in the world has shrunk.

"And what do you think?" she asks after a few minutes.

"I think I liked it better when I was anonymous. He's even put up a picture of me drinking RBuzz while I'm clearly trying to pretend it's prosecco."

We both laugh at that. The endorphins are coming. Boy, do I need them.

27

Walker pulls out a seat for Baz in the interview suite.

"Thank you, Mr Walker, sir," says Baz.

From regular members of the public, that kind of deference sounds insincere, but Baz Obi has done time inside and it's hardwired into him now.

Walker notices that the whites of Baz's eyes are more yellow than white. Walker wonders if he's noticed and has seen a doctor. Could be something badly amiss with his liver. Or is it gallbladder?

Anyway.

Walker looks at the set of questions Beaches has given him to ask all the potential witnesses. He puts his hands over it.

"So, you're aware of the night of the shooting, Baz?"

Baz nods.

"Why don't you tell me all about it?"

And Baz does. After ten minutes, Walker decides the Baz is no raconteur, although if he's got any young kids in his family he could use that monotone voice to send them off to the land of nod. But Walker lets him finish anyway.

"Wow. So you saw the guy?" says Walker.

"I did."

Walker shows him the file picture of Seamus Wollacott. "This him, right?"

"That's him. I don't know if I saw him clearly, but that's him."

"You're sure?"

"Uh-huh."

"Have you seen him at the casino before?"

Baz shakes his head.

"Name's Seamus Wollacott. You know the name?"

"No, sir."

"And you also saw the woman with him?"

"I did."

"You see her clearly?"

"She had long dark hair and a baseball cap. Like a fashion one. With sequins on it, I think."

"Coat?"

"It had a pattern. Spotty, like a cheetah."

Leopard pattern, cheetah pattern. Walker isn't about to dip into the distinction between the two. He's not even sure what the difference is.

"Like a fur coat," says Walker.

"Not actual fur," says Baz.

"No. And you saw them ... talking? Walking?"

"Esther reckoned they were arguing."

"Uh-huh. That's what Esther said? What did you see?"

"She pointed them out to me. I dunno. They looked like regular people. But she immediately pointed out that, like, the guy had a gun under his gilet jacket thing."

"Right. So she pointed out to you that he had a gun. Did you see the gun yourself?"

"Nah. It was like under his jacket in the top of his trousers."

"So, did she even see it?"

He mushes his lips to moisten them. "She said she could tell. I dunno. I knew what she was saying."

"But you didn't see it?"

"No, sir."

Walker nods and looks further down the questions. "So tell me what happened next."

28

I wasn't expecting the crap from the shooting to invade my professional life.

It starts like so many of the conversations I have at work. Someone who's had a bit too much to drink getting gobby with the staff. We have zero tolerance for that, so as soon as I see Orla give me a kissy signal from the bar, I go over to have a word with the punter.

"Sir, can I please ask you to step away from the bar?"

We always treat people with as much respect as we can. This guy's wobbling as he turns to face me. He's definitely had too much to drink.

"Oh, it's you!" he says.

I don't know this guy.

He has a strange expression in his eyes. Malice? Glee? I don't know him.

"I'm going to need you to make your way home now, sir," I say. "Can I call you a cab?"

"Ooh, you gonna get me shot are you?" he giggles as he stumbles across the carpet.

"I'm sorry?" I say, hearing my voice turn hard.

"Don't you follow me, bitch," he says.

Now he turns back towards me and his face has an oily sheen of sweat and contempt. I feel nauseous as he takes a step and closes the gap between us. Normally I can take command of these situations, assert myself with calm authority, but that's not happening.

"Oi, oi!" Baz appears.

I'm glad to see him. Baz is just what I need right now. He steers the man into the lift and downstairs. With a bit of luck he'll be on his way home in a cab inside five minutes.

"Hey." Orla leans across the bar. "You all right?"

I give her a nod, but she can see what's going on; she's no fool. I have less authority with punters. They think that I'm an unreliable flake who got a man shot by imagining he had a gun.

I take a seat for a few minutes, pretend I'm overseeing Camelia at the roulette pit.

It doesn't take Baz long to reappear. "All dealt with, boss."

"Thanks, Baz."

I'm grateful to Baz, but I don't like being in the position where I need him to rescue me.

That feeling of being diminished creeps over me again. I used to picture myself like one of those lizards that can make itself look big by lifting up its neck frill when it needs to assert itself. I'm small, but I can appear big. But that's not working. I'm filled with the creeping idea that there's less of me than there was before. It's horrifying. What if it keeps happening?

I realise that Baz is still standing there.

"Yes?"

"We had to go talk to the cops today."

"I heard." Gabe has also agreed with the police that they can film some sort of crime re-enactment from outside the casino. I'm not best pleased.

Baz seems excited by his chat with the police. Perhaps it's a small glimpse of celebrity, being spoke to by the detectives. He'll be telling his mates at his mum's restaurant. I'd have thought he'd had enough of the police. He's had more than enough run-ins with them over the years to be excited about chatting with the feds.

No, that's not it. He has something to say.

"The guy they shot. The police have a picture, and a name," he says.

"Yes. They showed me."

"You said you didn't know him, boss." He gives me a lop-sided grin. "It's fine. I didn't drop you in it."

"Sorry, what?" Baz isn't making any sense.

"You saying that you didn't know him," he says.

"Cos I don't."

"You do. I never told 'em though."

"Baz, what are you on about? I don't know that man."

"Boss?" His big face creases with confusion. "You do. Seamus Wollacott."

The name is utterly meaningless to me. I'm shaking my head.

"Lisa McNally."

Lisa used to be a cleaner at Meridian. Ages ago.

"Lisa McNally and the shitbag," says Baz. "That guy's the shitbag."

A cold shiver of fear runs through me.

Oh fuck.

I do.

I do know Seamus Wollacott. I absolutely do know the dead man.

"Don't worry, boss," says Baz and tries a wink. "I didn't tell no one."

29

Josie gets out of Rob's car and inspects the soles of her shoes. Every time they head out to the countryside, they seem to bring the smell back with them.

Josie wouldn't specifically call herself a city girl. Leicester's a fair-sized city, maybe tenth biggest in the country, but not big enough for someone to really feel like a city girl. She's been out into the countryside before. She's done walks, sure. But she doesn't think she's cut out to actually work in the countryside. Especially if it means bringing the countryside experience back to the office on your shoes.

As she closes the car door, she sees Greg Scabbard standing by his car.

"Sarge," she says to Rob. "All right if I catch up with you?"

Rob sees Scabbard. "Er, sure. I'll put the kettle on. We need to write up the logs."

As Rob heads one way, Josie makes straight for Scabbard.

This is a bad idea. It's definitely a bad idea. But part of her strongly feels that if she can just talk to him, outside of the office environment. then maybe she can get past the hierarchical bullshit and whatever else is going on.

They might have been drunk that night, but they talked to each other like human beings. Such things were possible.

"Sir," she says.

Greg turns and he doesn't exactly look pleased to see her.

"Can I talk to you a minute, sir?" she says.

He wants to say no but he doesn't. "A minute. I'm due in a meeting with Silver Command for updates on the Wollacott shooting."

She nods. "I want to talk about..." She pauses, rephrases. "Have I done something to offend you, sir?"

He laughs, spontaneously, and then rolls his eyes. "I thought this was going to be a proper conversation."

She doesn't respond to that. She gives half a beat of silence.

"I work hard. I have passion for the job. I'm actually good at what I do. I'm a good detective."

"Look, you're on Operation Chainlink—"

"It's not just about that, sir," she says, knowing the danger of interrupting him. "I want to get on in this career. I have ambitions. I'm a good member of your team. I don't slack. I don't fiddle the overtime. I'm not a moron like certain people. I'm a good detective."

"Yes?" he says.

"And then something happened between us." She makes a back and forth gesture that somehow tries to encompass the drunken fumbling, the attempted extra-marital sex (at least on his side) and the whole messiness of human interactions. "And you immediately drop me with the Duncans who, by the way, are really nice guys. I feel like I'm being punished when I should be given responsibilities within the most critical investigations you've got going."

He nods silently. He doesn't bawl her out. He doesn't leap in with a snide and hurtful remark.

"Is that it?" he says. "Are you finished?"

"Yes. I think so."

He makes a half-move to just walk away but stops. "Do you want to know what the problem is, DC Kaminski? Do you want to know what the issue is with you?"

This can only go badly but she needs to know. "Yes, sir."

"I would say that you're too impulsive, but that's not even half of it. I want to say that you're too eager, but that just sounds like a good thing."

"I am eager."

He exhales noisily out through his nose. "You open your mouth when you shouldn't, Josie. That's number one. You open your mouth when you shouldn't and when you do you speak too loudly. You actually have the fucking temerity to say what you think when no one gives a rat's arse what you think. That's number one."

"I see."

"You think you're important when you're not. You actually think you matter. All fur coat and no knickers. I may have morons on my team but they know their place. They're not too fucking big for their boots."

"I don't—"

"And then – this is the kicker – you think you can come onto me, a married man, and ensnare me."

"Ensnare...?"

"Ensnare. You think it will help you seize those career opportunities you're convinced you deserve. It's underhand. It's devious. It's pathetic."

He flings a hand at the towering brick police building.

"You're with the Duncans for good reason. You may think they're nice guys. But you should ask them, ask them both, what happens to supposedly good detectives when they get ideas above their station. You ask why DS Joseph wears glasses he doesn't need and is erasing the tattoos on his body like he can literally erase who he is. You ask Walker how come an educated copper in his fifties has spent the last twenty years as a detective constable without a single hope of promotion."

He breathes deeply like he's just got a massive weight off his chest.

"Things happen for a reason, Josie." He makes to go again and stops once more. "But you do want to be part of the Wollacott shooting investigation?"

She's too shocked and will be enraged when she's stopped being shocked, but she nods. Because she does. She wants to be part of the investigation.

"Good," says Scabbard. "Cos it's a pickle. We've either got to find that bloody gun or prove Esther Butler acted maliciously. And actually I've just been talking to the media team and we need someone like you—" he looks her up and down "—as part of the team."

She doesn't know what that means and she's not sure she likes the sound of it.

But Scabbard has delivered his piece and walks off.

She goes inside and slinks up to the office.

"How's things?" says Rob.

"Apparently they need someone like me on the Wollacott investigation," she says. "The media team and Scabbard."

Rob nods. Josie can see from his face that this is likely to prove disappointing.

"Cool," he says eventually.

30

The dead man is Seamus Wollacott.

I know who Seamus Wollacott is.

I called the police and Seamus Wollacott is dead.

I called the police and a man who I knew – or at least knew of – is dead.

I sleep that night but I have some frightening dreams. Baz is there in my dreams, and he's somehow also Kieran. The weird Baz-Kieran hybrid knows every terrible thing about me and wants to tell the world. I spend my time trying to stop him, but I can't. It's exhausting.

I wake up feeling more shattered than ever.

When I meet Jeety for a run she sees my face and shakes her head. "More shit, my love?"

I nod. "This one's a doozy. Seriously."

Jeety's presence is reassuring because she's so sure of herself. She's solid and present in a way that I'm not really feeling. She's wearing her t-shirt that declares she's a *Running*

Wanker. It's in an acid green colour and she's paired it with her pink skintight leggings.

I wonder if there's a way I could ask her for help in taking up my space in the world again properly. I'm not even sure what that question might look like.

"Come on then. Spill," she says. "There's something on your mind."

"Yeah. I need to get my thoughts in order."

We establish our pace and it helps. The rhythmic sound of our feet, and our breathing. It's a metronome that helps to soothe the mad panic that's suffused my entire body for days now. Half a mile down the road, I'm ready to speak.

"Right. First I need to tell you about Lisa." I glance across at Jeety. "Did I ever mention a Lisa?"

"Not in a way that I can recall," she says. "Like, big drama stuff? No."

"Big drama?" I sigh. "It's more like entirely predictable drama that happens all the time. Lisa's a nice young woman who hooked up with an abusive narcissist."

She makes a show of baring her teeth. "Fine. Buckling in. I hate him already."

I don't know if that's the energy I want from her, given what I'm about to tell her.

"Lisa. Lisa McNally. She worked at the casino as a cleaner. She worked hard. She could have done much better than being a cleaner. I think she had a degree, actually."

"Okay. We're blaming narcissist guy for holding her back, are we?" Jeety arches an eyebrow.

"He brought her down, yeah. Brought her down in every sense. By the way, I never met him, so this was all second-hand from Lisa, but what she didn't tell me I could just see in her face, you know? This is the story."

"I get it," says Jeety.

"By the time I understood what was going on I could see her unravelling in front of my eyes. She started at the casino young, smart, full of life. But this guy, he wanted to control everything that she did."

"Fucker."

"Uh-huh. She couldn't go out socially without him. He didn't really like her coming to work, but presumably he did like the money."

"What about family?"

I shake my head. "I don't know what happened there, but she's estranged from her parents. She'd never even talk about them. Don't think they're local. I don't remember all the details. This was at least a couple of years ago."

Jeety grunts in time with her feet hitting the pavement. "Feel like I've heard this story before. Fuck's sake. So he had a perfect setup for controlling her life."

"Yep. She stopped wearing makeup to work. Said he was convinced that she was flirting with someone. Dressing up nice for strangers was the same as being unfaithful, according to him."

"Because we're not even allowed to look nice for ourselves."

"Exactly."

"Fucking unacceptable." Jeety spits at the roadside. She says that she wants to reclaim spitting. I still think it's a bit gross, to be honest, but I admire the idea.

"Anyway," I say, "that was how it really stood out when she did wear makeup. She only wore concealer, to hide bruises."

"How did I somehow know that's where this was going?"

"It took a really long time to get her to talk to me – I'm talking months and months. I'd always ask her how things were and she'd always tell me that everything was fine. Then one day I found her in the toilets." I shake my head at the memory. "He'd driven her into work. That was another of his things. She could have caught the bus, but no. He wanted to give her a lift. People thought he was so caring; but it wasn't care, it was control."

Jeety's staring at me now, waiting to see what's coming. I'm slightly concerned that she's going to trip over something on the pavement so I hurry on.

"She said that he'd got annoyed with her, just before they arrived at the casino. Something trivial about what she'd got planned for their evening meal. He backhanded her across her face. Still driving, didn't even look what he was doing, just slammed his hand into her face. Split her lip, and she sprayed blood down her clothes. She was in the toilets trying to clean up the worst of it."

"Fuck."

"She was sure he hadn't even noticed the blood. He was just talking about his curly fucking fries or whatever. She got out the car and all she could think was how to get cleaned up before people saw her like that. She was embarrassed rather than mad. That's how low she was."

We jog on for a few moments while I line up the rest of the story.

"Once she'd started to tell me stuff, it all came out. I wanted her to get away from him, but she was scared stiff of leaving him. Apparently the slap thing wasn't the worst thing he'd done, and she was convinced he'd really hurt her if she left him. Kill her even."

"Yeah, but that's only if he finds her."

"Totally. You know though, it's complicated when women get stuck like that. What seems like a simple and obvious solution is anything but."

"Oh, don't I know it."

I glance sideways at Jeety, wondering what her experience is. She wouldn't be the first powerful, confident woman who had a horrific backstory.

"I worked on her for a long time. Gave her leaflets, contacts. She'd act like I'd given her something toxic or illegal. Frightened to death that he'd find it."

I spend a few minutes thinking about how I can phrase the next part.

"I realised that if I was going to help her, I needed to step in."

"Step in?"

Jeety stops. Jeety never stops when we're out for a run. Her face is a great big question.

I stop, panting.

"I got the police onto him," I say.

"You told them about the...?"

"No. Not that. No. Thing is, the guy was not only an abusive shit but was also a wrong un. He was into drugs. He'd already had convictions and another would put him in prison."

"You phoned the police."

"An anonymous tip-off," I say. "It was enough. The police got over there and arrested him. Um, drugs possession with intent to supply. He had a serious quantity of drugs in his house."

"Jesus Christ, Esther. I knew I was right about coming

round yours when that zombie apocalypse hits. You had that girl's back. She got out from under him then?"

"She did. I haven't heard from her for a bit. I managed to convince her to go to a refuge in Coventry. She started over."

"Think I'd want to get a bit further than Cov, personally," she grimaces. "Seriously though. Well done."

We head off again and run on in silence for a few minutes. I can tell Jeety's processing.

"Wait a minute. You said that first you had to tell me about Lisa. You told me about Lisa. There's more, right?"

I nod. "Yep. Here's the thing. Lisa's other half? Her abuser? I never met him. I didn't even know his name. By the time Lisa and I really got talking about it, she was just calling him the 'shitbag'."

Jeety snorts.

"His name was Seamus Wollacott."

"Right?"

"That guy? The one the police shot. That was Seamus Wollacott."

Jeety stops dead again.

"Oh fuck," she says.

"Yeah, oh, fuck is about right."

"Well, good riddance," says Jeety and then I wait. Her face slowly changes. "Oh."

"Yeah, exactly," I say. "You said you hated him even when I just started to tell you the story. For months I had nothing but burning contempt for a man I'd never met. I hated him too."

"And then you called the police and they shot him."

I put my hands to the sides of my head, feel fingers running through tangled hair.

"I'm going out of my mind. Think how this'll look when the police find out."

She shakes her head. “If the police find out. There’s nothing to link you.”

“It was Baz on the casino door who pointed it out to me. He knows.”

“You think anyone else is going to work it out?”

I stare at the sky. I have no idea.

31

When Josie sees the blonde wig on the table she assumes it's a joke.

"You're the same height and build as Esther Butler," says Scabbard. "I said you'd want to help."

He might want to rub it in further, but DI Gill and a woman from the media team are in the office.

"We're going to film a recreation of the incident," says Gill. "Night time shoot. Esther. Wollacott. The supposed mystery woman that no one but Esther and the doorman ever saw. We might get it on local TV, maybe jog some memories."

"Social media is the more powerful tool these days," says the media team woman. "Facebook groups. Neighbourhood Watch. The High Cross Business Improvement District people."

Scabbard raises his eyebrows and looks at the wig. "You said you wanted to be involved."

Josie does want to be involved. She doesn't want to be a laughing stock in a stupid wig and whatever Esther was wearing that night. But she wants to help. If anyone but Scabbard was asking, she'd say yes without hesitation.

So she says yes.

Scabbard smiles like he's won a point. Josie doesn't give him the satisfaction of responding.

Her attitude improves when she sees what they're doing for preparation the following day.

DI Gill has booked a large conference room which is packed with officers. They're a mixture of investigative officers on the shooting and those roped in for the re-enactment. Gill stands in front of the screen.

"For the purpose of prep for the crime scene recreation, we have a copy of some of the AFO bodycam footage from the night in question."

Josie can't help but be intrigued. A chance for a closer look. Rob and Walker sit next to her. They've been roped in to play the roles of the AFOs. The real AFOs are effectively a million miles away, all currently removed from front-line duties while the IOPC investigation into their actions takes place.

"Right," says Gill. "Let's familiarise ourselves with the material, shall we?"

She spends thirty seconds trying to get the video files to come up on screen.

"Bourbon?" says Walker, leaning over and offering Josie an opened pack.

Josie reaches for a biscuit with a smile.

Rob points to the files on the screen. "File names. Force, date, officer ID and case number. Six different officers there."

"Seamus Wollacott was shot at twelve minutes past one," says Gill. "We will look at the minutes leading up to that. Fair warning. We will see the moment when the suspect is shot."

Gill runs the video. The opening minutes are footage of the AFOs riding in the back of a van. They are suited up in black. Two sergeants, four constables, each camera showing different views inside the armoured van.

The AFOs have holstered pistols: police-standard Glocks. Josie knows that much. Two sit with assault rifles. Josie's done basic pistol training but nothing further.

On screen, the van pulls up and the officers move out. Now, the videos arranged across the screen start to tell separate stories.

Gill pauses the footage as the officers approach Esther Butler.

"This is Esther Butler who called the incident in."

One of the cameras is close to Esther. The identification in the corner labels it as *Ferguson*.

Esther has her phone pressed to her ear and looks stunned by what's unfolding.

Gill lets it play.

"*Name?*" says Ferguson. He's Scottish, by the sound of it. Josie doesn't know him.

"Esther Butler," says Esther.

"You made the call. Where is the gunman now?"

Josie wonders if Ferguson talks like this all the time, barking at people, or does he just do it in this sort of situation?

On the screen, Esther points. *"In there. The woman got away. It's just him, I think."*

Ferguson gets another AFO to take Esther towards the van, and he moves towards the fenced-off area. Another, marked as Grigson, is directing the officers. He's got a cone of light in front of him, illuminating the way.

"Is that a regular head torch?" Rob asks, taking a bourbon from the pack.

"Reckon so," says Walker. "They'd break out the infrared if they wanted stealth, but that's not the case here. One of these might have thermal imaging equipment."

"Cool."

"There's lights on their weapons too," says Josie, pointing at the screen. Ferguson leads the way, his assault rifle in front.

One of the feeds makes them wince as a bright light shines directly into the camera lens for a good few seconds.

"It's like driving at night with some nutter who won't dip their headlights," said Rob.

"Poor etiquette," agrees Walker.

Far from the others, they see PC Pike help Esther into the back of the van.

Grigson's directing the team as they advance into the dark space. A man becomes visible, but he's hidden behind a pallet stacked with bags. He was spotted by one of the team and now they are all advancing towards him.

"Armed police! Show me your hands! Drop the weapon!" yells Grigson.

The man behind the pallet makes a small movement. At the point where he should simply raise his hands really, really carefully, he either stumbles, or reaches for something near his ankle. It's not easy to tell.

"Drop the weapon!" yells an officer, Jinks.

Ferguson fires.

And it's over at that point. The man behind the pallet, Seamus Wollacott, is propelled back and doesn't move.

Josie doesn't look away. She needs to see it all.

That's how a man dies. It's as simple as that.

32

Josie watches the screen where the firearms team still advances slowly, fanning out.

"Okoye," says Grigson. *"You and Ferguson will approach the subject. Check his condition. Everyone else, search the area. Find the weapon."*

Ferguson approaches Wollacott, and taps him firmly on the shoulder, and runs through a brief series of checks. Okoye comes up behind and stands over him.

"Oof!" Rob says. "Tough call, that."

"It was." Josie nods along. "And there was no gun."

"Does that make Ferguson shooting him unlawful?" says Walker.

For a second she thinks he's genuinely asking the question, but then picks up on the inflection. A teachable moment. She tries to remember the exact wording taught at policing college but doesn't quite recall.

"If no weapon is recovered, it doesn't automatically make the shooting unlawful. It's down to what the individual officer honestly thought was happening in the situation," she says.

"There is no legal requirement for an officer to seek permission before using lethal force," says Rob. "It's judged on necessity, proportionality, reasonableness and..."

"...Honest held belief," says Walker.

"Having our own little meeting over there?" Gill asks.

"Sorry, ma'am," Walker calls back to her. "Refreshing ourselves on section three of the Criminal Law Act 1967."

From anyone else that would have sounded facetious, but somehow Walker makes it sound charming.

"Well, keep it down, Walker," she says.

On the video, while Grigson is calling for the ambulance, Ferguson's bodycam angles towards the ground. Josie wonders if that's retching she can hear. It must be a hell of a thing to take a person's life. As he straightens up, there's another moment of a dazzling light searing into the bodycam. A concerned colleague, perhaps. That so-called etiquette probably went out the window if you saw your colleague in distress.

Grigson approaches Ferguson. *"Ferguson."* He takes a moment. *"Feeling alright?"* Ferguson nods. *"We need to secure your weapon for the post incident procedure."*

Ferguson looks at him.

"I'll need your weapon, son," says Grigson.

Grigson checks in with the rest of the team, who continue the search for Wollacott's weapon.

"He's already prepping for the IOPC," Josie says with a shake of her head. "Politics."

"It's a standard part of their world," says Walker. "Shooter is Nick Ferguson. You know him?"

Both Rob and Josie shake their heads.

"Top bloke. Does a lot of work for charity. Served in Afghanistan."

"Walker," calls Gill.

"Sorry, ma'am," he says.

They watch the footage for a few more minutes, but the show is over. Gill brings it to an end.

"We will obviously not be doing a recreation of the shooting itself, but the moments leading up to it are key," says Gill. "Clive has scripts for those with acting roles."

Dean Beaches makes a wisecrack Josie doesn't hear and there is some laughter.

Scabbard claps his hands. "Right. Show's over folks. Get back to work. Dean, I want you to speak to the Butler woman again. Today."

Josie, Walker and Rob leave the room with the others and walk back to their desks.

As they sit down, Josie looks at the other two. "Has there ever been a situation where someone's got out of the Duncans by providing some kind of stellar insight into an ongoing investigation?" she asks. The thought is unrealistic but intoxicating.

The two of them look at each other, as if they're sharing a private joke.

"You know what that sounds like to me?" Walker says.

Rob nods. "Bargaining." He reaches for a magnet on the divider in front of him and moves it.

33

Vomiting out all the Seamus thing to Jeety is oddly therapeutic. That and the run itself leave me feeling a little lighter. This mood lasts until early afternoon, when I get a call from the police. It's the weasel-faced DS Beaches. He wants to speak to me again.

I agree to go back in on my way to work.

My stomach churns on the journey in, imagining the moment they say, "*So, why didn't you tell us you knew Seamus Wollacott?*"

"Many thanks for coming in, Esther," Beaches says, putting a hot drink in front of me.

The cup of sludge looks so disgusting I'm not even sure what it's supposed to be.

I give him a polite nod.

"I'm at work in forty minutes," I tell him, laying down how little time I can give him.

"Sure. Now, do you think we might go over a couple of things from the night of the shooting?" he asks.

I wonder briefly what might happen if I say no. "Sure."

"Great. Thanks." He settles into his chair as if he's really pleased with himself. "What we'd especially like to focus in on today is the woman that you reported seeing."

"The woman that I saw." If he's going to be a knob about this then I reserve the right to correct him.

"Indeed." He couldn't sound any less sincere. Is he doing it on purpose? "We're going to be filming a crime scene recreation this week. Like the old CrimeWatch on telly. So we need your account of her actions."

"Okay."

"Take us through it then, in your own words. Please describe everything about the woman that you can recall, and how she interacted with the gentleman she was with."

Interesting how she's a woman and he's a gentleman. Feels like it says more about Beaches than he realises. I inhale deeply, thinking back to my first glimpse of them.

"I saw him first. The way he was moving caught my eye. She was slightly further back and his body was across hers. She had the jacket on that I described. Leopard print. And a velvet baseball cap."

"I have some images of leopard print coats." He pushes a printed sheet across the table.

I'm briefly distracted by the thought that there's someone here in this police station whose job involves trawling Pinterest or shopping websites.

There's a variety of styles and lengths here.

"It was long, like these ones here," I say, pointing. "Pretty sure it had a collar too. I reckon this is the closest." My finger stabs an image, tapping for a moment while I ponder it. "But it's not quite right. See how this one looks like it's thick, like faux fur? I think the one she had on was thinner."

"Good work Esther," says Beaches. "Let's talk about the hat then, shall we?"

"Right."

He leaves a pause, as if I'm supposed to say something, but I have no idea what.

"I have a question about the hat. If it was dark, and you didn't see her well, how do you know it was velvet?"

He finishes with a smug grin, as though he's trapped me in a lie with his amazing question.

"Ah. You've got me." I give a rueful nod.

He leans forward.

"It could have been velour," I say.

I have no idea what the fucking difference is, but I'm not having this.

He has bags of unearned confidence, this man. It doesn't faze him. "Right. Can you please tell me what made you believe that the hat was made from velvet or velour?"

"The texture was clear enough. It's a thing, isn't it? A subtle sheen, and the way the colour looks."

"What colour?"

"Either a deep grey, a brown or maroon." I've said this before.

"So, just getting this straight – you could see the texture of the colour but not the actual colour?"

"Yes." I'm bristling with annoyance now. "That's what happens in the dark, isn't it? Colours seem more grey than in sunlight, but there's still texture."

He slides another sheet across the table with a bunch of hats. The variations are smaller than with the coat. The depth of the crown, the size of the peak. A button on top.

I exhale noisily. "Not so sure about this. They all look quite similar." My finger trails across the page. "No button on top. In fact, it wasn't dorky like some of these ones."

"Not dorky?" Beaches is pulling a face now.

"Listen, I don't know hat words, but I know fucking dorky when I see it."

He holds up his hands. "Fine. Put a line through the ones that you're discounting."

I put a vicious line through some of them, because he's pissing me off. I slide his picture back towards him when I'm done.

"What would you say the woman's mood was?"

"Nervous and annoyed."

"How does someone look both of those things?" he asks. "Tell me what visual cues told you that."

How to describe those impressions that come across in the tiniest, most subtle movements and expressions?

"It's like I could imagine her saying to him, 'Oh what the hell?' or something. Her face said it. The angle of her body said it."

"But you didn't hear any of their actual conversation?"

"No."

"And when they walked away, she was in front?"

"She was."

"Was she trying to get away from him?"

I'm wary of over-reaching. I don't know what was in her head. If she really wanted to get away from him, why didn't she head inside the casino?

"I don't know. She might have been trying to get away, or she might have been trying to make a point."

He leans back and nods. "As I say, we're working on a reconstruction of the scene. It will go out to the public, along with some of the outfit details that you've given us. I need to tell you now though that we've found no trace of this woman."

"What?"

"Sure, your mate Baz the bouncer, he's backing your story. He says he saw her."

"Says?"

Beaches shrugs. "Our analysts have searched CCTV images from all over the city, and there's no sign of a person matching your description either before or after the incident."

"How's that even possible?" I say.

"It's as if she never even existed," says Beaches. He's actually smiling as he says it.

34

Honestly, it feels like my world is unravelling.

I go into work and pretty much sleepwalk my way through the first half of my shift. Mrs Wan wants to show me pictures of her new granddaughter during a brief pause in their Mahjong game. I make the right noises but don't really pay attention. I check on the cashiers doing the cash count in the strong room. One of them has put her shopping in the inner room of the strongroom beyond, by the large older safe that gets almost zero use. Storing personal belongings in here is not good practice, but I let it slide. The pizza oven in the restaurant is on the blink again. I tell Orla Hawkes I'll get onto it.

I do the work but I'm not in any way present.

I take a long lunch break to clear my head. I wander further into the city centre, grab a sandwich and sit by the Clock Tower to try to pull myself back together.

I mentally lay down the facts in the case, the ones that the police might very soon put before me. I'd love to have someone to discuss all this with, but I've leaned on Jeety a lot recently. My husband should really be the person I can turn to with this stuff, but apparently he's too busy obsessing over how to use my horrid moment of fame to shift energy drinks whilst simultaneously "keeping an open mind".

What are the facts?

There was a cleaner at the casino, Lisa McNally, who had a 'shitbag' of a boyfriend.

I did what I could to help her and when the opportunity arose I made an anonymous call to the police that had the shitbag picked up for possession of cocaine with the intent to supply. I made the phone calls to the refuge in Coventry and Lisa departed.

That's not the whole truth. There are other details but that's the gist of it.

It was also long enough ago that it feels like ancient history.

Except the shitbag, Seamus Wollacott, clearly finished serving his time and came back to Leicester. For whatever reason, he was back outside the casino – my casino – with a gun on his hip and a woman by his side that no one else in the world saw. Sure, Baz saw her too, but I got the clear message from DS Beaches that the police think Baz is lying to back me up.

But I saw what I saw.

I chew my sandwich and try to picture the gun again.

I remember the bulge under his body warmer. I saw something in his hand as he walked ahead of me down that cut-through by the Novotel. And at the entrance to the building site where they shot him, I saw – I can mentally see – faintly gleaming light and his hand curled around something.

He had the gun on him. Didn't he? In my mind I can't quite see it now.

Fuck.

But then the police turned up. That one guy talked to me, barked at me. Nick. That was what the other officer called him. Ah, wait. And then... The words "*It's like Ferguson said, we need you out of harm's way*" pop into my head. Nick Ferguson.

The Ferguson guy and the others went in. They must have seen the gun – seen something because they don't just randomly shoot people. They must have seen something even if they can't find the gun now. I'm not the only witness in this thing.

I find a new sense of resolve as I think this. It's not my word against everyone else's. There were other people there. The firearms guys were there too.

And why the hell was Seamus Wollacott back at the casino anyway? He wasn't a gambler that I knew of. The casino has crazy strict policies about employers dating punters, even the cleaners. Lisa gave no indication he was a gambler.

Why would he be back at the casino where Lisa worked unless it was something to do with Lisa?

Was he looking for Lisa?

Why was he looking for Lisa and carrying a gun?

That's a chilling thought.

And who was the woman with him? A woman who hasn't dared come forward since the event?

His latest girlfriend? His latest victim?

A violent abuser turns up at his old girlfriend's workplace with a gun. Jesus Christ. Was he that desperate to find her again?

I have so many questions.

Why was Seamus at the casino with a gun?

What did the firearms officers, like Nick Ferguson, see that made them shoot him?

Does Lisa have any of the answers to this?

As I finish my sandwich I realise I've got things I can at least act on. I've got three names: Seamus Wollacott, Nick Ferguson, Lisa McNally. Two are alive and I can at least try to find out what they know. The other might be dead, but there are people out there who knew Seamus and might be able to offer answers.

If the police aren't going to investigate this properly, if they're just trying to make this all look like my fault, then maybe it's up to me to start uncovering the truth myself.

35

Josie is in her role of Esther in the recreation. She has deeply mixed feelings about this. It's a starring role, which is no bad thing. She's wearing a trashy blonde wig, which is fun, but it's not a good look on her.

They're in the office, getting ready. It's after nine at night, so that it's properly dark.

Rob and Walker keep giving her acting notes, in the manner of over-zealous film directors.

"You work in the service industry, you need to stop scowling."

"I never noticed before, but you walk like a farmer, Kaminski. Try taking smaller strides."

The two of them are dressed in tactical gear, so that they can play AFOs. Josie would have enjoyed that, but she tries to settle into the role of Esther. She's got the waistcoat and jacket on.

"I'm glad I don't need to wear this kind of stuff every day," she says, pulling the waistcoat down at the bottom. "It's so fucking lumpy and old-fashioned."

"Just look after it," says Walker. "The casino's lent it to us for this."

Josie gives it a sniff, wondering if it's been washed. Smells of some kind of cleaning solvent with a side note of despair.

The three of them look up as Beaches wanders into the other side of the open-plan office. He's showing off his outfit to the others.

"Jesus, look at him," mutters Rob.

"Hold on, just getting into role," says Josie, limbering up by flicking her arms and flexing her neck. "Oh look! I've spotted someone across the road who I think might be a fucking twat and a menace to society."

Rob and Walker laugh, but then Scabbard appears from the doorway of his office with Gill and they shut up.

"Right, all ready? Downstairs. Van's waiting."

When they get to the scene, the area's sealed off for this exercise. Naturally this has attracted some attention, but Josie ignores the onlookers, scoping out where she's going to walk, what she's going to do.

The casino's letting them use the foyer, so Josie begins there.

There's people here from the media team. A director is yakking in Josie's ear, telling her all about what she's thinking and feeling as Esther, but Josie knows all this. It was her who took Esther's statement.

She concentrates on stepping into those shoes and properly living the role.

By the time they begin the scene, Josie's almost prepared to believe that this is happening to her. She's at the door, talking to the big guy who's playing the security guard.

Her attention's caught by the man across the street, played by Beaches. She manages to suppress the annoyance she feels at Beaches, who's practically mugging for the camera. He's got a hand in his pocket like he's a bad conjuror, about to pull out a fucking dove.

She points him out to the security guard. He acts like it's nothing, but she's Esther, and she knows something's not right.

There's a woman out there too. Josie's really glad she didn't get to play that part. She hates the casino uniform, but the leopard print coat and velvet baseball cap would have been worse.

She steps out and follows the two people away from the casino.

The media team do several takes.

She hopes that the cameras are properly capturing how it looks in the darkness. There's a drone up there somewhere. She knows that drone footage often has a way of making things look clean and neat. Down here it's grubby, bleak and unpleasant.

They film the part when Esther calls the emergency services. She has her phone to her ear when they get to the construction site.

As nobody knows what happened to the woman in the leopard print coat, the team has made the decision that she would exit the scene at this point, by running away down Great Central Street. They film Josie looking around once the woman has gone.

She's now engaged in the conversation with the fictional operator. This is closely scripted, from the recording of the actual conversation. It goes on for what feels like a really long time, but Josie wonders how it felt for Esther, whose stress levels must have been through the roof.

Eventually, the van arrives with the AFOs. Josie stays in

character. She sees the van disgorge black-clad figures with guns.

Esther must have been shitting herself at this point. Josie's heard the recording, and the operator was getting no response from Esther until she managed to get her to say her name. Josie follows the script. It's easy to channel that feeling of confused fear. These are her colleagues playing dress-up, but she can't even tell who's who and she doesn't like it.

One of the officers, the one playing AFO Pike, steers Esther into the back of the van.

Josie's role in the filming extravaganza is over, but outside she knows that Wollacott is about to get shot.

Rob and Walker get to take part in that final action scene, not that they are going to recreate those very final moments. The police don't need to share what might be a terrible error of judgement.

The police need the narrative to show that Wollacott was a credible threat. That or somehow pin the whole thing on Esther Butler's lies. That's the harsh reality of things.

36

Kieran is not in when I get home.

Kieran, his car and a box of RBuzz energy drinks are gone. Maybe he'd mentioned something about a sales pitch meeting in Lincoln. I tune a lot of it out.

I feel relieved to have the house to myself for a bit which, in turn, makes me feel guilty. What state must my marriage be in if I'm happy to discover my husband is not home?

I love Kieran. I do love him. I think I do. We're pleasant to each other. We're civil. He's never been cruel or unkind or unfaithful. At least not that I know of. And yet ... I have my life and he has his. I work and keep this house going. His work isn't bringing in any money but he puts a lot of energy into it and he does some of the chores around the house. We rarely spend time together doing something we both enjoy. We share a bed but I can't remember the last time we had sex.

Sometimes it feels like we're just two best friends who live together except I'm not sure he's my best friend anymore. Nothing horrific has happened to us, yet it seems like we're happiest apart. And then that voice pipes up in my head, saying that most married couples are probably like this and maybe if we'd had children there'd be something to tie us together, give us focus.

I can't imagine having kids with Kieran. I just can't. Sometimes – most of the time – it feels like I'm the only adult in the house.

And when I really need Kieran to have my back, like over this shooting business, he carefully positions himself so that he doesn't have to say he believes me. People who love each other should surely have each other's backs?

I grab a drink (in a house full of luminous energy drinks, I have to search for five minutes to find a carton of orange juice) and I sit on the sofa to work on my problems.

The police think I was mistaken when I said I saw a gun. They're going to think something else entirely if they discover I knew Seamus Wollacott had been beating one of my colleagues and it was my phone call that put him in prison. I need to track down some people. I need to find some answers.

I've got three names. Lisa McNally, Seamus Wollacott, and the firearms officer Nick Ferguson. First stop, I simply google them. Most people in the world today you can look them up on Google. If they're old, they have Facebook accounts. If they're younger, they have Instagram or TikTok. If they're career-minded, they're probably on LinkedIn. A lot of women are conscious about putting their true identities on-line, but most people are there somewhere.

The results are disappointing.

Lisa McNally can't be found. At least that makes sense. She went to a refuge to escape an abusive partner. Absolutely the kind of person who would be keeping a low digital profile. If she was on-line, it would be under a false name.

No sign of Nick Ferguson on-line either. A bit more surprising. I wonder if I've got the firearms officer's name wrong. Nick. Short for Nicholas? I try Nicholas. I try Fergusson with two 's's. Nothing. Maybe police officers are also cagey about making themselves known on-line.

Seamus Wollacott has a Facebook account. Whoop-de-doo. I click on it. Without being his Facebook friend, I can only see public posts and that amounts to the various profile picture changes he's made. There's a couple that are just of him. There are several of an older man, maybe a deceased dad or uncle. There's one of Seamus himself with a bunch of other men, most of them bald, outside a pub with an unclear mural on the wall behind them.

Internet searching has provided me with very little.

Next step. I know where Lisa went, the last I saw of her a couple of years ago. A women's refuge in Coventry. I don't one hundred percent remember the name so I do some searching. Progress Haven. That was it.

I put a ready meal in the microwave for my dinner and give them a call.

It rings out unanswered the first time I call. The second time, it gets picked up immediately.

"Hello," says a woman. She sounds frazzled, out of breath.

"Is that Progress Haven?" I say.

"Yes."

"I'm trying to get in contact with a woman who might be there. Lisa McNally."

"Who is this?"

"My name is Esther."

"Are you family?"

"We used to work together. In Leicester."

"Uh-huh. Let me go check."

There is the clunk of the phone being put down on a surface and silence for a good long while. The woman comes back.

"Sorry, can't help you," she says.

"As in she's not there at the moment or she doesn't want to talk to me?"

"She's not here." The woman pauses. *"She left us a while ago."*

"Can you tell me where she went?"

There's not quite a laugh on the line. *"I wouldn't be able to tell you that."*

"Are you able to contact her? Do you have a number?"

"I can't give that information out."

"No, but could you possibly get a message to her? It's important."

She sighs like I'm really taking up her time. *"Fine. What's the message?"*

"Just to give me a call. It's Esther. From Meridian Casino. That's where we used to work." I give the woman my number. I get a strong impression that she's not even writing it down.

"Thanks," I say and she ends the call.

Well, that was a fat lot of use. Sitting on my arse and googling things and phoning women's shelters isn't going to get me answers.

In the kitchen, the microwave pings. I got get my dinner and plan next steps.

37

Kieran comes home later that night when I'm already in bed.

I'm half asleep when he gets in. He does it quietly like he doesn't want to wake me, doesn't want to even disturb my half of the bed. I'm filled with the impression that he, like me, knows we're two polite strangers occupying the same space. He gets under the covers without us even touching and soon he's asleep and I'm fully awake.

When I get up in the morning, he's already downstairs, busying himself in the kitchen.

"You were in late," I say.

"Roadworks on the A46. But a really good meeting in Lincoln."

"Yeah?"

"The company that runs the gyms on the university campus. Very promising leads. A good energy."

I've put a quid in the slot now and Kieran regales me with the whole story of how he and Trey pitched hard to the gym management guys and maybe they'd be getting RBuzz in all the facilities across the uni. There were a lot of 'maybe's and 'hopefully's. Things were universally 'promising' and 'positive'. Nothing concrete. Nothing that would actually make him some money. It doesn't seem to bother him.

"And they've got links to De Monfort," he continues, "so that might mean word will spread. Lincoln, Leicester, Loughborough. We get right in at ground level, become the sports drink choice for a new generation."

"Right," I say, not interested.

The doorbell rings and I go to answer it, just to get away.

I recognise the newspaper before I recognise the woman holding it.

It's the Leicester Mercury. The front-page headline reads: *Leicestershire Police admit 'gunman' unarmed.*

I recognise the woman a second later. It's the young journalist, Kayleigh Chandler, who came into the casino. And now she's doorstepping me. My hackles rise.

"What the hell are you doing here?" I say.

"Police say he was unarmed," she says.

"I'm not talking to you."

"I just wonder how you reconcile that with your account."

There's something about the word 'reconcile' that makes me even more angry. Maybe because it's a big word dropped by a little shit who is really sticking her nose in where it's not wanted.

"I saw what I saw," I say. "I don't want to talk to you."

"You need to get your version of events out," says Kayleigh. "Even if you were mistaken, you were driven by public spiritedness, right? Lone women, walking the streets of Leicester at night. It's not safe. And you did what you thought was right."

"Didn't you hear me?" I'm getting close to shouting now.

"I told the police what happened. It's not my fault they can't find the stupid gun. Take it up with them."

"So you think the police are incompetent?"

I scoff. "Even if he wasn't armed, it wasn't my decision to shoot him."

"But he was armed."

"He's a dangerous man. That woman looked scared."

"Right. And your actions probably saved her life, right?"

I can see what she's doing. With her half-accusatory, half-supportive phrases and that constant rising inflection like she's turning everything into a question, she wants to tease comments out of me.

"No fucking comment," I say. "Now get off my property."

"I just want to help," she says.

I slam the door in her face.

"Who was that?" Kieran calls from the kitchen.

"The bloody press!"

"What? About your nine-nine-nine thing?"

He says it like he's surprised it's still a thing. A man is dead. The police can't do their bloody job right. I can feel a sword hanging over me. And Kieran ... Kieran seems to think it's all blown over and no one could possibly be interested anymore.

I dress in a rage and go into work. I'm not due in until the evening but there's something I've got to do.

I go up to Gabe's office. He's not in, which is good. Our staff personnel records are in filing cabinets on the back wall. Yes, in the twenty-first century, Meridian Casino keeps its staff records in actual paper files. It's quaint, bordering on crazy, but it's how Gabe likes it. It's a one casino operation (though who knows what other pies the owners have their fingers in?) and Gabe likes to keep things close at hand.

Gabe's also a bit of a hoarder when it comes to information. Says he never knows when he might need something again.

This is all good for me. I open a drawer, looked at the hanging files and then go to the next. *M* for *McNally*. If I know Gabe, Lisa's records will still be in here. They won't have moved since I first hired her. And those records will have her mobile phone number, her old home address, and maybe even something else that might help me.

I find the file and start to look through. There's the ID photo of Lisa glued to the front page. She's smiling at the camera, one strand of mousey blonde hair coming forward over her ear. She might be smiling, but part of me thinks I can now see some of the sadness in her eyes that become more and more pronounced over the months I knew her. She was a clever woman. Thought on her feet. She was curious. Too curious in the end...

The door opens and Gabe comes in. My natural reaction is to flinch, to try to hide the file, but that would just look suspicious. I don't need to lie to Gabe.

He frowns at me.

"Just checking an old personnel record," I say. "Someone I want to catch up with."

"Is that the McNally woman?" he says. His eyesight is better than I imagined.

"It is," I say slowly.

A faint queasiness seems to come over Gabe. I know exactly what he's thinking.

"Why are you looking at her records? We should not even still have them."

"It's your filing system, Gabe."

He holds out his hand for it. I get a good look at the address – 32 Oakchurch Road – before passing it over.

He grasps the three stapled sheets.

"We do not need this. We got rid of her ages ago."

"We did," I agree.

He clenches his jaw and makes several unhappy expressions with his mouth before saying, "I know how useful you've been over the years, Esther. You've always been good at your work when it comes to the crunch."

I nod. His understanding of the story of Lisa McNally as it relates to the abusive boyfriend and why she left Meridian is very different to the actual truth. It's a truth I've not shared with anyone fully. Definitely not Kieran. And that story I told Jeety about the boyfriend and an anonymous tip to the police, while true, is the tiniest tip of the iceberg. There's a whole dark underbelly to that story that I've never told anyone and, until recent events, I'd hoped I'd never have to tell anyone.

If the real truth came out, I'd be in prison for sure.

38

The Leicester Mercury is not Rob's regular choice of newspaper.

He buys the Times and the Guardian at the weekend and tries to cultivate the habit of reading them as part of his weekend morning routine. There's an artisanal bakery café not far from home, and on his free weekend mornings he sits there and forces himself to read the whole lot. He feels it gives him a more cultured view of the world. Occasionally, he wishes he lived closer to London, to see some of the exhibitions and plays that are mentioned.

The Leicester Mercury is much more digestible, and a number of officers have passed this particular edition around the office, moaning at the front page.

He reads it in the car as Josie drives.

"*Leicestershire Police admit 'gunman' unarmed,*" he reads to Josie. "That's the headline, but the quotes underneath say no such thing."

"Uh-huh," she says, only half paying attention.

"Down here we've got a quote from Superintendent

Becky Ayres. '*Police officers reacted to what was reported to be a credible threat to life. Our investigation and search of the local area is still ongoing. We understand that this must be a distressing time for Mr Wollacott's family and we are keeping them informed of developments.*' That is not admitting there was no gun."

"But there was no gun," says Josie simply.

"You think Esther Butler is lying?"

"Doesn't matter what I think. Doesn't matter what she says. If there was a gun, they'd have found it. They've brought in dogs and metal detectors. If the gun was there then they'd have found it."

He folds the paper up. "Somehow I thought you'd take the woman's side in this."

She scoffs. "There are no sides. There's the truth. The question you need to ask yourself is: did Esther lie to the police in her statement, and if so, why?"

She indicates and turns off the A50. The day's list includes two farms nears Ulverscroft. Neither of them are signed up to the Operation Chainlink community chat, but with recent thefts from farms not far from here, they're going to check in and see if the places are likely targets.

"Why did she lie then?" he says.

"I didn't say she lied. She might have been mistaken. She might have been mistaken and then doubled down on it. Maybe she thought she saw something and utterly convinced herself. People can get to a point where they have convinced themselves something is true. People are unreliable. You know that."

"I guess," he says.

"However," she continues, "maybe she lied for a reason."

"Such as?"

She shrugs. "Not my case. I've been told that several times."

She drives into the entrance to Whitwick Farm and the track underneath immediately becomes rough and uneven.

"My job is visiting shitty farms in the middle of nowhere and telling farmers to make sure their tractors are safely locked up."

Rob gives a pretend gasp. "Is that a note of acceptance, I hear?"

She smirks, perfectly aware of how he's tracking her through the stages of grief. "No fucking way. I'm still thinking I can bargain my way back into regular CID work."

She grips the wheel tight as the track worsens. The fences to either side are rotting, mostly held together with barbed wire and sagging into the road under the thickly growing grass on either side.

Ahead there is a yard, a vehicle shed with only two sides, and a low, miserable looking farmhouse.

"This really is a shithole," she says.

Rob has visited the full range of farms that can be found within a ten mile radius of the city. A few – a select few – are like children's drawings of farms, with animals and crops in the fields, watched over by a stout stone-built farmhouse. The kinds of places families would spend good money to stay in on a countryside holiday. Most of the farms though are exactly what business demands: industrial outposts with great sheds for crops or machinery; concrete yards full of vehicles and trailers. There's a space in which the farmhouse just happens to be. It's the place where the workers and their family live. Far from any sort of rural idyll, but functional and possibly profitable.

And then there are places like this. The farmhouse

windows are dark. There are tiles missing from the roof in several places. Anything of value on this farm has probably been sold to pay off debts. As the average age of farmers goes up and few from the younger generation show any inclination to take up the thankless work, this kind of thing becomes more common.

Rob's not been to Whitwick Farm before, but this looks like a farm that is either dying or has died.

"I don't think these people are gonna have anything worth stealing," says Josie.

"Lead from the roof, copper piping," suggests Rob and he's not necessarily joking. He points at a camera mounted on a post near the farmyard. "At least they've got CCTV."

They get out and he looks at the paperwork. "Whitwick farm. Mr Bashford. Aaron Bashford."

Josie turns, hands on hips to inspect the whole place. "Shithole," she concludes.

"Shush. He might hear you."

He goes to the uPVC front door and raps on the frosted glass. He waits. There's no reply.

"He might be out working the land," he says.

Josie gives him a look.

The fields nearest the house are all wild meadow with sprouting grasses and brambles. Farmers can get payouts from the government for devoting a percentage of their land to wild meadow. Rob suspects that this isn't necessarily what's going on here.

He knocks again.

"Take a look around," he says.

Josie nods and heads off towards the shed and the outhouses.

Rob looks up and around for any more CCTV. There's none he can spot.

He knocks a third time and takes a wander round the house in the opposite direction. The windows are streaked with thin mud, run through with the tracks of previous rainfall. It's daytime but the interior is gloomy.

He can see into a living room where old-fashioned furniture bunches together in front of a TV on a stand. There are bookcases, crammed with papers or magazines overflowing on the lower shelves.

He goes round further and finds a kitchen window.

He barely has a glance in before he jerks his head back in surprise. There's a man sitting at the kitchen table, facing the window, but his head is tilted back and to the side as though he has fallen asleep at the most uncomfortable angle. His mouth is open to the ceiling.

Gathering himself a second, Rob knocks on the window.

"Mr Bashford?"

The man doesn't move. Rob knocks again, but the man's pose is truly unnatural for a conscious human being and he starts to get a bad feeling. He peers in, hand shielding his eyes. The man's unshaven. He's wearing a dark knitted jumper and has his head fully thrown back. Shadows in the room make things unclear, but there's a large, dark, irregular shape on his temple. He can't see clearly, but it looks like a wound.

39

Rob hammers on the kitchen window. "Mr Bashford! Aaron!"

There's no movement within.

"Shit." He shouts: "Josie! Get over here!"

Even with his experience, it takes a moment to decide on the right course of action. He calls into central command.

"Control, urgent. Tango-Four-Two-Four at Whitwick Farm, Ulverscroft. I have a male inside the farm building with a head wound. Maybe a gunshot. No visible weapon in hand. I'm requesting ambulance and uniformed support ASAP. I may have to make entry. Over."

As control responds, Josie comes running from round the building.

"What is it?"

"Man, inside. Appears to have a head wound."

She takes a look. "Dead?"

"I don't think I can make that call looking through a window."

Josie goes to a door a few feet along and tries the handle,

without success. She turns around looking at the ground, then picks up a concrete garden ornament. It might have been a frog or hedgehog, but the paint and outer layers have been weathered away.

"Dynamic risk assessment?" she says to Rob.

"Do it."

She smashes the door glass above the handle, then sweeps the ornament around the frame to clear shards away. She reaches in and a moment later the door is unlocked and open.

"Let's go," he says, then calls out. "Police! We're coming in to help you!"

He leads the way. Josie follows close behind. She looks up the stairs and out towards the living room area as he heads straight into the kitchen.

He hears her shout. "Armed police are on their way! If anyone's inside, make yourself known and keep your hands visible!"

Rob enters the kitchen behind the seated man and sees the injury directly. It's not new. The blood covering his temple and cheek has poured onto his shoulder. The floor is dry.

There's a handgun on the floor, a foot to the side of his dangling right hand.

Rob goes in, watching where he treads and takes the man's pulse. He's cool to the touch.

"Fuck," he whispers.

"Dead?" says Josie in the doorway.

He nods.

His first thought is that it's a suicide. The injury looks self-inflicted. Suicides in the farming community are far from uncommon. But right now this is simply a suspicious death and the area a potential crime scene.

"Check the rest of the house," Rob tells her, "then we step outside and wait for backup."

She goes without a word and Rob gets onto central command to request further assistance.

40

As I drive down the Narborough Road from work to Lisa's old address, a little voice tells me over and over again that this is wrong, this is a bad idea.

I argue back that I'm just going to visit the house and maybe speak to the neighbours or the new occupants. They might know what Lisa is up to these days. If I'm really lucky they can put me in contact with her, and Lisa can help me understand why Seamus came back to the casino where she'd once worked.

That's my chain of reasoning, but the little voice keeps saying it's a bad idea. And I know why. Up until Baz pointed out the link between me and Seamus I was able to tell the police honestly, hand on heart, that I didn't know the man with the gun and I certainly didn't wish him any harm.

Right now, with knowledge of that connection in my head, I can still say the same thing to the police. I'd be lying, but I can say it. I just have – what's the phrase Americans use in political dramas? – 'plausible deniability'. That.

If I go looking for Lisa, try to pick up that thread again,

then I'm making the connection between me and Seamus more real. The little voice flings questions at me.

Why are you looking for Lisa McNally, Esther?

Why are you looking for an old employee?

What do you know about her relationship with Seamus Wollacott?

What do you know about the circumstances surrounding his arrest prior to his two year prison sentence?

Why were you so very keen to help Lisa escape that abusive relationship? Was it really out of the goodness of your own heart?

Why did you put all that effort into getting her out of Leicester and into a refuge miles away?

Why were you and Gabe Savage so keen to get rid of her so quickly?

What secrets are you hiding?

How desperate are you to keep those secrets? Are those secrets so important, you'd be willing to kill someone?

If Seamus turned up at the door of the Meridian Casino would you actually phone the police and tell them he was carrying a gun, in the hope that they would permanently silence him?

The accusing little voice is unfair. It knows things that only I know. The events of the past are a jigsaw, and though lots of people hold pieces of the puzzle – Lisa, Gabe, Baz – no one but me can see all of them.

I turn on the radio and play music loud enough to drown out the voice.

I take the turning down Braunstone Lane. I follow the satnav. I know Leicester well, but I don't know this area. Apart from some low flat-roofed blocks of flats, most homes here are detached houses, probably former council houses. The area is laid out with the curving crescents and cul-de-sacs of a housing estate. I pass a little park with charity collecting bins by the entrance. St George's flags flutter from several lampposts.

Oakchurch Road. I count door numbers and come to an apartment block, two storeys high. It's a boxy building. There are little balconies cut into the wall for the flats on the first floor. Many are full of hanging washing or used to store bikes.

I park and go up to the building. There's an access door at the front, propped open with a brick. I look up. Thirty-two is on the first floor and I climb stairs that lead to a balcony corridor at the back of the building. Here, front doors overlook a narrow strip of grass, a row of towering laburnum trees, and the houses on the next road over.

A TV is playing in a nearby flat.

I go along to number thirty-two. Someone has taped a piece of cardboard over the letter box with a messy crisscross of brown parcel tape.

I knock at the door.

There's no reply. The TV in the nearby flat goes quiet.

I knock again and a door opens, but it's the next flat along, number thirty.

An older woman with a shock of grey hair, like she's just stuck her fingers in an electric socket, looks out. "Who you after, me duck?" she says in a gravelly voice.

"Oh," I say and point at the door. "I was trying to find Lisa. Lisa McNally. I think she lived here."

The woman scratches her face. "She's not been there for years, me duck. Two tenants since then. Last ones moved out by the council for using their flat as a drugs drop."

"Ah – right." I honestly hadn't expected Lisa to still be there. "I've been trying to get in touch with her. She used to work for me."

"Yeah?"

"At the casino. Very hard worker. You knew her?"

"Knew her," the woman says. "Kept all kinds of hours."

"You don't know if she had family in the area? Friends? I'm just trying to get back in touch."

"No family. I don't think so," she sniffs. "Reckon Sorcha knew her. She works the bar at the Kingsway Social."

"Right?"

The woman points back through her flat to indicate the world beyond the front. "Just at the other end of the cut-through. Blue hair. She and Lisa were good friends."

"Okay," I say. "That's very helpful."

The woman nods and gestures back to the flat. "Heard the council wanted to put a woman with one of them disabilities in that flat, but there's no lift so I don't know what they're thinking."

I nod and smile as I might to a customer. "Thanks again," I say and go down.

Out front, two young teenagers are sitting on a telecoms box by the pavement and watching me with bored eyes. I can see the cut-through the old neighbour was referring to. A path across the road goes between two houses and into a wider park area.

I decide I might as well leave my car where it is and head over the road.

41

The park area is small, maybe just big enough to walk a lazy dog. There's no playground. There's one bench and a litter bin with its plastic top missing. On the far side the park comes out by a wider road. There's quite a bit of open space here. I guess the planners who designed this area thought more open space would make the place look attractive. It doesn't. It just makes it look like something is missing.

The Kingsway Social Club is a flat-roofed pub joined onto another similar building with a Leicester City Council Community and Housing Office sign on it. There are picnic bench tables outside the social club, but no one's sitting there. I recognise the mural on the wall behind the tables; it only takes me a moment to recall that I saw it on one of Seamus Wollacott's Facebook profiles: a photo of him and a bunch of men drinking there.

It makes sense that Seamus would live here, near Lisa's old place, so why does it take me by surprise?

I go inside and it takes my eyes a few seconds to adjust to the lower lighting.

A cushioned bench runs around the inner wall of the bar, and the seating is otherwise low stools and little round tables. There's a stage at one end, set up for karaoke, with a curtain of silver foil ribbon behind it. The bar occupies the opposite end of the room.

There's a dozen people in here in mid-afternoon. A few committed daytime drinkers, but also some more social knots of older men and women. In many ways this isn't so different to the kind of daytime clientele we might get at the casino – just different kinds of money, different proclivities.

I go up to the bar. A big woman with her hair in oiled curls looks to me.

"Is Sorcha around?" I ask.

Her eyebrows dip in a momentary frown. "Not on shift for another half hour. Can I help?"

"I was told to ask for Sorcha. I'm actually trying to get in touch with a Lisa McNally."

The barwoman shakes her head. "Don't know her. You'll have to ask Sorcha."

"Right. I'll have a coke then."

She pours. I pay. It's half the price we charge at the casino.

I take my drink and sit at an empty table. While I wait, I look at my phone. It's the standard thing when there's time to kill. I try to imagine what people did with empty time before smartphones. Did they just stare into space?

Kieran is still trying to make social capital from the flicker of attention my news story has drawn to his energy drink business. There are several posts trying to hint at the idea that RBuzz is the next big major trend, but even I can see there's just no momentum. It's embarrassing. Not for the first time, I wonder if it's socially acceptable to unfollow and unfriend your husband.

I move away from social media and try searching for the firearms officer again. I'm only looking for him because I heard his name. Nick Ferguson. That was definitely one single officer, right? Nick Ferguson? I've not got one called Nick and one called Ferguson and accidentally mushed them together?

Nick Ferguson got no results. The search for Nicholas Ferguson brings up an American journalist, a New Zealand footballer and the LinkedIn profile of a pub manager. Maybe I misheard. Maybe Nick is Nic? I search variants and eventually ask internet AI to suggest possibilities. It throws back Nico, Nikolai and Dominic among other less sensible ideas.

I search further, sipping my coke.

Dominic Ferguson brings something up. A photo on a news website. A link to a charity event for a Leicester youth rugby club. I'm about to click on it when I'm distracted by a sudden flicker of light.

Across the bar someone's lit a cigarette lighter. Smoking indoors is illegal and the floor manager in me immediately looks to see what's going on. A dark-haired woman is lighting a tea light candle. She places it on a table I'd not noticed before, even though it's in plain sight by the wall. The table is small but it's crowded. There's a large framed photo leaned up against the wall and several smaller photos in front of it, all on top of a Leicester City football club scarf that drapes over the sides. There's a small bunch of flowers, and now a lit candle.

The photographs are of Seamus Wollacott.

It's a shrine.

A chill runs through me.

How did I not spot that before?

A man stands next to the woman who lit the candle. The people at the nearby tables are speaking softly. Words of comfort. Kind words for the dead.

Family or friends of the man killed because of what I said are standing by a shrine to him, maybe ten feet from where I'm scrolling the internet and drinking coke.

This is not good. I do not feel good.

"There she is," I hear the woman at the bar say.

I look. A woman with hair dyed a vivid blue is now behind the bar. Sorcha. She's looking at me.

"Can I help, love?" she says.

I stand. I glance at the shrine and the folks nearest it. I can't stay here.

"You were looking for Lisa?" she says.

Out of the corner of my eye, I think I can see someone glancing over.

"I'll come back another time," I say quietly but stumble noisily as I try to move round my table.

A voice says something as I leave. I have no idea if it's even directed at me. I'm straight out the door. I can't stay. I don't want to trample on other people's grief, but more pressing than that, I don't want to put myself in the midst of people who are quite possibly angry over Seamus's death.

I blink in the brightness of daylight and momentarily forget which way my car is. It's over there, through that bit of park and down an alleyway to the next road over. I'm immediately cursing myself for having parked what now feels like a very long way away.

I stride towards the little park. I put real energy into it. Any faster and I'll be breaking into a jog.

Just through the park entrance, there's a loud shout behind me.

"Hey! Hey, you!"

42

I'm standing by the bench. I'm grateful for the natural barrier as I turn to face the three people who've followed me. I often need to judge people and situations quickly. I already knew this was a bad situation, which is why I made a hasty exit.

Now I can see these three, I wish I'd left sooner. They look more than hostile. They are carrying themselves like they'd sooner throw punches than talk.

I spot what I reckon is a family resemblance to Seamus in two of them. I decide that they could well be his mother and brother. The third is a younger man, incredibly pale.

"Yes?" I don't want to look like I'm on the back foot. Any confrontation is worse if you act like a victim.

The mother raises a finger and points at me. "How dare you. How fucking dare you?"

I give a little shake of my head. "I'm sorry. I don't know what you're talking about."

"Fucking bitch!"

The woman's eyes are red, as though she has been crying, but they seem to be rapidly drying up now.

"Can you back off please?" I hold up my hand, as if I'm stopping traffic. Sometimes that does actually work, but not in this case. They ignore it.

"You're the bitch that did it, aren't you?" says the mother.

The brother bares his teeth. "You got our Seamus shot."

I need to slow my breathing and remain calm, even though there's a part of my brain that's screaming at me to run.

There's no good reply to his accusation. I keep quiet but meet his gaze.

"You've got the wrong woman," I say.

"It was fucking you. I've seen the pictures. You and your stupid energy drink shit," says the mother.

"Please," I say. "You have nothing but my sympathy."

"You said he had a gun," says the mother, taking half a step forward. "Why would you say that?"

"He had a gun," I hear myself say.

I also take half a step forward. I grasp the back of the bench in front of me so that I can lean forward and meet the mother eye to eye. We're very close now. It's a gamble, but I need to do something.

She recoils slightly. I hope this signals a shift.

"Who does that?" she hisses. "Who calls the cops and tells them that?"

"Fucking feds," spits the brother.

The question's answered by the pale kid. "She wanted him dead." He cocks his head to one side and looks at me.

I'm not about to join in with this.

I push off the bench and step back, still keeping eye contact.

"I'm sorry for your loss. I'm leaving now."

"Don't you fucking come back here neither," said the mother. "Show your face here again and you'll know about it. Not fit to breathe the same air."

I wonder why she chose that phrasing.

Breathe the same air as who?

Definitely not Seamus.

As I walk off I hear her sobbing. I force myself to walk tall, back to the car.

43

Josie and Rob wait outside Whitwick Farm for colleagues to arrive.

"What's the chances we might get to actually investigate this one?" Josie says, as they unfurl crime scene tape across the entrance to the yard.

"A murder? Yeah, no. Not a chance," says Rob. He pauses, leaning on the gate. Josie reckons he's one step away from having a piece of grass in his mouth and talking about milk yields.

"Everyone's flat out on the shooting. Why not us?" says Josie. "We could just have a quick look round."

He gives her a look. "That's the bargaining talking, that is. You're about to say it makes sense for us to be involved, because we found the body."

"Was not," lies Josie.

"Listen, I've been there. Really."

"Right? And what? You're about to tell me that I should just give up on everything?"

"Absolutely not. We all need our own goals."

Josie knows that a polite person would ask what Rob's goals are at this point, but her temper's rising again. "That's the problem. What if our goals are incompatible with being relegated to the fucking Duncans?"

He gives her a grin.

"What?" she says. "Now you're laughing at me?"

"No, mate. Not at all. Do you think anyone's goals are compatible with being a Duncan?"

She jabs the ground with her boot. "God, no. Unless your goal was just to get through the day, earn some money and go home. Some people are like that."

"Way I see it, is like this." He walks over to where she is, picking up a stick on the way. "Here's you, and here's your goal. One of your goals, yeah?"

He makes two marks in the dirt with the stick, some distance apart.

Josie rolls her eyes. "Right?"

"The only way you're seeing of getting from here to there is like this." He draws a straight line, connecting the two points.

"That's because I'm not a lunatic." Josie doesn't want to hiss in such a bitchy way, but he's being patronising.

He continues, without reacting. "Being a Duncan – joining our noble brethren – is a setback. You're going to be heading towards your goal. You gotta keep it in your mind. But it won't be a direct path, and that's fine." He creates a line that wobbles and deviates.

Josie looks hard at Rob. Something about the way he's telling it... She waits until he raises his eyes and looks at her.

"Did a fucking therapist say all this stuff to you?"

He nods. "Yeah..."

"And you don't really believe it yourself, do you?"

He gives a half-smile. "I'm trying hard to believe it. Otherwise I'll go stark raving bonkers."

She joins him in laughing at the absurdity of it all.

Thirty minutes later, the crime scene is secured. Uniformed colleagues, the forensic medical examiner and the SOCOs have arrived.

"Here we go," says Rob, checking a message. "DI Gill's taking primacy on this." He looks up. "And that's Sanjee the crime scene manager. We're to assist until Gill arrives and tells us to stand down."

Josie sees Sanjee Baksh walking over. He has one of the smiliest faces she's ever known – like he should be a children's entertainer, not a CSM. His face is a series of circles and semi-circles. Round face, round-framed glasses, permanent grin. He approaches the two of them before he enters.

"Afternoon all! Tell me the story of this scene."

"Visit was in relation to Operation Chainlink. We couldn't get any response, spotted someone unresponsive in the kitchen," says Rob.

"Performed a dynamic risk assessment," adds Josie.

Sanjee pulls a face as if she's got to the exciting part. "What did you do?"

"Smashed a pane on the door to gain access."

"Noted. Talk me through what you found."

"We found the victim, very clearly deceased, gun present. We swept the premises to be sure that nobody else was present. We called it in and withdrew."

"Nice. Very good." Sanjee beams at them both. "Nevertheless, I would like you both to put on suits and accompany me inside. We will step through where you went. It's important that I know this stuff."

Josie tries not to show how pleased she is to be invited back into the thick of things, even if it's just a fleeting glimpse. She and Rob climb into suits and put on bootees over their shoes before entering the house with Sanjee.

"Here we go. We'll step over the glass, so we don't track that inside." Sanjee takes it slowly, which is fine with Josie.

She looks properly round at the kitchen. It's functional, grubby. It's like being at one of those living museums. Nothing in here belongs in the twenty-first century. Even the kettle on the hob, decorated with stylised mushrooms, has got to be decades old.

"Hey, Rob. That kettle."

"Yeah. Who has time to boil water on the hob?"

"Handle's to the left," Josie says.

"Fuck, yeah. Gun's by the right hand."

"Intriguing detail," says Sanjee. "Obviously, you'll let DI Gill know your observation."

"Obviously," says Rob."

44

My trip to Braunstone makes me late for work.

I'm never late, even though nobody's keeping tabs.

I don't like it.

I take a walk around the casino, letting the familiar rhythms of the job bring me back to earth a little. I have the jitters after my run-in with Seamus Wollacott's family.

Still. I managed to de-escalate that situation. Calm authority is still within my grasp, I just have to reach for it.

Orla Hawkes gives me a smile as I pass by where she's serving. It's not her usual greeting, it's more like sympathy. Pity, even. I don't like that.

I need to get that calm authority properly back in my life. It grinds my gears that the staff feel that they have to protect me. It's supposed to be the other way round. I am the rock that anchors things here.

I fling myself into routine.

Having the police borrow some of our spare uniforms last

night has left a mess in the break room, where a lot of storage tends to get dumped.

I launch into it, dragging things out of boxes and organising as I go.

I end up with a massive bin bag full of ancient lost property and uniforms from before our last re-branding. All of that can go.

There's a load of uniforms that needs to go to the cleaners, either because it was used last night or it smells funny from being at the bottom of this funky pile. I bag it up, ready to go.

"Thought I paid you to walk the floor?" Gabe's here. Again.

"Having a purge. The police thing." I wave an arm at the room.

"Yeah?"

"Who's going to wear uniforms that the cops have borrowed?"

He concedes the point with a nod. "We should put this behind us."

His meaning is clear. Me looking at Lisa McNally's records has rattled him. He's had enough of this shooting thing now, he wants it back in its box.

I'll second that.

Things are unusually quiet into the early evening, so I take break and pull out my phone. I want to check out that link I found relating to Dominic Ferguson. If Nick Ferguson could be Dominic, then it's the only trace I can find of someone who was there on the night.

I pause and check in with myself.

Gabe has made it clear that he wants the casino to move on.

The healthy thing for me to do would be to move on, too.

Trouble is, I tried that already, and then it came looking for me. That stupid post of Kieran's told the world that I did this.

I went and stirred up trouble with Seamus Wollacott's family, which wasn't what I set out to do, but I can't deny that it felt good to be doing something.

I'm not someone who sits back and waits for things to happen, I like to be the one who's making them happen.

I click on the link. It's a news story from last year about a fundraiser for kitting out a junior rugby team: the Oadby Cubs. The photo shows a beaming row of kids wearing their new kit, along with their coaches. One of those coaches is Dominic Ferguson. I zoom in on his face, but of course there's no way I can know if he's the right person. Those police shooters looked like robots piling out of the van in the dark.

Does he look the right age and build to be an armed police officer? He's probably mid-thirties, and he looks fit, so yes.

I don't know what to do with this information, so I sit back in my chair and sip my tea.

The thing is, I do know what to do.

I look up where the Oadby Cubs are based, and their fixtures.

They have a game in a couple of days.

It couldn't hurt to take a look. Could it?

45

I have no idea why my mood is so much more buoyant as I make my way home after my shift. I think it's because I'm taking action, even though it's got me precisely nowhere.

I'm even thinking about cooking an actual meal, although it's close to midnight. My body hasn't seen a green vegetable in days.

I let myself into the house and call out for Kieran. His car's in the driveway, so I know he's here.

"In the lounge, Babe!" he calls.

His tone is odd, but I go through to find him.

"Come and sit by me," he says, patting the sofa.

I take in the scene. It might be late at night but he's got things set up for filming. A tripod faces the sofa, his phone on top, recording video.

"What are you doing?"

"Come on, sit down." He beams at the camera.

I join him. "What's the camera for, Kieran?"

"We'll just sit here and have a chat. Husband and wife, just come home from work. Normal, everyday stuff."

"We can do that." We never do that. "But why would we film it?"

Kieran hands me a can of RBuzz, but I'm not drinking that crap. I put it down on the floor.

"That other video was so popular, we need to put out a follow-up." He makes a goofy face at the camera. "Conversational stuff, nothing heavy."

I look at him. Has he gone completely mad?

"It's the brand, see?" He glances at the camera. "People think that a brand is all about fancy logos and that, but it's not. The brand is the people. You and me." He gestures between us, and then makes one of those hand gestures in the shape of a heart, directing it towards the camera.

I shake my head. "It's your brand, Kieran."

"No, Babe. It's us. You're the one who's generating all the interest."

I can feel my temper rising. "Can you turn the camera off please?"

"Will do in a moment. Just before I do, how's the past few days been for you? In your own words. Bit of a rollercoaster, eh?"

My spidey sense is bawling at me. I get off the sofa so I can check the phone. As I look at the screen, my throat tightens. It's not just taking a simple video. He's gone fucking live on social media. Whatever we were just talking about, we were apparently sharing it with the world. Little thumb emojis fly up the screen and questions scroll past too quickly to read. I stab the button to stop this horror show.

"Aw, what you do that for? Did you see how many people were watching?"

"I did not expect this kind of low trick from you, Kieran!" I keep my voice under control, but I am very close to losing my temper completely. "What the fuck were you thinking?"

"It's called making a silk purse out of a cow's ear," he says.

I cannot be correcting his stupid fucking grasp of the English language at this point, but my mouth's on autopilot.

"Sow's ear."

"Eh?"

"The saying is that you're making a silk purse out of a sow's ear."

"I agree!" He beams as if the thought is mine. "It's a win-win."

"It's not a win-win when you broadcast someone on the internet without their knowledge or consent. It's just a really shitty thing to do."

"Fuck's sake, Esther. You've been so wrapped up in yourself, what was I supposed to do?"

I ignore him. Stupid things coming out of his mouth shouldn't surprise me anymore.

"I'm sure you believe your version of things, but the world's moved on. You need to keep up."

I screw my face up in an effort to process what he's just said. "You what?"

"You need to keep up. There's no gun. You were wrong. Suck it up and move on."

He's standing there with that look on his face, like he knows he's said something unacceptable but it's his duty to say it to me.

Where do I start? Where do I even start?

He doesn't believe me about the shooting.

He's put that gormless fucking conversation out on the internet, which is going to make both of us look like idiots.

He sincerely believes that he's somehow doing the right thing.

I give up even trying to make sense of it and I leave the room.

46

The following morning I get up early enough to avoid any conversation with Kieran.

Today needs to have a 'fuck you' energy to it, so I start strong by making myself a bacon sandwich and taking it out with me to eat in the park.

Jeety's on a rest day, so I'm not running, but a walk around the park with a stop off for a bacon sandwich sounds like a decent substitute.

I decide that I might as well switch things up properly, so I drive into the city centre and park up near Abbey Park. I'll be closer to work when I finish my walk, and there's geese here. I can save a few crusts for them. Bread's not good for them, but I'm only talking tiny crumbs, and who doesn't love seeing a goose run?

It's a decent morning, and I'm here before most people. Life is good walking the paths here, as long as I don't slip on goose shit.

I sit down on a bench to eat my sandwich and I check my phone.

I wasn't going to do it while I was still in the house, but now I'm here in the lovely greenery, I can handle the crap.

Except ... I'm not sure I can.

However bad I thought it might be after Kieran's stupid video's gone out, this is worse.

I'm not on that many platforms, but notifications and messages on them all are on a scale I've never seen before.

I'm tagged in hundreds of posts, and most of them feature the same clip of me shaking my head at Kieran, looking like some uptight headmistress. Somehow I have also managed to turn my gaze directly to the camera right after that, glaring with my angriest face, as if I'm hating on every single person on the internet. I think it was the moment when I got an inkling of what might be happening.

"Fuck." I breathe.

The one I look at is captioned *Guys: here's how this bitch is to her husband. She got a guy SHOT!!! She's coming for you next!*

Most of the people sharing this are men.

I realise that Kieran's gym-bunny followers will mostly be men, but surely there are some nice people amongst them?

I only read a handful of comments, and I want to throw up.

My hands are shaking as I turn off my phone.

Out of the twenty-odd comments I read, there are four that mention how they'd violently rape me and two death threats.

I put my phone in my bag, and throw the foil-wrapped bacon sandwich in a nearby bin. I can't imagine eating.

I look around at the park that felt safe a few short minutes ago. It was a source of peace and tranquillity, and now all I can see are hiding places for people who want to attack and harm me.

I pick up my things and hurry to the car park. I don't know what's happened to my lung capacity, but I can't get enough air into my body. I have to stop twice to draw some extra breaths. I feel light-headed, as if I might keel over at any time.

When I reach my car, it feels like a sanctuary. I lock myself inside and feel the protection of the steel doors.

I try to steady my breathing and figure out what to do next.

Do I go to the police?

This stuff is illegal, definitely, but I have an idea that they won't be all that interested in stuff that's online.

Right now, I need to get somewhere safe, and that's not home.

I wait another ten minutes, until I convince myself that I'm not going to pass out, and I start the engine and drive to work.

47

Rob enjoys the drive to Whitwick Farm. The approach is leafy and pleasant, but Whitwick Farm itself is still a tumbledown mess.

He wonders what will happen to it. It will get sold, but will it remain a farm? The fields might be absorbed by another farm and the farmhouse transformed into a posh family home. It's a pattern that's happened elsewhere, and he's not sure how he feels about it.

An empty farm is an even bigger target for equipment thieves. The investigation into the farm owner's death and the aim of Operation Chainlink overlap considerably here. That's what Rob told Josie when he said they'd be going back to make a full tally of the items of value on the farm.

In the passenger seat, Josie stares across the fields. "For this inventory, do we have to look in all the fields as well?"

He turns to her. She knows the answer, she's just looking for extra material to sulk about.

"Consider it a challenge, detective."

"Ooh, spot the fucking tractor. They should make a kids'

puzzle book out of that." She makes massive comedy bug eyes as she pouts.

Rob laughs. "Come on."

They leave the car and approach the yard. It's still an active crime scene. DI Neelam Gill is there with her hair tied back in a ready-for-action bun.

"Rob," she says. "Can't keep away from this place, huh?"

"It's our well-known fascination for agricultural machinery," says Rob, deadpan. "We're doing the inventory. Kaminski is hoping to complete her bingo sheet."

"Operation Chainlink is our life," says Josie, hand on heart.

"Some probate solicitor will thank us too, I reckon," says Rob, with a heavy sigh. "Found anything of interest, ma'am?"

Josie eyes him, but he pretends not to see her noticing that he's looking for a sniff of the case.

Gill nods. "Want to take a look?" She glances at Josie. "You the one noticed that the kettle was positioned for a left-hander?"

"That's right, ma'am."

"Good eyes."

Both of them are keen to take a further look inside. Josie almost falls over her own feet, gleefully hauling herself into a onesie.

The body has been removed for post-mortem, but the rest of the room is frozen in time. Only the markers added by Sanjee's team indicate that anyone else has been here since the death of the man that they discovered yesterday.

No, that's not true. Rob sees that the gun has also been removed, but he can picture where it was.

The crime scene manager, Sanjee Baksh, is still there with a couple of members of his forensics team.

He might be wearing a face mask, but Rob can still see his grin of greeting around the edges.

"We've bagged and removed the firearm," says Sanjee. "Plenty testing we can do on that back in the lab." His hands come together, as if he can't wait to play with the gun.

"Cool," says Rob because he feels as if he should. He's never quite seen the fascination for guns. Sometimes he wonders what the world would be like if they didn't exist. Would there be some other small, portable killing device? Something else that would arise to take its place because people simply had to kill each other?

"So," announces Sanjee. "There are a couple of things I've told DI Gill here."

"Does one of them relate to the victim being left-handed?" Josie asks.

Sanjee makes wide eyes. "Ooh, an eager beaver, aren't we? Yes." He moves around the table to a grubby book. "Know what this is?"

"An old-fashioned ledger," says Josie.

"A perfectly functional ledger," corrects Sanjee. "Not everything needs to be digital. Our victim had been working on his accounts, as you can see from the date."

Josie peers at the page. "It's smudged where he leaned his hand on his own work," she says. "It's what lefties do."

Rob holds his hand out and mimes the motion, nodding along.

"Correct!" says Sanjee. "And do you know what's the icing on the cake?"

Josie looks at him. "You found ink on his hand, didn't you?"

Rob's not sure whether this is some sort of burgeoning mentoring relationship, or weird flirtation between the two of them. Probably both. Kaminski can do charm when she wants to.

"So a leftie shoots himself with a gun in his right hand," says Rob. "Suspicious. A set up?"

Gill pulls a face and tilts her head. "I don't know."

"You don't know?" says Rob. "That's suspicious, right?"

She looks at her notebook. "Aaron Bashford. Thirty-three years old. Born in Northumberland. No family left up there. Took on Whitwick Farm from a great uncle, now deceased, a few years ago after serving several years in the British Army."

"A soldier?"

Gill nods slowly. "Left-handed soldiers are trained to shoot right-handed."

"Is that a fact?" says Rob.

Gill is still nodding. "I googled it."

She gives a tight brief smile to Josie. "Good spot on the kettle thing. But suicide is still the likely scenario."

"What about the gun, ma'am?" says Josie.

"What about it?"

"It was a handgun. Why did a farmer – an ex-army farmer – have an illegal firearm?"

"That is a good question," says Gill in the manner of a woman who has been thinking the same thing. "I will ponder on it while you two count tractors."

48

I spend the entire day at the casino successfully avoiding people. It's a bit too easy. Perhaps too late, I wonder if the staff are all talking about me. Telling each other to leave me to my own devices.

The pity and the underhandedness piss me off in equal measure.

When I go home that evening, Kieran's there. I'm slightly surprised to see him packing up boxes of RBuzz. The RBuzz boxes are like furniture. They rarely move.

"Get some orders?" I ask. It's a light, functional question that doesn't touch on any of the other stuff.

"You not see my messages? He looks put out. "It's proper blown up. I've been flat out, packing and delivering. I was hoping you might be able to swing half a day, give me a hand."

"I've been busy," I tell him flatly. I don't tell him that I shouldn't be the one 'swinging half a day' to help him since I'm the only one bringing money into this household.

I leave the room before he can say any more.

What's going on?

I lock myself in the bathroom and look at my phone. I need to check it sooner or later.

I see a series of messages from Kieran.

Better mood today? Well, you will be later – only got some bloody orders from a gym up the road!

Then an hour later...

It's all coming home now Babe! Ten orders in the past HOUR. Be a fine thing to get all this stock sold. A band of fitness brothers out there want to support me. Coolio!

Two further messages indicate rising panic.

Babe, I could do with some admin help here. Any chance?

I'm drowning. Seriously. Come home will you?

Even in text form, I read a whining tone in his messages. He gives no further clue about what's prompted these sales. And why Trey, his actual business partner, can't come and help out with some admin.

I could do with knowing, but I hesitate to look on the internet. That was a nightmare last time.

I go to an empty browser and search for RBuzz Leicester, see what comes up. After all, I don't need to click on anything if I don't want to.

I don't know what I expected to happen, but the first hit I get is a YouTube news story on a channel called the Leicester Whisperer.

Of course, it's written by Kayleigh Chandler.

I click onto the headline.

"It's not my fault they can't find the stupid gun," says Leicester Woman at heart of shooting scandal.

My words. Feels like a lifetime ago that I said them, but they're my words.

The rest of the article is built around those other tiny

soundbites that I gave her. She's stood outside here and made a video about what I said.

"I saw what I saw" says Esther Butler.

It then shows parts of Kieran's video and talks about the tensions that have arisen in the Butler home.

"Fucks sake," I mutter.

I can hear Kieran starting to look for me, calling through the house.

I flush the toilet to buy myself a minute, while I watch the rest of this stuff. It all makes me sound like a complete psycho who's getting even with the world because my 'story' isn't being believed. And yes, the word 'story' is getting air quotes, now.

As I reach the end of the article I want to curl up and shut down until this has all gone away.

Then I realise that I haven't yet seen why this showed up in the search results for RBuzz. I scroll down to look at the comments.

Fuck.

The comments have not been moderated. It's all the same stuff as I saw earlier, just so much more of it. And it's even worse. I try to block out the awful ones, and focus in on the words I'm looking for, but I can't help myself seeing them from the edges of my vision.

I put a hand over my mouth as I scroll down, and then I find what I'm looking for.

It's from a user called TommyTruthTeller.

This man of hers needs a pass out of there. Join the call to action and buy his RBuzz drinks.

There's an impenetrable cluster of emojis and then a link.

I press to follow.

It's something called MRALeics.TV, but it tells me I need to create an account to join the live chat.

I'm pretty sure I don't want to do that.

I run the water and leave the bathroom.

49

When I come out of the bathroom, Kieran's waiting on the landing. "So? Yes or no? Can you take care of it?"

I don't know what he's talking about.

"You're not checking your messages at all are you?" He rolls his eyes. "Fine. I need to go out and make these deliveries. Can you be in for the next two hours? There's more stock coming this evening. Delivery from the wholesaler."

All I hear is that I have the place to myself for a couple of hours. I nod, hoping I don't look too eager.

Kieran leaves and the house is quiet. The house is quiet and most of the RBuzz boxes have gone. It's the one glimmer of light in a shitty day, and I walk around, trying to enjoy the space.

When the doorbell rings, I know it's going to be this massive delivery of new stock that's going to rob me of this lovely space.

I open the door and there's a guy with a clipboard. He's checking something on his form, and then he looks up at me.

He says nothing for a long moment, just stares.

"Sorry, can I help?" I ask.

"It's you."

"What?"

He thrusts the clipboard at me.

"You're the man-hater, right?"

Fuck. This can't be real. My hands shake.

"You want me to sign for the delivery."

He stamps a finger on the clipboard so hard he nearly knocks it from my hand.

"Fucking disgrace," he mutters.

I sign for the delivery. I want him to go.

He silently takes the clipboard and goes to his van. He removes a box from the side door and hurls it onto the drive.

"Hey! Don't do that. You'll damage –"

Another box follows. I can see liquid seeping from the first.

"Stop that! What's wrong with you?" I yell.

"What's wrong with me?" he asks, advancing towards me.

I shrink back. He's a large man. His angry eyes and gnarly beard make him look wild.

"I'll tell you what's wrong with me," he snarls. "I work hard. Every day. Me and every bloke I know. Peters-Mouldon gets it. He's the one that showed us what you did. Makes me sick to know that any time someone like you sees a man that makes them 'uncomfortable', you can snuff us out. Just like that."

I'm frozen to the spot in horror. He's using wild arm movements to display his disgust. Every move he throws, I flinch.

He stands there for a moment more and then returns to the van. He's got more of Kieran's stock to destroy. He throws some more boxes onto the drive, but now his focus is elsewhere, I can move. I go back inside and slam the door. I lean against the door, grateful that I am safe from harm, at least for now.

I can hear the crashing sound of the RBuzz drinks being thrown around, but I retreat into the house.

He mentioned Peters-Mouldon. *The* Peters-Mouldon. Paul Peters-Mouldon. I'm sure there are other people in the world called Peters-Mouldon, but he's the one who seems to hold sway over people who really ought to know better. TV presenter, column journalist, professional shit-stirrer.

Do I look? Can I bear to?

I put the kettle on while I think about it.

Peters-fucking-Mouldon. If he's talking about me, then this is mainstream now. It will be everywhere.

I need to know what he's said.

It's on YouTube on someone else's channel, but it's Paul Peters-Mouldon and he's doing that thing where he makes out he's being completely reasonable. Just asking questions. My picture's there. That video's there. There's a shot of the Meridian Casino.

Fuck.

"There is now a cultural presumption of guilt about all men," Peters-Mouldon says as the video cuts away to direct footage of him talking in a TV studio. *"All men are awful until they can prove otherwise. This shows what happens when a society loses grip of the idea of 'innocent until proven guilty' and decides always believe the alleged victim."*

He has that posh bloke thing. He must be right because

we've all been conditioned to listen to middle-aged white guys with posh voices.

The video cuts to a photo of Seamus Wollacott and then to the actual damned tea-lights and photos shrines in the Kingsway Social Club.

"*Let's emasculate men*," he continues. "*Let's strip away everything they are and tell them they're the problem. We've become so obsessed with virtue-signalling and demonising men, we've lost sight of basic fairness.*"

The images roll. Stock images of armed police, some random woman on a phone, a chalk corpse outline from some US crime show.

"Young men in particular feel put upon by this radical feminist agenda."

"Radical feminist agenda?" I whisper. "He had a fucking gun."

But I'm talking to myself.

I glance down at the comments section. I'm tempted to look. There's hundreds, but I know that they'll be horrendous.

KentonW: *The police didn't act on intelligence, they acted on fear.*

BensDad404: *A woman says 'danger' and suddenly all men are potential monsters.*

MRALeics: *What's truly dangerous is a society where accountability can't be probed for fear of antagonising the woke brigade.*

I can already feel my heart racing. My whole body's gone into fight or flight mode, but I have no idea how I might do either of those things when the problem is so intangible and pervasive.

I've been cancelled. That's what's happened. I've actually been cancelled. I honestly thought that only happened to celebrities.

I slam the laptop shut.

50

I wake the next day feeling just as bad as when I went to bed.

How is it possible that I had zero sleep and yet I was also plagued by terrifying dreams?

Those things can't both be true. I guess I drifted off.

In my dream I was in a tiny boat. The only other passenger was Lisa. We were on something like a wide canal, where the water should have been flat and calm. The ride should have been uneventful – pleasant, even. But I could see an enormous, unnatural surge of water coming. It was the size of a house, this bulge of water. It wouldn't even be possible in any scenario other than dream logic. I called out to Lisa to hold on, but when I turned away for a second, she was in the water, floundering.

I don't know what happened after that, but the terror seeps into my waking mind. I lie in bed, trying to re-work the dream, give it a happy ending.

Then I remember all of the real world terrors and the dream fades.

Kieran had spent his evening hosing down the drive and rescuing his precious stock. I left him to it after I realised I was getting nothing from him in the way of support or empathy, even though I'd been threatened on my own property.

It's really early when I crowbar my way out of bed. Just after five. There's no way I'm getting any rest.

I wonder if Jeety is up? Sometimes she's a proper early bird. To my relief, she answers my text and within ten minutes, we're jogging along together.

Day breaks as we run and that feels good.

"Have you seen how crazy this shit's got?" I ask her.

She nods. "You're on the BBC website now, did you know that?"

It seems as though I still have the capacity to be floored. "You what?"

"Yep. It's a story about the controversy around the shooting."

"There's only a controversy because fucking Peters-Mouldon made it into one!" I howl.

"It fucking stinks." Jeety's face is set into a fearsome glare. I'm suddenly glad that she's on my side.

"It's coming right to my door, Jeety."

"What do you mean?"

I tell her about the delivery driver.

"Surely the police need to step in?" she says. "It's like a hate crime, isn't it?"

"Is it?"

"Yes, it fucking is!"

I'm not so sure that the police will see it that way. A bunch of people don't like what I did. The police are hardly likely to slap me in witness protection, are they? Especially when they don't believe me either.

I blow out a long breath. "The police didn't find the gun and they didn't find the woman. If either one turned up, maybe they'd have my back. I dunno."

"Well I can't imagine you'd find the gun. What about the woman? You remember anything about her?"

"The police asked me all about the coat and hat she was wearing." I laugh at the recollection of all the pictures. "You know what caught me by surprise? Someone at the police must have the job of going round the shopping websites and grabbing pictures of different kinds of clothing. They had some that were not far off, to be fair."

"Jesus H Christ, Esther." Jeety gives me her widest smile, which has a manic shark-like intensity. "You do know that shopping is like my super-power, don't you? Let's go back to mine and sleuth the ever-loving fuck out of this thing."

I almost double up with laughter.

"What? What's the matter, you mad twat?" Jeety stops, hands on hips.

"I have no idea." I gasp for breath. "I think I just needed to laugh to stop me from crying, if the truth's told. But you're funny sometimes."

"Damn right."

"And I'm so grateful for you trying to help me."

"Less of the trying. More of the doing. Let's hit those online shops and hit them hard. I'm free now."

"I've got work," I say. "But later. I'll come over."

We run on. Jeety's enthusiasm and ideas lift me a little. But not enough. I've been cancelled. I've been called a liar. If my life isn't currently in ruins, I don't know what ruins looks like because it surely can't sink any lower than this.

51

I go to work. I cast around for all sorts of reasons not to. I could call in sick, but nobody will believe that. I decide that I'll go in and just avoid people. Easier said than done when you're the floor manager.

Once I'm in the casino that morning, I can begin to imagine how I might survive the day. I just need to find an excuse to be safe inside the building, but keep everyone at arm's length.

It occurs to me that I've been doing that for a few days now. When I was sorting out the storage in the break room, was I just using it as an excuse to hide?

Totally.

I force myself to walk around the casino. I smile at everyone, but avoid any talking. I'm just not capable of acting normal right now.

Orla Hawkes isn't having that. She looks as if she's been waiting for me, and she comes round the bar to stop me walking straight past.

"Nasty business you've got yourself wrapped up in." She has her phone in her hand, but I avoid looking at it.

I nod an acknowledgement.

She looks me over, perhaps seeing how rattled I am.

It would be so easy to meet Orla's gaze. If she has the slightest hint of sympathy in her eyes, I'll just lose it. I'll break down like a baby and sob into her shoulder. I can't afford to do that. I'm losing face at work, and I just can't afford to do that.

"Gotta go," I mumble and I walk away. I don't walk like a normal person either. Some sort of droopy stumble is the best I can do.

I make my way to the break room, intending to do more sorting. My phone buzzes with notifications.

One of them's from Kieran. I'm not even going to be looking at that.

The other is an e-mail from someone called Hannah Douglas-Jones who I've never heard of.

Dear Esther,

I hope you are holding up well at this difficult time. Right now, social media and the mainstream media are commenting on you in a way that must be very hurtful. I run a boutique PR consultancy firm in Leicester and I would like to offer you our services—

I close it down. Shit. I'm not looking at that. I'd do well to ignore my phone completely.

I get a call from Georgette on reception. *"Can you come down?"*

"Sure. What's the problem?"

"It's a bit hard to say right now."

"So, the problem's listening then?"

"Uh-huh."

"Is Baz there?"

"No."

"On my way."

I walk into reception and I have to suppress a groan. The person standing there is someone I last saw threatening me in a park over at Braunston. It's the pale guy who was with Seamus's mother and brother. This day continues to deliver huge steaming piles of crap.

I give him a brief, professional smile and then turn to Georgette. "Hi there, how can I help?"

"This gentleman wanted to speak with you."

I can tell by Georgette's intonation that she doesn't think he's a gentleman and that he didn't use those words. I act as if I know none of that and I turn to the newcomer.

"Let's take a seat." I wave him over to the bench seat.

"I'm Esther Butler. And you are?" If nothing else, I want to get his name.

"Mac." His flat, dead eyes meet mine. "You killed my brother. Remember?"

"You're Mac Wollacott then?" I'm not entering into the conversation about killing his brother. I'm doing this conversation in the foyer of our casino, effectively in public. I must summon all the steely professionalism I have left.

He doesn't look like the other Wollacotts, but I'm not doing their family tree.

"What can I do for you, Mac?" I glance up and I see that Baz has appeared and positioned himself close by, but he's looking away, maintaining a discreet distance.

"Thought I might join up. Come here and play the machines, you know?"

I nod. "I'm sure that Georgette explained to you how that works. You're very welcome to join."

He lounges on the seat, spreading himself out, luxuriating in the space he's taking up. "Yeah. Gonna need a line of credit. That part's not standard, apparently."

Is this an attempt to shake me down?

"No, sorry. There's no credit available."

"I think you're wrong."

His eyes slide sideways and bore into me. His gaze has an intensity that's exaggerated by his pale, thin face. It slides into a sneer, and he pushes his head forward. I'm put in mind of a snake.

"I think that there's a point at which you'd extend me some credit. It just needs me to push. The. Right. Buttons."

He uses his forefinger to grind into the bench seat as he stresses each word. His eyes never leave mine.

52

I'm supposed to be intimidated.

To be clear, I am intimidated, but I'm on home turf and Baz is right here, so it's not a serious threat.

"You don't get any credit at our casino, Mr Wollacott. You have my sympathies though."

He laughs, breathily, disbelieving.

"You see, I got thinking... Seamus used to date a girl here, didn't she? Lisa. Did you know her?"

I say nothing.

"Cos I asked Sorcha and Jenny at the club. They said you came in asking about Lisa. So you knew Lisa?"

"I didn't know Seamus," I say automatically, which isn't exactly wise since that's the line he's trying to draw.

I knew Lisa. Lisa dated Seamus. My phone call had Seamus killed. It's not a good look.

"I could just tell the world what I know," says Mac, with a grin.

That's enough.

I stand up, and glance at Baz. He's been watching, and he ambles over.

"Gonna be off now," says Mac, getting up. He takes his time, as though he's choosing this time to leave. "I'll be seeing you around, Esther."

I wait until he's left the building, then I smile my thanks to Georgette and Baz, and I attempt to withdraw again. Every member of staff that I pass eyes me nervously. How am I supposed to do my job like this? Nobody wants to talk about the shit that's going down, but they all know about it.

Is that fucking freak Mac declaring himself to be my stalker now? I kind of wish he had, because that would give me something to take to the police.

I go back to the break room to hide. Yes, to hide. Two seconds later, the door opens again. Baz comes in and I'm immediately wary.

Baz has always been easy enough to manage. The only unpredictable thing about Baz is where his fists might land if he gets physical. Day-to-day he's straightforward enough. But now, I'm viewing everything with suspicion.

"Hey Baz."

He sits down, looking troubled. "My cousin said I should talk to you."

This sounds like a red flag.

Baz, I can deal with. The moment he starts outsourcing his thinking, it's probably bad news.

"Yeah? What prompted that, Baz?"

"My cousin saw you on the news. Says you hate men."

I lean in towards him. "Have I always been there for you, Baz?"

"Sure."

"When things have been a bit sticky, have I always had your back?"

"You did, boss."

"Do you think I hate you, Baz?"

"No, not me."

"You're a man, Baz. I don't hate you and I definitely don't hate men." I sit on my hands to stop any air quotes happening. They'd weaken what I'm saying. "I don't like to see people treated badly, you know that."

He nods.

"Now, did your cousin say anything else that we need to deal with?"

"He said I should ask for a raise."

This is bad.

Baz knows I knew Seamus Wollacott, however tangentially. Baz is in possession of information that could make things very difficult for me, which gives him power. I don't know if Baz knows that, or knows what to do with it, but it makes me wary.

Baz might not know what to do with the power of information, but his cousin does.

This means that Baz has told him that I knew the shooter.

"Your request is noted, Baz," I tell him. "And I'm going to give it some careful thought."

Like hell I am.

53

Jeety has so many tabs open on her laptop, it's dizzying. She uses touchscreen and keyboard with such speed that I can barely keep up. All this is an effort to locate the mysterious vanishing woman via the clothes I saw her wearing that night.

I'm sitting on her sofa with a glass of Co-op Rosé in my hand. Jeety's husband Joel and the kids are out for the evening. Some Marvel superhero film followed by Drive-Thru KFC apparently. Nice for them.

Right now, I'm jealous of the simple calm of her home life. I feel safer here than anywhere else at the moment. I'm a ball of anxieties held together by my tension. In the last twenty-four hours I've been cancelled by internet trolls, featured on global news websites, threatened by Seamus's pasty-faced brother, Mac, and had Baz attempt to blackmail me in a way that, given all I've experienced recently, was quite sweet and naïve.

I've told Jeety everything. Well, almost everything. I still haven't come clean to her about exactly how well I knew

Seamus and how much I was involved in his arrest for drugs possession. But she knows enough to show the right kind of sympathy.

Searching for the mystery woman I saw with Seamus gives us purpose and, fuelled by really tasty budget wine and kettle chips, I am able to return slightly to my old self again.

Jeety is in her element, searching for the leopard print coat and baseball cap. She speaks the language of fashion like a native, and she's not limiting her searches to the new stuff in the shops. She's all over Vinted and Ebay too.

We've been at it for an hour and I've seen so many hats that I'm a bit dizzy and hat-blind.

But then she asks me about logos and marks, and while I'm not certain, I can visualise something in the shading of the mystery woman's hat that's like one of the styles she brings up.

"Fucking knew it!" Jeety kicks her chair backwards on its wheels, and slams the table with her hands. "Juicy Couture, bitch!"

"Good?" I say. I have no idea why she's excited. It's still just a hat, isn't it?

She gets in my face, impatient. "Don't you get it?" She waves a hand at the screen as if it's obvious. "Those hats were all the rage in the early noughties. If she's wearing one of those, at that time of the night, she's might have been at one of those nostalgia club nights, dancing to Britney or Sophie Ellis-Bextor."

"Huh. I must have not been paying attention when we did fashion hats at school."

"Don't mock my expertise," she says, giving me a playful punch. "The leopard skin coat matches too. Pure Indie Sleaze. Think Kate Moss, back in the day."

"Sure. So I now need to find out who had a nineties night last Sunday and then..." I shake my head.

"Ask if people knew her?" says Jeety. "Want me to get AI to do an e-fit thing?"

"You can do that?"

"AI can do anything," she says with a grin. "Seriously. I love my job but AI will swallow up nearly every graphic design job in the next five years. Less."

"And what will you do then?"

She tilts her head. "Wait for the apocalypse. The whole Skynet, Matrix thing. Collapse of civilisation. I think they'll need sign painters in the post-apocalyptic world."

"You think about the end of the world a lot, my friend."

"Bring it on," she says and tops up my glass.

We spend the next half hour mucking about with her AI assistant, getting all manner of images that sort of look like the woman I saw. I thought hat-blindness was bad, but now I can't tell if this woman or *this* woman is closer to the truth. I say as much.

"Memory's a funny thing," she says. "There comes a point where you don't know if you're remembering the actual event, or just referencing the last time you thought about it."

Our eyes meet for just a moment and I see exactly what she's thinking.

She doesn't think I saw a gun either.

She's trying to tell me without telling me. She's offering me a chance to come clean.

Fucking hell.

54

My best friend in the whole world doesn't think I saw a gun.

I feel both anger and anxiety come rushing in like a tsunami. She sees it too and grasps my hand tightly.

"I will *always* believe you, Esther," she says in a furious but controlled voice.

She says it with such ferocity and seriousness that her words punch right through me. And I feel like this woman is literally the only person I can trust in the whole wide world. It's enough to make me burst into tears.

I cry. I blubber. Big messy tears. Jeety holds me close and I want to protest that I'm dribbling all over her nice sweatshirt but I'm too busy sobbing.

We stay like that for maybe five minutes, but it feels like hours. I don't want to leave the comfort of her embrace.

And then the front door opens and her family spill in, chatting noisily. We separate quickly and Jeety passes me a tissue to blot my eyes and cheeks.

Joel and the kids come over. He sees my face and freezes awkwardly.

"Everything okay?" he says, which is a stupid bloody question and just a reflex.

"Having the best time," I say in the most unconvincing voice.

He nods, gives me a look that's mostly sympathy but framed with mild distaste, then puts on a cheery tone. "Come on, kids. Teeth clean, jimjams, and then kiss mummy good night!"

There's only two children but they make enough noise for twenty as he shepherds them upstairs.

I make sure I leave before they come down.

I go home. I don't want to go home. Home is the place where some brute of a delivery driver who spends too much time on the internet threatened me. Home is where Kieran tries to weaponise my nightmare and turn it into a marketing campaign. Home is where I should feel safe and supported and I feel no such thing.

Kieran is overnight somewhere in East Anglia, supposedly following up on another energy drinks sale lead. There was a time when I wondered if he was cheating on me, using these sales trips to hook up with someone. Now, I literally don't care. At this point, it would be a convenience to discover he was having an affair, an excuse to get rid of his spineless carcass.

I sleep alone and it would be a lie to say I'm not afraid. I'm afraid. I shouldn't be afraid but I am.

I wake to a quiet house and a cool grey day and I realise it has been a full week since Seamus died. That's it. One week. I get dressed and leave for work as soon as possible. Better to be at work than here.

I've got my regular work today, but it's not enough. I want to bury myself in activity.

I tackle the cupboard in the drinks area. Emptying and washing all the mugs, wiping down the cupboard and putting them back is the closest thing I can manage to meditation.

I peel back the layers of pain. It doesn't seem possible that a week ago, everything was so very normal. A week ago, I was doing my job, living my life and feeling fine.

Now, I'm hiding from the world and doing work that someone on minimum wage would normally do. I'm losing myself, in every sense. I hold up my hands, and almost expect to see my bones through the skin.

All because I saw a gun.

Everything hinges on that.

If I had a time machine and I could go back and look more carefully, what detail might I observe? What extra evidence could I get?

I feel utterly certain that if I'd whipped out my phone and tried to take a picture, I'd have ended up with an out-of-focus picture that showed nothing.

It's all in the context. In the body language.

It's all in the things that are impossible to explain or prove...

Which does beg the question: could I be completely wrong?

Kieran thinks I am.

Rochell thinks it's a possibility.

Of course I could be wrong.

If I was the police, I'd have questions too.

A thought lands in my head. It's so sudden and beguiling that I step away from the sink and first look inside my purse and then feel in my waistcoat pocket.

I pull out DC Josie Kaminski's business card.

55

Josie steps away from the final house on the row in Copt Oak. It's one of the nearest villages to Whitwick Farm, and with the tenuous Operation Chainlink connection, she, Rob and Walker have been drafted in to assist DI Gill's investigation into the death of Aaron Bashford.

She walks back along the B road to where Walker stands. He makes a hand gesture she doesn't understand, then realises he's gesturing questioningly at the pub.

"Bit early for a pint?" she says.

"I was thinking more a soya latte and a KitKat," he says with a smile.

Walker is a very likeable man. Okay, maybe his middle-aged dad shtick is a bit too smooth. Josie is sure his children both love him and groan at him in equal measure.

"A drink of some sort," she agrees.

"Compare notes?" he says as they head across the car park of the white-painted country pub. On the far side of the car park fence, there's a track that runs into the fields and woodland beyond the village.

"So basically, almost no one knows this guy," says Josie. "Woman who worked at the local CostCutter saw him there a couple of times. Beans, bread, lager."

"That his entire diet?"

"She thought he was a miserable sod."

"That a direct quote?"

"Yep."

He nods. At the bar they order drinks. Josie decides to go for a coffee to join Walker. She orders crisps too.

"Cheese and onion," he notes. "Prefer prawn cocktail myself."

"That's a psycho's choice."

"I'm a connoisseur."

After the drinks arrive he says, "Dora at the bar there says Bashford came in some nights. Her diagnosis was that he was suffering from depression."

Josie opens her crisps. "Can bar staff give psychological diagnoses?"

"They are students of the human condition. She reckons he had no social life, was a total introvert."

"Who came to the pub?"

"Reaching out? Trying to connect?"

She pulls a face.

"You like the murder angle because of your left-handed insight," he says, and he's right. "Very *Murder She Wrote*."

"You think it was just suicide?"

He see-saws his hand. "The gun thing is interesting. In days gone by, half the demobbed soldiers had a service gun secreted away at home. Half the guns on the street used to be old World War Two issued weapons. Nowadays...?" He sips his coffee. "It's weird."

"It is."

"The gun was a Glock 17," he says.

"I saw it."

"Recognise them by sight, do you?"

"I could see it was a Glock."

"Right."

"How'd you know it was a 17? Seen a report?"

"Just asked Neelam Gill. She knows me of old: from the pre-Duncan days, when I was working in the Drugs Squad."

"Glocks are very common," says Josie.

She's read police reports on seized firearms. There are a lot of homemade pistols out there in the criminal fraternity. Hideous one-shot zip guns that are as likely to kill the user as the target. There's been a steady rise in homemade 3D printed weapons. Converted sports starting pistols feature too. But actual firearms made by a recognised firearms company – Glock handguns currently top the charts in the British criminal fraternity.

"Maybe he had organised crime connections," she says.

"Two arrests for public order offences, both linked to alcohol?" Walker wrinkles his nose. "Hardly looks it. What I'm seeing is a former soldier with a poor social support network who – however he got hold of that gun – decided that ending his life was the right thing to do."

"Wow," she says. "You trying to make me suicidal?"

"It's a genuine tragedy," Walker says in a firm tone. "He wasn't the first. Won't be the last. You're buzzing."

"Huh?"

He nods at her. "Phone. Buzzing."

He's right. Josie doesn't recognise the number. She picks up.

"Hello?"

"Is ... is that Detective Constable Kaminski?"

She recognises the voice. "Esther?"

Butler? Walker mouths, curious.

"I have a question."

"Yeah? Is this about the incident? You should really be talking to DS Beaches about this case."

"It's a hypothetical question. About police stuff generally."

"Uh huh. Go on."

She pauses. Josie can hear her licking her lips nervously. And then Esther asks, *"Do the police hypnotise people? To help them remember more stuff?"*

Josie blinks. This is more than unexpected.

"Like, you could hypnotise me, couldn't you?" says Esther.

"Fuck," Josie says under her breath and hopes Esther didn't hear it. "Hang on," she says and mutes the call. She looks at Walker. "Esther Butler wants to know if we can hypnotise her to..." She waves her hand.

"Uncover her true memories of that night? Jesus. She wants to change her statement?"

"Maybe."

"That's TV detective nonsense. And it won't save her from a perverting the course of justice charge."

Josie nods and unmutes the call. "Yeah, Esther?"

"Yeah?"

"That's not something we do. Apparently, it's not reliable. Looks good on the telly, but it's not given credence by the courts."

Maybe she sighs on the other end of the line. *"Right. Thanks. Just thought I'd ask."*

"Is there anything else, Esther?" says Josie.

"And there's been these messages. On-line. I..."

"What messages?"

There's a long pause. *"Never mind,"* she says and hangs up.

Josie looks at her phone. "That woman sounds like she's in a world of pain."

"The woman who cried wolf?" says Walker but it's an open question not an accusation.

56

As I'm walking to work through the Highcross pedestrianised area, I see movement from the corner of my eye. As I turn to see what it is, my face is hit with wetness. It's not pain that I feel, but a deep sense of shock.

My hand reaches up to wipe it away and I see that it's the filling from an egg mayo roll. Someone has thrown it in my face.

"Who did that?"

It's embarrassing to yell like that, but my heart's banging in my chest and the words just erupt from me.

All around me, people – shoppers, pensioners, young people who should be at college – stare at me. No one owns up. No one shouts at me. They look at me with faint interest and disdain, like I'm a yapping dog whose owner can't control it.

"Who the fuck did that?" I scream.

No response, just stares. I can feel tears welling. I run

away. I literally run away, to the end of the pedestrianised bit, over the road and into the Meridian Casino.

I stumble in. Orla's on shift at the food and drink counter.

My breath is coming in heaving gasps.

She comes round onto the floor and takes me by my elbow.

"Come on. Let's go and get you cleaned up."

"Some fucker just threw this at me."

"Shush. Come on."

I'm being led away like a child. I'm supposed to be in fucking charge here.

She steers me to the break room, sits me down and finds a cloth for me to wipe my face.

Orla wants me to sit down for a bit, but I need the air. I have that sensation of just not being able to breathe the oxygen out of the air. Obviously, I can breathe, but why isn't it working? I'm light-headed, but I feel sure that the real air outside will help.

"Stay here a minute," she says.

"I don't want to be here," I say.

I don't want to be here. I don't want to be at home. I don't want to be in the streets where people think they can assault and abuse me. Places of safety are few in number now. At least the people here are trying to show me sympathy.

My phone rings. It's an unknown number but I wonder if it's that detective, Kaminski, phoning me back in response to my call earlier.

"Hello?"

"Ms Butler? Glad I caught you," says a woman with a well-educated accent. *"It's Hannah Douglas-Jones here. Just following up on my e-mail yesterday."*

"What e-mail?" I say.

"I run a PR and image management business in Leicester and, as I outlined in my e-mail, I really wanted to reach out and help you with all that's going on in your life right now."

Now I remember the e-mail. "I'm not talking to journalists," I say.

"I'm not a journalist," she says quickly. *"Image management. Literally here to help you and, let me be clear, at zero cost to you."*

"I don't need help. I'm not talking to anyone," I say and kill the call.

I look at Orla, a tension in my chest. "People won't leave me alone."

The break room door opens and Georgette from reception comes in.

"Ah, Esther—" she begins.

"Esther needs some space," says Orla.

"Gabe wants to see you."

"She needs a moment."

"It seemed urgent."

I gently push Orla's hands away. If Gabe wants me, he's the boss. I look in the full length mirror by the staff lockers. The mess has been wiped from my face and the fringes of my hair. There's a pale stain on my waistcoat but there's nothing I can do with that. I smell of egg and damp cloth.

"It's fine," I say in a weak voice.

I use the climb to the second floor to take deep breaths and reassert my professional mood and demeanour. I'm only partly successful. I knock on Gabe's open office door as I enter.

There's an unhappy wariness on his face which is not Gabe.

He can do difficult emotions. He can do anger. He can do worry. But like his hand gestures, he favours big and obvious emotions; slightly larger than life. This expression is something else.

I point at my face. “It’s okay. It was just an egg sandwich.”

“A what?”

“Egg sandwich. You heard?”

He half shakes his head.

“Someone threw an egg sandwich at me. Par for the course in my life, right now.”

He nods as though that makes sense. Which it doesn’t.

“I’m gonna cut to the chase, Esther,” he says. “We’re gonna have to let you go.”

I’m too shocked to be shocked. You can only hit a person so many times before they just stay down.

He’s firing me.

57

"What?" I manage to say.

Gabe waves his hands to indicate everything around him, not just his office but the casino beyond. "You know Meridian. We exist for the customers. We are a community, a family. People come here to be entertained, to get away from their own lives, to be the person they want to be in this ... haven. And we exist to create that space for them."

I know what he's saying and I want him to stop. I've spun this line before, especially when we've had to let someone go for unacceptable behaviour. Arguing with customers. Going beyond acceptable levels of flirting with the customers. There are plenty of people who come into the casino business and then cross that line.

I know it. I've dealt with those situations.

But this is me. I've done nothing wrong.

"Gabe, you can't fire me."

"Letting you go."

"You're firing me. How long have I been here?"

His mouth opens, like a goldfish.

"Fifteen years," I tell him. "I've been here fifteen sodding years. You can't just cast me aside."

"I'm not – I'm not doing that, Esther." He looks wretched, heartbroken, but I've only got sympathy for myself right now. "This business you've got yourself into. It tarnishes the image of the casino and, more than that, it draws all manner of eyes on us. We're not here to be seen."

I could scoff at that. Casinos are all about the glitter, the allure, the razzmatazz. But I know what he means. We – the people in the casino world – we're like those swanky high class butlers. We make it all work, but we should glide silently in the shadows, as serene as swans. In the casino, the customer is always the star.

But maybe he means more than that. Because Gabe's business is not squeaky clean. Never has been.

"The things I've seen," I hear myself say. "The things I know."

His miserable pity for me almost entirely dries up in an instant. "What of them?"

"I know what really happens here. I mean *really*. I know what the owners do apart from owning casinos."

"You expect to do something with that information?"

I shake my head earnestly. I'm not that kind of person. "When things got too close, when things got dangerous, like with—"

"Like Lisa McNally," he says, tapping his desk.

"Like that," I agree. "I helped. I straightened it out. I made sure she was gone with no trouble at all. I have been a team player throughout. My loyalty and service—"

"Beyond question," he says with a sigh. "Listen, Esther. I

am going to keep paying your salary. Two months. No, three months. Something to tide you over."

I feel cold inside now because this is really happening.

"But you've got to go," says Gabe. "We can't have this image. This kind of attention on us. It's not acceptable. I will write you the most glowing reference you've ever seen. I've got contacts in other casinos. Nottingham. Birmingham."

"Who'd want to live in Birmingham?" I say hollowly and I can't help but let a bitter smile burst through.

He tries a smile on for size too, but he's genuinely unhappy about this. "This is a done deal and I'm sorry. I'm so very, very sorry."

I nod slowly. "Orders from on high?"

He doesn't quite agree. The owners of the casino are like gods on a mountain top, inscrutable and rarely spoken of.

It's over. Fifteen years of the best job I've ever known. All because the world thinks I'm a man-hating liar. A murderer even.

What's there to say? I'd shake Gabe's hand but despite his evident affection for me, I can't forgive him.

I go downstairs.

"Everything okay?" says Orla.

"I'm heading off," I tell her.

"You thought of wearing some sunnies when you go out?" She holds out a pair of large sunglasses, and I realise what she's saying to me.

She's concerned that if I go out without obscuring my face, I'm just going to run into more trouble. She's right. My face spells danger.

"Thanks," I say and take them on my way to the door.

I don't let her know that she's never going to see them or me again.

58

"Esther! Get in here!"

I can hear Gabe's shout as clearly today as when I actually heard it two years ago. I've never heard him shout with such urgency before or since.

Two years ago.

I remember the moment clearly.

It's about six o'clock on a Tuesday morning. The Meridian Casino is open twenty-four hours a day, seven days a week, but there are some dead times, and early morning mid-week is one of them. It's a low energy time, a quiet time, a cleaning and taking stock time.

"Esther! Get in here!"

Gabe's shout pulls me from the reception area and down the rear staff corridor.

The door to the strong room is open.

I go in. Lisa McNally, with her cleaning tabard on, stands facing the corner like a naughty schoolchild. I can recognise her from behind – there are very few people with hair a natural copper orange like that. Her head is bowed and her shoulders shake as she cries.

I go straight to her, put hands on her shoulders.

"Hey, hey," I say softly. "What's going on here?"

"I didn't mean ... I didn't mean to look..." she manages to say between sniffles.

"Look?"

"Esther," says Gabe tersely. He's in the inner room, by the safe.

Time was when the cash room at the casino would be manned around the clock and thousands of pounds in cash would pass through here daily. The world has turned cashless since that time and the cash business has shrunk to near zero. The inner room and the big safe fell out of use. Official use.

The safe door is slightly ajar. There's a gym bag on the floor and I can see a bundle of bank notes in there. But more importantly, I can see the shelves of the safe. Packages of white powder. Cellophane-wrapped bricks and small baggies.

It's all cocaine. I know this. I know exactly what the casino owners have Gabe Savage keep in his safe. They've been using the casino safe as secure storage for their product for over a decade, and I've known for most of that time. I'm not even sure when I found out. It just sort of happened by osmosis, crept over me. I knew the owners were secretive, I knew they were dodgy. It's only a hop, skip and a jump from there to just accepting that they were in the illegal drugs business.

Gabe and I had spoken about it rarely, and in those conversations I always said the same thing – I didn't want to know. I understood the reality of the situation. I morally disapproved of it. No way was Gabe going to involve me in any of it. I wasn't going to allow any drugs use on the premises of a place where I worked. But I understood that the owners of the casino had made Class A drugs their business. I could compartmentalise my life enough that I could function as a casino floor manager – and love it – while the owners and the manager used an otherwise useless room to manage that side of the business.

"She saw!" Gabe hisses at me.

"I didn't mean to..." Lisa says, head turned away. "I was just walking by. I was polishing."

I realise she still has a duster and a can of spray polish in her hands. It feels ridiculous.

I step into the inner room. Gabe shoves the gym bag with the money inside the safe and shuts the door. It gives an electronic trill as it automatically locks.

"She didn't see anything, Gabe," I say.

His face contorts in anger. Gabe is very rarely angry. Honestly, getting angry requires energy and Gabe is, at heart, a lazy man. But this side of the business, I think it frightens him. I suspect that if he had his way, he'd just be a casino manager. This side of the work is something he had no choice over and the demands of the owners versus the legality of what he's doing makes him afraid. And that fear can turn into anger.

"You get rid of her!" he says in a tight and supressed whisper.

"Get rid—?"

"Get rid! Gone. Vanish. Finito."

I nod in understanding, if not agreement. "I'll deal with it."

59

I take Lisa to the break room. I sit her down. I make her a coffee. The coffee we have in the break room at that time isn't great, but it's the act of making it that counts.

I put two cups down on the table and sit.

I look her in the face.

I've spent a lot of time with Lisa over the previous year, more than I would with many members of staff. At first she'd been just one of the regular cleaning staff. I remember my first impressions of her were not positive. She was young, white and British – I made the prejudiced assumption that she wouldn't stick it out for long and be gone within weeks, if not days. I was wrong. She kept at it. Not brilliant, not awful, but always there.

And then I spotted the bruises and the behaviour and, yes, at first, briefly, I told myself it was none of my business; that I was probably making assumptions. But eventually I had to say something and, bit by bit, over weeks it came out. She had an absolute bastard of a boyfriend. The 'shitbag' she called him. It gave her some power to call him that, at least in this place of safety.

Sometimes I saw his car dropping her off. His black BMW with the rattling exhaust. He dropped her off for every shift and picked her up afterwards. Door to door, her life sealed from end to end.

For a specific period of time, I paid special attention to Lisa. With the benefit of hindsight, I recognise that she became a hobby of mine. I wasn't just angry on her behalf: I became enthusiastic about helping her. She was my pet project. If her only freedom was during the hours of work then I gave her that freedom. I took her out for lunch or breakfast, depending on how the shifts fell, and in those moments I tried to be a doorway into a better life. She was younger than me, maybe only six or seven years, and it was clear that she saw me as the wiser older woman. Not a mother figure as such, but something caring and protective.

Lisa's real mum was hundreds of miles away and seemingly didn't give a shit. Lisa's surname and copper hair made me think that mother might be in Scotland or Ireland, even though Lisa didn't have an accompanying accent. We never discussed her family.

On those meals out, I probed her for information and said all the right things about her poisoned abusive relationship with the shitbag. And she told me everything. How he 'worked from home' doing a mixture of decorating work and dealing weed to make ends meet – which meant he never kept regular hours and could be at her flat whenever he fancied. She told me about the controlling behaviour, the 'occasional slap' he gave her because 'women crave discipline'. Whatever she'd felt in the beginning for him had turned into hate and fear – she was with him because she was with him. It was a pattern and there was no escape. And no matter how many domestic abuse helplines I passed to her or women's refuges I tried to interest her in, there was no changing her mind. She wanted to leave. She really wanted to leave. But, in her head, this was something the universe would not allow.

And now this. She's seen inside the safe.

I hold my coffee cup between my hands on the break room table. "What you saw back there—"

"I didn't see nothing," she says very quickly and sniffs. Her tears are drying.

"Correct," I say. "You saw nothing at all."

"I'm sorry. It won't happen again."

I shake my head. "There's a line. You didn't know it was there, but you crossed it."

She blinks in wild surprise. "You're firing me."

"We'll make things right," I say. "We'll pay you to the end of the week."

"I can't lose this job." There's sudden fire in her voice. "Do you know what will happen if I lose this job?"

And I suddenly do. She'd intimated it before. Her income goes straight into the shitbag's pocket. He's the big man. All things go to him and he buys her what he thinks she needs. This job is part of his income stream.

"We'll work something out," I say.

"No. No." She's shaking her head, gripping the table and would be backing away if she wasn't sitting down with the wall behind her. "It can't change. If it changes..."

I grab her hand and squeeze it. "You can't live like this, Lisa."

"I can't..." She's fearful. People use the expression 'like a rabbit caught in headlights' but that's what she looks like. She's lived her life as a creature of prey. She has no responses to danger except flee or freeze.

"You can't be here any longer, but you can't return to that," I say.

"Then what do I do?"

"You leave."

"He'll find me."

"You leave and you go to a refuge. I was only speaking to that, er, Haven one in Coventry the other day. They have a room for a single woman. I don't know how long they can keep it open."

"He'll find me."

"He won't."

"He will. Unless he's dead or locked away, he'll find me."

And then an idea strikes me. It's both magical and terrible. It's insane and yet very, very workable.

"Then we lock him away," I say.

60

I leave Lisa in the break room and go look for Gabe. He's still in the strong room. The safe is shut. He's leaning on one of the old wall-mounted work counters next to it, staring at nothing and seething gently.

"Is she gone?" he says.

"Nearly," I say.

He sighs. He's pissed off.

"It's my fault," he says. "I was sloppy."

"You're human."

"Sloppy," he repeated.

I nod. He's right. "You need this to go away."

"I do. We pay her off."

"My thoughts exactly," I say. "How much are you willing to pay?"

He shrugs. He's not even thought about this.

"Give me one of the baggies."

Gabe looks at me. "What?"

"You can give me one and make it straight with the—" I

gesture airily to indicate people I never want to meet. "—with the guys?"

"She wants paying off with white?"

I nod. It's almost true. "And some cash."

He shakes his head but opens the safe. I know the code as well as him. It's not been changed in all the time I've been here.

He takes out a baggy and some cash held together with an elastic band.

"That's a forty gram baggy," he says. "Maybe worth a thousand on the street." He slaps the drugs and the cash into my hand. "A thousand in cash." He grips my fingers before letting go. "You're making this go away?"

"Absolutely," I say. "Close the safe. Be on with your day."

I pocket the drugs. I did a bit of recreational weed and E in my wilder days, but this is the first time I've held cocaine. I'm not happy about it. I'm not happy about any of this, but this wild, crazy perfect idea in my head carries me aloft.

I go back to the break room.

I tell Lisa the plan and she's shocked for maybe a minute, then I can see she's as entranced by it as I am. I get her to confirm the shitbag's car registration number and where he parks at night. And then I phone the women's refuge in Coventry. If Lisa can be there tomorrow afternoon then they can guarantee her a room for at least three weeks.

Lisa takes the cash and drugs, barely even noticing them. We go over the plan. The more we plan and double check, the more her emotions settle until she becomes strangely empowered with confidence: a woman on a mission.

She leaves at the regular time at the end of her shift as though nothing unusual has happened. I am tempted to go out and see her picked up, but I don't want to jinx anything with unusual behaviour.

I try to get through the rest of the day but I'm thoroughly preoccupied. I go home and let Kieran's monologue about how his fledgling business with Trey is going wash over me. At nine o'clock, I declare I'm going for a jog.

"At this hour?" says Kieran but doesn't comment any further.

I leave the house in my jogging gear and only go down the road to the corner where the Aberdale Pub stands. I stand beneath a street light, google the Crimestoppers number and phone them. I can't call the emergency services direct without them having my number and that won't do.

I'm nervous as the number rings and then a man answers. I give him all the details.

"There's a man dealing drugs. He's got all this cocaine in his car. Cash too." I give him the address and the car details. "I think I saw him threatening a woman with a knife," I add. "Hurry."

I only stay on the line long enough to be sure I've conveyed the details and the sense of urgency. Lisa's already told me that the shitbag's got a record for drugs possession and for carrying a blade. Forty grams of cocaine. If the police bother to act then that's got to be enough to secure a conviction, surely?

I put the phone away, continue my run and then go home.

If all goes to plan, I'm driving Lisa to Coventry tomorrow.

61

Lisa, the shitbag and the planted cocaine in his car. That was all two years ago. And, though it's hard to believe, I'd managed to push it almost entirely from my mind.

It was a crazy episode, a situation to which the equally crazy solution had presented itself so easily. Everything had slotted into place so simply that I'd just been able to get on with my life afterwards and, yes, forget about it.

But now, with all the other shit raining down on me, that incident has the potential to come back and bite me. Seamus Wollacott is dead. The police can't find the gun that I was so sure I'd seen. Seamus's creepy brother and casino security Baz both know enough of the truth to cause me real trouble. The internet, particularly those hate-spewing misogynist keyboard warriors, have turned on me. I've had abuse – and egg sandwiches, for fuck's sake! – thrown at me in the street. And now I've been fired.

If this isn't rock bottom, I don't know how I could sink any lower.

I make my way home. Kieran is in the front room, sitting on the sofa in his shirt, tie and underpants. His trousers, neatly pressed, hang over the arm of a chair. He's eating a protein bar and doing something on his laptop. By the state of his clothing, I'm guessing he's on his way out to another work thing. I could almost laugh. His work is actually turning into real work now, actual money-in-pocket sales of the luminous RBuzz drinks, fuelled by my misery.

He looks at me, surprised, almost affronted that I've turned up a home early.

"Aren't you meant to be at work?" he says.

I could lie to save me pain but I don't have the energy.

"I've been fired," I say.

"You what?"

"I've been fired."

He doesn't get up to comfort me. His expression of surprise hasn't changed.

"What for?" he says.

"Huh?"

"What for? Why did they fire you?"

My whole head and shoulders do a shrugging shake. "Because of the Seamus Wollacott thing. Because of the negative publicity."

"Can they do that?"

The question never even occurred to me until that moment and I'm irritated by it more than anything else.

"I don't know," I say hollowly.

He sniffs and scratches his cheek. "Understandable though, really."

For a second his gaze goes back to the laptop as though he thinks this conversation is over.

"I've been fucking fired, Kieran," I say. "Gabe fired me. I loved that job."

"Been there a long time," he agrees.

"And you think it's understandable."

"I'm just saying..." He spreads his hands and fails to explain what he is 'just saying'.

"What? What?" I demand. "What's understandable?"

"Well, the man's dead, isn't he? And people are looking round to see who's to blame."

"I didn't fucking shoot him, Kieran!"

"No, but you told the police he was armed."

"He had a fucking gun!"

"So you say."

"So..." I knew Kieran felt this way about the matter. For the past week he's been – at best! – a spineless fence-sitter about the whole matter. And now he's creeping down from the fence and he's on the other side of it. I'm about ready to explode.

"You're my husband!" I shout.

He tries to shush me and waves his hands. "The neighbours will hear!"

"Sod the bloody neighbours!" I yell. "You're my husband! You're meant to be on my side!"

"I am on your side!" he squeaks. "I'll always be on your side, no matter what you've done!"

"No matter what I've done? You're meant to believe me! Taking my side means believing me! If you've not got my back then what's the point?"

"But I don't believe you." He says it calmly and clearly, like this nugget of personal opinion has been waiting inside him for days. It comes out clear, well-rounded and unambiguous.

"What?" I whisper.

He gives me a rare honest look. "Esther, I'm sorry, but I don't believe you. I want to but I don't. I don't know what happened that night. I think it was dark and you were maybe scared or excited or got caught up in the moment, but I don't believe you saw a gun. If you had, the police would have found it by now. They just would. I don't know why you did it. I'm not convinced that you hate all men. Maybe you've got an axe to grind. I know things can be tough. I'm sure you've put up with a load of crap in your time and maybe this was the moment when you decided to do something about it." He shrugs. "I made marriage vows to you. To love you. To care for you. To stand by you. And I will do that, no matter what you've done."

I can't bear to listen to any more of this. I don't know what's worse, the fact that he thinks I deliberately called the police on an unarmed man or the fact that he thinks he's being reasonable and loving by taking this attitude. Does he actually think that this is what a loving husband says or does?

"Fuck you," I say simply. "I'm not putting up with this. This—" I say, waving a hand between us two "—and all this," I add, gesturing around at our house: our half-formed life filled with boxes of vile second-rate sports drinks. "We're done."

I leave and go upstairs. I don't know what I'm going to do up there because I can't picture myself staying here for a minute longer.

"I've supported you!" he calls after me. He's at the foot of the stairs. I look down on him. "I've supported you, Esther," he says. "Frankly, I've bloody carried you this week. I've done all you could ask of me. And maybe – yeah – maybe I've bloody tired of being the one who does all the carrying round here."

I'm not even going to dignify that bollocks with a response. I go to our bedroom and slam the door.

62

Emotionally, socially, I've backed myself into a corner. I don't have many options left.

I change into non-work clothes and then I pack a bag. I pack two bags. I throw enough clothes and toiletries into the big suitcase and the travel rucksack we've had since that three week trip to Thailand we took before the pandemic.

"Oh, come on!" says Kieran as I lug them downstairs and out to the car.

That is, apparently, the sum total of his argument.

He watches me from the door as I put the bags in the car. His mouth hangs open, not because he is stunned, but because he has nothing else he can say and that stupid expression is the only thing he's got left.

"And your drink tastes like piss!" I snap at him before getting in and driving off.

Any sense of victory at flouncing out on a douchebag husband doesn't even last until the end of the road. I've got nowhere to go. At some point I'll ask Jeety if I can crash at her place for a while, but I don't want to cash that chip in right now because it will be calling in a favour with possibly my one last ally in the world.

Right now, I just need to go somewhere. And I need to be doing something.

As I drive through the city with no particular destination in mind, I think through the options. I try to ignore the fact that two men are trying to blackmail me over this matter. If I can prove there was a gun, if I can prove there was a woman in danger, then despite the links between me and Seamus Wollacott, I can salvage my public image and get everyone that matters back on my side. I've got two angles I can follow. I know the name of the one of the firearms officers – Nick Ferguson – and I can try to find out if the mystery unknown woman was at some nineties nostalgia night in the city somewhere.

I could try and contact the copper, Ferguson, through the rugby club he's done charity work for. I'm not quite sure what I'd say to him.

"Er, hi, I'm the woman who called the police over that guy you shot. Any chance you did actually see a gun and, dunno, lost it somewhere?"

That's not going to be an easy conversation. Searching down a mystery woman at one of the dozens of nightclubs or hundreds of bars in Leicester is not going to be any easier, but at least that doesn't come pre-loaded with awkward conversations. I'm going to get straight onto that.

I park up on a side road and decide to do this on foot. I pull up my hoodie and put on the sunglasses Orla gave me. I glance at my reflection in the window of a disused shop. I still look a lot like me, but I'm not a master of disguise.

I head over to the Novotel. I've decided that's where I'll start.

Very occasionally I will take leaflets to some of the hotels. Never hurts to grab visitors to the town. As a result, I have a paper-thin relationship with some of the managers. The Novotel is close to the casino and it puts on various events and has its finger on the pulse.

I walk in and recognise the woman on reception. She's always been a friendly face.

"Hey," I say as I walk over.

"Esther," she says, remembering despite me being out of work gear. She glances around. The reception area is quiet, so we can talk. "Why do I see your face wherever I look?"

"It's not through choice, Elaine," I say with breezy honesty. "It's been a nightmare."

People use that phrase very readily. 'It's been a nightmare.' I vow never to misuse it ever again for mundane inconveniences like the car insurance going up, or the washing machine breaking. This has been an actual nightmare, like one of those horrible dreams where you can't move or breathe while some malignant force gets closer and closer.

"I bet," says Elaine, as if I've indeed just told her that my washing machine has broken.

"I have a question that you might be able to answer," I say.

"Sure! Fire away," she says.

"If someone had been out on Sunday night at a club, where might they have gone? Something with a nostalgia thing going on. Early noughties."

"Yeah." She tilts her head. "Sunday, you say? 2Funky. Or maybe the Grotto."

I must have looked like I didn't recognise the names. "2Funky's pretty close by. Over by the big Tesco. The Grotto's on the way to Abbey Park."

I briefly wonder if it makes me officially old that I can navigate fine using supermarkets and public amenities. Probably.

"Hey, wait a minute. Is this to do with the, um, thing?" asks Elaine.

I start to speak, but think better of it. "No. Not really. Thanks Elaine."

As I leave she calls after me. "We need some more leaflets. And take care out there, Esther."

I wave a goodbye and head over towards the big Tesco.

2Funky turns out to be a large venue made from modern brick with what looks like several different function spaces.

I walk around, but it's all closed up.

"Reckon they're not open for a few hours yet."

I turn and see someone washing the sign for the Tesco car park.

I huff mildly. "Thanks. I'll come back."

As I'm about to leave, I cross the road and ask the sign-cleaner, "Any idea what was happening there on Sunday night?"

The cleaner has a head of unruly curls that bob as he moves.

"Oh yeah! Whole place was hired out for a wedding. Bollywood themed. Should have seen the cars that turned up."

"The whole place?"

He nods. "Deliveries all day. Massive thing."

He turns back to the sign, which is already really clean.

He buffs it with a separate cloth. I wonder how many times a day he wipes this sign.

"Thank you."

I cross back over the road.

I guess it's not 2Funky then.

I head over towards Abbey Park, in search of The Grotto.

By the time I've walked there, I've found their Instagram account. They post regularly, which is great for me.

I come upon the building, which is very different to 2Funky. It's concrete and a little grim from outside.

I can see from the Instagram pictures that it's all dramatic neon tunnels and vibey atmosphere on party nights. We can all overlook a grim exterior if the inside is fun.

It's also closed, so I lean against the door and flick through their social media pictures. They have nineties nostalgia nights every Sunday and Wednesday night. I pore over the six pictures they posted from the night of the shooting, zooming in on every single one, to see if I can find the mystery woman, but there's no sign of her.

I look up from my phone and stare up and down the road, as if I might expect to see her, which is ridiculous.

But still. I reckon she was here.

I just need to come back when they're open and flash around the mocked-up AI images Jeety made on her laptop.

It's progress of a sort.

63

I head back to my car.

It will be dark soon and I crave its protection, rather than walking the city streets wondering who might attack me next. I've not looked at any news or social media content all day. Who knows what crap is circulating?

What else am I to do? I'm burning with an energy to find answers; to make this whole mess I'm in move in a direction that I want it to go.

I drive to Oadby and the grounds of the Oadby Town Rugby Club. It's on Wigston Road, not far from where Kieran and I live. Lived – past tense. If I'm lucky, Dominic Ferguson will be there or someone can put me in touch with him and – if I'm really lucky – he'll turn out to be the Nick Ferguson who was on the firearms team that shot Seamus Wollacott.

There's a large car park, so I pull up and try to decide how I'm going to do this. I can see kids and parents piling out of cars all around me, so it's easy enough to get pulled along in the group, who are all heading past the brick-built clubhouse to the pitch.

The pitch is floodlit. It seems like a very professional setup.

I don't know who's the home team and who's the away team.

There's ranch-style fencing around the edges, and parents are watching from the other side.

I'm wearing the sunglasses, even though it's dark now, and nobody accosts me with accusations or threats. It's possible, for a short while, to imagine that I am a normal person who's just here to watch some sport. Possibly with a fictional child who's there in the thick of it.

I'm standing next to a dad who's murmuring a commentary to himself.

He's declared his expertise, so I reckon he's fair game for my questions.

"What team is this?" I wave my hand in a deliberately vague manner.

"This one's the Cubs, and the ones in red and black are the away team, from Moseley." He turns to look at me. "Which one's yours?"

I point at a cluster of kids and don't give him a chance to question me any further. "Are the coaches any good? I've never met them."

He claps his hands together, as if he's been waiting a long time for someone to ask him that very question.

"Your Cubs have got that chap, Ferguson. He's not as technically on point as our Barlow, but he can really motivate the youngsters. They adore him. Barlow might well out-manoeuvre him today though."

These kids are so small. I'm slightly surprised at the seriousness.

"Where is Ferguson?" I ask, as if I have failed to spot someone I know well.

He looks around. "Obviously not on the field during a match. He'll be along here somewhere." After scanning the crowd he points to a tall man, very focused on the play. "There you go."

"Oh, yeah."

I drift backwards and make my way over to Ferguson. This is going well.

I stand behind him for a short while.

Nothing in his appearance would make you think he'd have a job where he could take someone's life, or that he was someone who'd wade into a dangerous situation knowing he might die. He's large and physically fit, but he looks like a regular person.

My phone rings. It interrupts me in my pursuit of Ferguson but I answer anyway.

"Esther?"

"Uh-huh?"

"Hannah Douglas-Jones again. Please don't hang up."

I'd have blocked her number if she'd seemed like a threat. She's more of a nuisance. "Why though?" I'm shaking my head.

"You probably don't realise that I can actually help you."

"What?"

"I really can. I can be of immeasurable use to you."

"How?" She'd said she was in PR. An image person, she'd said. "An image person? What even is that?"

"PR and image management," says Hannah. *"It's my job to turn the tide of public opinion. Seems to me that you could use that."*

I pause, thinking.

She takes that as her cue to continue. "*There are some powerful voices who've aligned against you, but it's not a lost cause. Come and see me. We can plot a course to get you your life back.*"

"I don't think you're in a position to do that."

"*Try me. Ten o'clock tomorrow morning. I'll text you the address.*"

"Whatever."

Did I just agree to go and speak to this woman?

I have clearly become desperate.

64

I focus on my mission again.

I squeeze forward and stand next to Nick Ferguson as the noise of the rugby game in progress plays beside us. His eyes are on the match.

I could wait until the end, or until there's a break, but I don't. I remove my sunglasses and turn to look directly at him.

"Nick Ferguson?"

He looks at me. It takes him a long moment, but I see recognition dawn. His mouth forms the beginning of an expletive, but he checks himself.

"What are you doing here?" he says. It's that same soft Scottish accent I heard him use that night by the old train station.

"I came to talk to you," I say.

"You can't be here."

I raise my eyebrows. "And yet I am. I've literally come to—"

"No, no, no." His eyes flicker across the people to his left and his right. He's not happy about what he sees.

He withdraws from the edge of the pitch and gives a tiny hand gesture, beckoning me to follow.

A dozen feet back from the edge of the pitch he stops and faces me. "What are you doing? We cannot talk to each other. This is not okay."

"I just need to talk to someone."

"There's a live investigation."

"Yes, I know. It's properly messed up my life. I need—"

"I don't mean that investigation."

He hisses in irritation and glances at the crowds of people lining the pitch. None are looking our way.

"I mean there's an investigation into *me*," he says in a harsh whisper. "Do you know what happens after the police shoot someone?"

I want to say yes but I realise I don't.

"We're all suspended from duty. The IOPC... Every day more questions. Which is why you can't be here. You're a part of it."

"I *am* a part of it," I hiss-whisper back. "Like you wouldn't believe. My life's fallen apart because of this."

Something in my tone makes his face change. Is that a flicker of empathy?

"How do you mean?"

I'm so hungry for another human to care about me that the simple act of him asking the question prompts a rogue tear to fall from my eye. It surprises me as much as it surprises him and I quickly wipe it away.

"Lost my job. I've had to walk away from my marriage. My home. And the threats... It's been bad."

His poker face shifts. I see conflict there. He's trying to

keep his mask in place, but that small shake of his head tells me that he's bothered by what I just said.

"I just need some answers." I want to press it home. He must help me.

He puts his hands on my shoulders. It's a weird, macho move. Proprietorial, even. So why does it feel so good?

I wonder if I've sunk so low that any kind of caveman move that makes me feel protected is enough to fill me a with a warm glow. Is it because this sports coach is treating me with the same comforting paternalism he probably shows to his youngsters?

I'm confused, delighted and horrified at myself, in equal measure.

"Please," I say.

"We all want answers," he says. "But the thing is—"

"No. Don't wheel out mealy-mouthed fucking 'buts'. If you wanted answers, you'd work with me." I give him the full wattage of my most determined glare.

"Work with you? What does that even mean?"

His hands are still on my shoulders, which is making me want to trust him. "The woman. I'm going to find her."

He grins. "The woman that my colleagues can't find? You're going to find her, are you?"

"I am very motivated. And I have a lead."

"What's your lead?"

"Oh right, yeah. I'm going to tell you and you're gonna go off and do your own thing. No. Not a chance."

He releases my shoulders. I feel bereft.

"Tell me what you know," he says simply.

"It's pretty flimsy, to be honest. Noughties nostalgia night at Grotto nightclub. Reckon she goes to it."

"You know this?"

"I suspect it."

He looks at me as if he's expecting more. "And that's it? That's your lead? What, were you just going to go along and hang around?"

"Yes."

It does sound like a rubbish idea, now that he's said it out loud.

He blows out a long breath, as though I'm trying his patience.

"I cannot help you. I cannot be seen talking to you," he says and now his voice is suddenly formal.

"But we both want answers."

He steps back and shakes his head. He waves his hand at the game going on beside us.

"This is a family event. Children. You have no reason to be here. I can call security."

I stare at him.

"We can do this loudly or you can just leave," he says, and waits.

I go back to my car and drive out of the car park as quickly as I can.

65

I wrestle with various conflicting thoughts about where I might spend the night. I really want to go to Jeety's. I want to feel safe in her house with her domestic clutter and her kids.

But I decide to splurge on a couple of nights in a hotel. I crave the anonymity of a place where nobody knows me. For that reason, I avoid the Novotel, as it's much too close to work.

The Premier Inn over by the station will suit me fine, and I can check in without talking to a human.

I get something that almost resembles a decent night's sleep. Almost. I'm still haunted by vivid dreams, and I wake up several times; but I sleep.

I decide that I am going to meet Hannah Douglas-Jones. I've thought several times about not turning up, but she sounded so certain that she could help me that I need to give her a chance.

Her office is over on New Walk. It's an upscale area. It

speaks of gravitas. Pushy little hustlers like Kayleigh Chandler wouldn't have an office on New Walk.

The thought cheers me.

The area around New Walk has that slightly university campus vibe. Pedestrianised streets, upmarket coffee shops, leafy trees overhanging the paths. Hannah's office is in a smart Georgian building. I push through the gate in the railings and find the button with her name. She only has a small part of the building, so I guess she's a one-woman operation.

The door buzzes open and I turn left into an office that is nicer than any office has a right to be. The walls are the palest green and the massive windows have blinds that let through a muted haze of light.

"Welcome," says Hannah. She shakes my hand.

There's a desk, but it's away up a corner. Hannah ushers me over to a pair of old leather Chesterfield sofas that face each other. A tiny lounge area, with a coffee table between them.

Hannah herself is the most striking thing in the room. I'm not sure how tall she is, but man, she's tall. Tall and blonde and imposing, like some Viking warrior goddess. She carries herself like a dancer, as if she aspires to be even taller. With high heels on, too. She's an impressive sight.

"So glad you came, Esther," she says as I take a seat.

She positions herself opposite and picks up a teapot. "Can I pour you a cup?"

I nod and watch as she pours tea as if she's in an advert. Everything she does is poised and controlled.

She hands me a cup with a wide smile.

I don't know what I expected, but Hannah is not it. She

looks as if she should be the editor of *Vogue*, or reading the news on the BBC.

"Do try one of these biscuits," she says, pushing a plate forward. "One of my small indulgences is fancy, artisanal biscuits. Some people would put fresh flowers on the table. I like something you can eat."

Her obvious pleasure as she takes a fancy iced biscuit is infectious and it forces me to take one too.

"Now, Esther. I've seen lots of coverage of your story," she says. "I've seen it in regular news outlets and some highly irregular corners of the internet. People are very interested in you."

I crunch down on the biscuit. It's very good. "Well, I wish they weren't." I think on what she just said. "What do you mean by irregular corners of the internet?"

Hannah waves the last part of her biscuit. "Those horrid, unregulated places where you and I would never go."

I wonder how she knows, if she never goes there.

She sees my confusion. "I have someone who does a little detective work for me."

"Oh." This is all making me quite uncomfortable, even though it's not very surprising. "Detective?"

"That's right."

"Oh."

"What I would really like, is for you to tell me everything. In your own words." She leans back into the sofa.

"It's a lot." I imagine she must have appointments.

"Don't care," she says. "If it takes all morning, that's fine. I have more biscuits."

And as simple as that, I launch into the story. I describe what made me follow Wollacott in the first place. Hannah stops me to clarify certain points.

"So, it was a mixture of instinct, and a soupcon of bloody-mindedness?" she asks, after I tell her about Baz trying to stop me.

"Yeah, I guess so!" I laugh at the idea. It feels so good. Not only is she listening closely, she's giving me a different perspective.

I describe the police arriving, them hustling me into their van, and then hearing the shot.

She's interested in the interview.

"Kaminski's not on the investigating team?"

"No. I think she was just filling in because she was available. A guy called Beaches is investigating, and he seemed a bit pissed off when Kaminski showed up again, asking questions."

Hannah jots down some notes. "Useful to know. If we have police officers with a difference of opinion, we might be able to use that."

I have no idea what she might mean by that, but I continue.

66

"So I went home," I tell Hannah, "and I expected that I'd be able to move on. That there'd be questions and stuff afterwards, but that I'd get over it all and move on."

Hannah gives me a moment. She can see me looking back to that version of myself when I thought the only worry I faced was getting over a violent confrontation. I shake my head at how unprepared I was for the coming shitstorm.

"But it didn't go that way?" she prompts.

"No." I sigh heavily. "Let me tell you about my husband."

I go back and re-live all of the stuff with Kieran. Getting this stuff out of my head feels so good. It removes some of its power over me. Kieran's a knob. End of.

Hannah sucks her teeth as she jots some notes. "Makes sense, everything you've just told me." She raises her eyes to meet mine. "Not that it makes sense that he behaved that way – but I can see that he's got support from some unsavoury groups, whether he knows it or not."

"Unsavoury groups." I echo her words. I wonder if I can

reduce the terror that they've induced in me by reducing them to a dismissive two-word description. It would be nice to think so. "And from them to Peters-Mouldon."

She pulls a face. "Yes. Peters-Mouldon has lots of opinions on things, doesn't he?"

She's tapping her pen on the page, thinking over what I've just told her.

I take another biscuit. They are very nice.

"Is there anything else that you think I should know, Esther?"

She raises her eyes and smiles. Her kindness and her poise take me by surprise.

This Hannah Douglas-Jones is the kind of woman I perhaps wouldn't naturally trust. She talks like she went to private school and then some posh university. She has the bearing of a woman who might spend her weekends playing polo, or on a yacht in the south of France. She has the looks and elegance of someone on her way to a debutante ball. This whole set up in this grand Georgian building in this part of the city speaks of money and privilege and someone who has absolutely nothing in common with me.

And yet, bizarrely, she speaks and acts with such direct honesty that I actually think I might trust her. I want to confide in her. I want to tell her all of the things that are bothering me.

"You know this?" I point between us, trying to indicate that *this* is the discussion, the relationship; whatever we're calling it.

"Yes?"

"Are you bound by a code? The things that I say to you, they'll remain confidential, yes?"

She puts her hands over her heart. If anyone else did that,

I'd think they were taking the piss, but she makes it look heartfelt and genuine. "Absolutely, Esther. You have my word."

"Right. Good."

I think about it some more.

"Maybe there are some more things that I ought to add, but first of all, why don't you tell me what it is that you can do? And, more importantly, why you would do it? You said you weren't going to charge me, right?"

"That is a very valid and sensible question," she says. "First of all, let me describe my business in broad terms. Mostly what I deal with day-to-day is publicity and reputation management for people who have some considerable influence. Politicians, celebrities. Maybe the odd Leicester City footballer or two. Increasingly, I get internet influencers who want to expand their activities in different directions."

I nod along. That all sounds like stuff that I'd assumed. Stuff that's a million miles away from me and my experiences.

"What I would normally do for them depends very much on the individual situation, but I tackle things in a multi-pronged approach." She counts off on elegant, manicured fingers. "Controlling the narrative means that outbound communication must be agreed and carefully managed." Another finger. "I'll create opportunities for positive exposure. Creating reputational capital, if you like. Aligning your name with values that matter." She grabs hold of her finger and waggles it for emphasis. "And most importantly, in your case, we have crisis management. It's like a dance where we need to grab hold of the choreography."

She grabs the imaginary choreography by the scruff of its neck and gives it a shake.

For a moment, I dare to believe that this woman can do the things she says.

"And as for your question about pro bono work..." She inhales deeply, painting a picture of thoughtfulness. I'm beginning to see how she succeeds with people. Everything she does is like a mini performance. "I do this from time to time. I call it strategic altruism."

"Strategic altruism." I try out the words. They are words that I understand, but the concept feels slightly alien. "Do you mean that you get a load of high-profile brownie points if you manage to turn around my kind of shitshow?"

"Yes! Exactly that." She claps her hands with delight. "And some personal satisfaction, of course. And if, at the end of this, you get a book deal or a Netflix documentary, then I'll take my fifteen percent." She smiles to indicate that this is incredibly unlikely.

I start to relax. It's a self-serving reason, but it's one that makes complete sense. And it shouldn't harm me.

"Happy?" she asks.

I laugh. "I'm struggling to imagine ever being happy again, if I'm honest. But if you mean, am I satisfied with this as an arrangement, then yes."

She tips her head in understanding. "Now what was it you want to tell me? What do you really want to tell me?"

67

I sit across from Hannah, a tea cup in my hands. I'm telling her *everything*.

"I was backed into a corner," I say.

I've told her about the threats, about leaving Kieran, about being sacked.

"You know how sometimes, doing nothing is just not an option?"

"Very much my area of expertise," she says. "You're preaching to the converted."

"I know that I had to act. I had to try and get to the truth myself. Nobody was believing me about the gun. The police haven't found it, they haven't found the woman; I'm pretty sure they think I made all that stuff up. I decided to do some digging of my own."

She spreads her hands. "Entirely understandable."

"To understand some of the things I'm about to tell you, it's important that I should let you know something. It turns out I knew the man who was shot."

She leans backwards, surprised. "Do go on."

"I didn't know I knew him – not until afterwards. It's messy and weird."

I spill the whole story. I tell her about Lisa, about how Seamus abused her and about how I set him up.

"I went over there a couple of days ago. I tried to find Lisa, but I found the Wollacott family instead."

She nods. "You were following leads, very understandable."

I tell her about the family. About Mac following me, trying to shake me down. And how he's not the only one. Baz, in his dumb, ham-fisted way is also trying to do the same thing.

Hannah's making more notes, nodding encouragement.

"Is there anything else?" she asks.

"Yes." I'm going all-in now. "I tracked down one of the police marksmen who shot Seamus. And I think I know where to find the mystery woman."

She blinks her surprise. "Good lord, Esther. You've been very busy."

I feel a tiny swelling of pride. It's true. I've achieved a lot, and it's nice to have someone acknowledge that.

I tell her about Ferguson, and about the clothing that the mystery woman wore. I show her the AI images on my phone.

Part of me expects her to instruct me to tell the police what I know, but she doesn't.

"More tea I think. Back in a moment."

We drained the teapot some time ago.

Hannah disappears into a small kitchen area where I can hear water running. She strides back into the room with a fresh pot and sets it down.

"You've got a lot going on, Esther."

A momentary horror clutches me. She's going to say that this is all too messy and she can't help.

"But it's all addressable."

I give a small bark of laughter, as relief almost chokes me. "Sorry. I mean, good. Thank you." I'm making no sense.

She smiles. "I will work up a formal strategy for you. Now, that sounds ponderous and dull, I know, but you'll see how important it is that we agree on some key basics. Having them written down is essential."

"Yeah." That makes sense.

"Now, from what you've just said, there are some true statements that we can make. For example, you never actually met Seamus Wollacott ahead of that evening. Is that correct?"

"It is true."

I knew of him. Knew what a monster he was, but I'd never clapped eyes on him.

"Then that is the line we're going to draw in the sand," Hannah says. "You never met him. If it turns out you had a mutual acquaintance, then that's something to deal with separately. The stuff about the drugs at the casino – that never comes out."

"Obviously," I say.

"Obviously."

I nod. I like what she's doing.

"I think what we might want to do is craft a press release and put it out through some hand-selected outlets. You can express remorse for what happened, but we can frame it heavily with the idea that you were looking out for another human being. That your role as protector is part of your job and one that you take very seriously. Leicester's night-time economy is in your blood."

She pauses to think.

"Do you think there would be some people who might give us some quotes about how you're an important part of it? We can paint you as a beacon in the dark."

"Yeah." I mention Elaine at the Novotel, and a couple of others in similar positions. I'm wary of asking anyone in the casino. Gabe might close it down.

"Good. I'll start to work something up."

"What do I need to do?" I ask.

"You have one job. It's very important. You do not speak to any press without me there. Where are you living at the moment?"

"The Premier Inn in the city."

She nods. "Stay there. Keep yourself to yourself. Do not make any kind of public statement. You do not leak anything about a relationship with Seamus Wollacott. That's it."

"I can do that."

68

Keeping my head down is not easy. I'm living out of a suitcase in a city centre hotel. I can't spend my whole life in there.

But I try.

I stay indoors a lot and when I do go out, I put my hoodie up and wear Orla's sunglasses. I realise that I need to change my appearance. Just enough that maybe people will take a second look before recognising me.

I go to the city centre market and drift around the stalls selling hair dyes and make up. I would rather leave my hair colouring to Sophie's Hair Studio in Wigston, but I'm not going to put myself in such a public scene right now. I pick out some easy application dark brown hair colour and then look at switching up my make up. Casino work is customer facing but super professional. I always wear make-up but keep it restrained.

As I look over the mascara and eyeshadow, I think of the nineties nostalgia night at The Grotto. The next one is tomorrow night. I told Hannah Douglas-Jones that I was keeping my head down but maybe – maybe – I can go along to that night, try my hand at finding my mystery nineties woman.

So, some nineties style make-up, perhaps?

And clothes too. Leicester Market occupies a space bordered on all sides by tall buildings, but within that confined area there's all manner of clothes stalls. And if I'm going retro, the places round here could be just the ticket.

After an hour's searching and a bit of haggling with a woman whose English was limited to only numbers, I bought some wide cargo trousers, a bomber jacket, and a bucket hat. I was born in the nineties so my knowledge of the era is poor, but I think I can rock some sort of All-Saints/garage look. Maybe I'll just look like one the Spice Girls' mums. Whatever, it's a change.

On the way back to the Premier Inn, I pop into an offy to buy white wine and chocolate. It's been a decisive day in a crappy week and I deserve endorphins.

Back at the hotel, I apply the dye to my hair over the small bathroom sink.

While I'm doing it, there's a message from Kieran on my phone. It's the third one since I left.

The first one asked when I was going to be back.

The second said he was worried that something had happened to me. I sent him a curt reply as proof of life so he didn't do something daft like call the police.

The third message could have been an apology, or a plea to come to my senses, or a declaration of his love for me and his commitment to the marriage. It was none of those. The third message was him asking if I knew where the contract agreements with the RBuzz manufacturers were, and if I'd put them in 'the filing'. I've no idea what secret filing system he thinks I have or why I might have put his business files there.

I ignore the message and sit around the room, waiting for the dye to take and watching daytime TV. Once I've washed and dried my hair, I run a brush through. I'm surprised that it looks okay. It looks cheap and the colour is flat, but it looks like the hair of a woman who's decided to try brunette for a while.

I get into my running gear and decide to road-test my new hair in public. I go for a jog around Victoria Park and the university buildings, turning back as the evening sky darkens. I don't expect my new hair to be some sort of invisibility shield, but I also don't expect people to recognise some random jogging woman as that man-hater off the news. The jog in public is a declaration to myself. I'm changing things, I'm being active, and I'm not going to be afraid.

Back at the hotel, I shower.

I can't stay off social media completely, so I go and see what's happening.

The news stories are still there and, even at a tiny glance, I can see that the hate is still spewing out at me. Of course it is.

There's a weird article that's gained some traction in which a female commentator, who appears to think she is defending my actions, has suggested that the mystery woman I 'claimed to have seen' was a mental projection. That I had pictured myself, other women, every woman, in that space, next to the dangerous and toxic man. And (the weirdo goes on) it doesn't matter that there wasn't a woman there – the danger represented by male nighttime predators is a universal reality.

As anyone could have predicted, that commentary draws ridicule from every side. And the worst part is that it feeds into the growing assumption that I must have invented the woman, just as I 'invented' the gun.

I go to bed without even opening the wine. I'm suddenly miserable, my brief optimism severely dented.

I wake up in the morning to a buzz from my phone. It's a WhatsApp from Hannah Douglas-Jones with a link to a press statement, carried by a news website I've never heard of. It is the press statement we'd agreed upon – my sorrow at the man's death, my understanding of the difficult work the police do, my concern for a very real woman I saw in danger. It reads well. I can see how it avoids certain matters, but it strikes all the right notes.

Another message follows from Hannah.

Call me when you can. I've got good news.

69

I call Hannah.

"Your statement is out in the wild," says the PR woman.

"I see."

"And there are people who like it enough to want to hear your side."

"Uh-huh."

"I'm going to line up a couple of interviews with sympathetic and trustworthy journalists."

"Really? We want to do this?"

"I've got Minnie Shroeder at the New York Times chomping at the bit."

I'm sure I've misheard her. "The New York Times?"

"Yes, indeed. American newspaper journalism is still something to be respected. Minnie worked alongside the reporters who broke the Harvey Weinstein story. She's really interested in women who are targeted by internet pile-ons, particularly on gender issues."

"Right, but..." I run my hand through my hair, dazed. "How is the New York Times going to help me here?"

"This is a battle on many fronts. Doing an interview with Minnie will be good for you. Trust me."

I don't understand, but I think I do trust her.

"Okay. I guess."

"And—" her tone changes suddenly *"—you should be aware that there are going to be some other news stories coming out over here. The Wollacott family have spoken to the tabloids. 'Our heartache at the unlawful killing of our son' et cetera, et cetera. You're going to be named."*

"Fuck."

"Yep. I know."

"What are we doing about that?"

"We let it ride. You don't challenge it. You don't comment on it. We fight your battles – the fight to be believed and to be able to protect women when they are threatened. Let the police tie themselves in knots with details. Let the family grieve as is their right. We focus on you."

"Okay."

"I'll get onto Minnie and tell her it's a yes. You keep living a very quiet life. Don't do anything we haven't agreed on."

It's Thursday. I think about the nineties night tonight at the Grotto. I shouldn't go but, like my grandma used to say, I was "a girl who won't be telt".

"I won't do anything we haven't agreed on," I say.

70

"Huh," says Rob.

Josie spins in her chair to look his way.

She's been in the Duncans' corner of the CID office for just over a week and she's getting familiar with her new colleagues. A strong part of her still doesn't want to. She knows she's not going to get out of this sin bin for a long time, if ever, but she doesn't want to become institutionalised best buddies with Rob and Walker.

But despite her intentions, she is getting to know them. She knows that Walker loves his kids but wonders if they've become distant, having mentally flown the nest, even though one of them is still living at home. She knows that Rob's latest tattoo removal session hasn't gone as well as he'd wished and he's already planning to book in the next session to eradicate his personal ink.

She also knows that when Rob says, "Huh", it's a conversation opener.

"What is it, Sarge?" she says.

He gestures to the computer screen. "Looking through the Aaron Bashford investigation files."

"Yeah?"

"Financial reports show several large cash deposits paid into his personal account over the past six months."

"Yeah?"

"Thousand pounds. Thousand pounds. Thousand pounds."

Josie thinks about this then shrugs. "So, our farmer does some cash in hand trading."

"Do you think any farming actually went on at Whitwick Farm?"

"He was selling stuff off? Maybe our farmer sold the tractor, sold the cow? That was how he was supporting himself. Maybe he ran out of things to sell and that's why he shot himself?"

Rob rocks in his chair as he considers this. "You buy the suicide angle now?"

"It is, annoyingly, the most obvious answer. Except..."

"Except?"

"He used an illegal firearm. Maybe it wasn't the farm equipment he was selling. He was ex-military. He knew guns. He could have been operating as an illegal firearms dealer. That's where the money came from. That's where the handgun came from."

"And yet it's a thousand pound a time," says Rob. "Very specific."

"Gill asked you to look at that?"

He wrinkles his nose. "No. Just bored." He looks around. "And hungry."

"Want me to grab lunch?" she says.

Walker and Rob favour a halal sandwich shop a way up

Belgrave Gate for lunch. Josie agreed to have one from there on Friday and now they are locked into some sort of rota from which she might never escape.

"Salmon and cream cheese bagel, sure," says Rob.

Walker is not at his desk. He's spent the morning trying to contact some sort of ex-soldiers' welfare liaison person to talk about Aaron Bashford. Josie doesn't know where he is now.

"Turkey ham and salad. All the pickles," says Rob.

"Always the same."

"He likes what he likes."

She needs the walk. Josie slips her jacket on and makes her way out. She's halfway down the corridor to the stairs when Scabbard leans out of a meeting room door.

"Kaminski." He clicks his fingers and beckons her in. He's back inside before he even sees if she's obeying.

She sighs and walks back along the corridor and into the room.

It's a long meeting room, but there's only two people in it. She doesn't recognise the woman in a suit opposite Scabbard.

"Sir?" she says.

Scabbard gestures at the woman. "This is Khadija Ali, CPS area lawyer. This is DC Kaminski – no need to sit, Josie. You're not staying." He addresses the Crown Prosecution Service lawyer. "Kaminski took the initial witness statement from Esther Butler and questioned her further when the gun issue first came to light."

Josie's not quite sure what this is about. The lawyer is nodding and making notes.

"The CPS has seen the interview transcripts from that Sunday night," says Khadija.

"Actually Monday morning when we spoke to her," says Josie.

"Everything seems to have been handled correctly and Mrs Butler was given ample opportunity to amend her statement while she was here. Is that correct?"

"It is. She was. She said she saw a gun before she called the police. She said she was sure Seamus Wollacott had one on him when he went into that building site."

More notes.

"The CPS is considering charges of Perverting the Course of Justice against Mrs Butler."

"Oh." Josie is not sure what else there is to be said.

Scabbard half turns to Josie but doesn't actually look at her. "We're taking the Wollacott family's claim that she acted maliciously very seriously."

Khadija Ali raises her eyes to Josie. "We need to know if there's any part of that interview process where appropriate procedures were neglected or overlooked."

"Not at all," Josie replies instantly.

"Mrs Butler's mental state. Her capacity to answer the questions put to her. She looks very composed on the tapes."

"She's a very confident woman," nods Josie. "A lot of spirit."

"Was there any sense that she was glad the man was dead?"

"None whatsoever."

"If this was malicious and we get Perverting the Course of Justice," says Scabbard, "can we go for Manslaughter by Unlawful Act."

Khadija's head wobbles with a suppressed laugh. "The CPS is unlikely to pursue that. Rarely used and very difficult to prove."

"But you are going to charge her with Perverting the Course of Justice?" asks Josie.

"We're weighing it up. We would need to show intent."

"There is no gun," says Scabbard. "She lied."

"We need to show intent," the lawyer repeats. "A connection between Mrs Butler and Mr Wollacott."

They're seriously considering legally pinning this on Esther. Josie is surprised but shouldn't be. If they do, and they get a conviction, Esther could be looking at several years in prison.

71

After dark, I walk to the Grotto nightclub. It's straight down Charles Street for a mile and a bit from the hotel. It's drizzling but not proper rain.

I'm wearing my cargo trousers and the bomber jacket over a plain T-shirt. I have the bucket hat wedged firmly on my head. It's not a great look. I look like I'm a mum having a mid-life crisis, but the important thing is that I don't look like me.

Being out in the city after dark feels unpleasant, given everything that's happened. For the longest time I have the feeling that I'm being watched. I look round but the only person in sight is a woman walking on the opposite pavement some way behind me. I force away the stupid feeling and press on.

The doors to Grotto are open and there's pink lighting and some pumping music from within.

I wouldn't call myself a nineties aficionado, but I recognise *Rhythm of the Night* by Corona. Maybe it's a night of cheesy dancefloor fillers.

I pay my seven quid on the door to get in and go through.

The place is buzzing, considering it's nine o'clock on a Wednesday. I step inside, buy a bottle of something blue at the bar and take a stroll around the place. There are several rooms. There are private booths and waitress service in some. It's a trad club in other spaces. More women than men, mostly thirties and forties. There's a cheesy girls' night out feel to the place, mixed with a general here-to-get-smashed-and-make-bad-choices vibe.

There's no place from where I can view the whole club. I either need to keep circulating or find somewhere to hang out for a bit.

There's a gang of women on shiny sofas on a raised area opposite the DJ. There's a spare chair.

"Can I sit here for a bit?" I ask one of them.

"Sure, love," says one and doesn't pay me a moment's further notice.

I sit and nurse my blue drink and watch. The DJ slides from *Rhythm of the Night* into *What is Love?* and I find myself unavoidably singing along.

A small blonde woman stands by the rails and looks at me for a minute. I look back at her.

"You okay?" I say.

"Do I know you?" she asks. She has a foreign accent, maybe Scandinavian or something, and she lands on each syllable with exactly the same stress.

"No," I say.

She raises her eyebrows, simultaneously curious and bored. "You look like you're waiting for someone..."

"Maybe," I say and get up.

I'm not hanging around to wait for this woman to recognise me from the news. My dye-job and bucket hat are not a perfect disguise.

I do another tour of the club. The dance floors are starting to fill. As I cross through the main room again, I look across in case the small blonde woman is watching me. She's not where I left her.

And then, as I go through a chill room, lit by blue neon tubes, I see a baseball cap. It's so blatantly *the* cap that I am frozen to the spot for a moment. I literally blink and look again. It is the woman.

I am seized by sudden self-doubt. I have thought about this woman so often over the past days that maybe I am ready to latch onto any woman as a possible candidate.

But it's her. It really is.

She's not wearing the leopard print coat, but that hat and that hair… I recognise the shape of her face, now that I see it. I would bet a million quid on her being the woman.

She's standing by the bar and chatting to a man. She has a glowstick bracelet around her wrist while she drinks from a tall glass with a straw. I can't tell if she knows the man or if it's a casual meeting. I can't read the body language between them in this light and noise.

And while I'm staring at her, she glances across and sees me. Not only does she see me but she recognises me. I can just tell. She stares long enough that the man looks round too. He's got an unruly mop of dark hair and a firm jaw that partly makes up for the deficiencies in the rest of his face.

I take a step forward and the woman says something to the man and turns away quickly, leaving her drink on the shelf table. I want to call out to her, but I can't afford to draw attention. Also, how will shouting bring her back? She saw me and ducked out.

I step after her.

The Grotto club is dark and loud and I lose her almost

instantly, only to find her again as she steps into a lighter corridor near the main entrance.

She's leaving. She's seen me and she's running like she's seen the devil.

"Wait!" I call out, a reflex action.

She doesn't look back.

I want to know why she's done that. I want to know and I want to ask her. I have to give chase.

I'm running fast enough towards the exit that the bouncer holds out his hands to stop me.

"Whoa, whoa, whoa. You can't take that out with you."

I have no idea what he's talking about, then realise he means my drink. I look at it like I've never seen it before, thrust it into his gloved hand and run outside.

The drizzle has turned into a full-on downpour. I'm going to be soaked within seconds.

I stumble away from the light press of people by the door and look around to see which way the mystery woman has gone.

Grotto sits at the corner of a four-way junction with a dual carriageway running through it. Car lights in the rain confuse my vision as I try to locate her. There are people: silhouettes in the streetlight. I look from place to place.

There's the orange light of a black cab across the road. I'm not sure if there's a taxi rank, but maybe it is. I move in that direction.

I see a head, a hat.

"I just want to talk!" I call out, no idea if it's her.

She could be anywhere, disappeared into the night. I go to the pedestrian crossing to cross to the taxi rank. Unless she's just walked straight back into the city centre. That might be an obvious direction to go in.

I stab the button for the crossing lights even though I've already pressed it once and I put my hand up by the brim of my hat to give my face a little more shelter. The cargo trousers are starting to stick to my legs.

I'm thinking about just running across in the next gap in the traffic when a man's voice right next to me says, "Hello. Fancy meeting you here?"

I look round. In the dark, his pale-as-a-sheet face is almost ghostly.

It's Mac Wollacott. Seamus's brother.

72

Mac Wollacott stands there, a black hoodie framing his white face like he's the Grim Reaper.

I don't say a thing.

"This is a coincidence, isn't it?" he says, making it very clear that it is nothing of the sort.

Has he been following me? Has he been watching me?

"I like your new hair," he says.

That both angers and terrifies me. He doesn't get to comment on my hair. He doesn't get to comment on any of me. And yet here he is, less than a foot away, staring intently right at me.

"I went by your work a couple of times," he goes on. "You weren't there. Someone said you'd left."

The lights change. I make to step out to cross the road but Mac's hand is suddenly on my elbow, holding me back.

"How are we going to sort out our arrangement if you're not there?"

"Getting your fucking hand off me!" I hiss and violently shrug my arm away from his.

"Don't raise your voice to me, bitch!"

Streetlights and headlights make bright stars of the falling rain, but there's another glint of light. In his other hand, held down low, there is a blade. It's not a big knife but you don't need a big knife to kill people.

I look around, but there's no one in the immediate vicinity. Maybe ten, twenty metres away, there is the doorway to Grotto. There are the outlines of the bouncers against the pink light, sheltering inside from the sudden downpour.

And in a moment of stark, insane clarity, I think to myself that I am dead and this is hell.

It's that fateful night all over again, but things have swapped.

I am the woman, dressed to go clubbing, with the angry man who is ready to kill. And close – so close – the protectors of the nighttime economy look out of their little doorway, maybe even seeing us. I can imagine them talking.

"Him. Over there."

"What about him?"

"He's got a weapon."

"You saw it?"

My heart pounding, I weigh up my options. I could run into the street. The little crossing man is still green. I could run back to Grotto. I could yell. I could scream. A truly rational part of me thinks that if I yell – not scream but yell at the top of my voice – yell and scream "He's got a knife! This man! He's got a knife!" then people will look and Mac won't know what to do. But I don't do that. I don't know why. Am I the woman who cried wolf one too many times?

Mac's hand snakes round my waist and I feel a finger hook through one of the waistband loops of my cargo trousers. He pulls me close with a sudden tug, my hip into his crotch.

"You and I need to talk, don't we, Esther?" he says.

He inhales noisily through his nose like he's breathing me in.

This man, this nothing of a man, this pasty evil fucker, has hold of me with one hand and a knife twelve inches away from my stomach with the other.

"Come on," he says.

He presses even closer, grinding himself against me before steering me along the pavement, away from Grotto, vaguely towards the city centre. I walk with him because I can't think what else to do in this moment. I know there is something to be done but I can't seem to find it. I know that when I find it, I will be able to act.

He guides me across a road, propelling me on.

He's talking, muttering, and I have to tune in to hear him.

"I just want what's due to me. I lost a brother and that's not fair. And the fucking cops, they've not even offered an apology. It's fucking shit. I just need some mark of... I just want an apology and some compensation. You know that, Esther? You know that right? You owe me. You owe me big time."

The shops and businesses on either side of the road here are almost all closed. There's a fried chicken shop on the other side of the road, but I can't see anyone in it.

"What are you going to do for me, Esther?" he says. "How are you going to earn my forgiveness?"

There's a beep of a horn from a car going past and a yell of "Oi! Oi!" from one person to another. For a second, Mac turns, grinning, watching the interaction of people passing through the nighttime city.

I don't know why I decide that is distraction enough. I think my brain has calmed down enough to realise that if I do nothing, my situation here is only going to get worse. Maybe I realise I don't need much, apart from some distance. He has a knife but he's only a man, capable of stupidity and doubt and fear. It's enough.

As he turns a little, I rotate the other way, unfurling the arm he has around my waist. And I run back the way we've come. Too surprised to yell out, he tries to hold onto the loop of fabric at my waist and it snaps apart instantly.

I run.

73

"Hey!" yells Mac and comes after me.

I run along the pavement. I could dash into the road, maybe thrust myself in front of a car, a taxi, a bus, and force a member of public into this drama. But in this weather there's a chance they wouldn't see me and simply run me down.

I just peg it. I run. I can hear him giving chase.

I go jogging three, four times a week. I can run. I rarely sprint, but I can run. Turns out the pasty bastard can run too. His feet slap the pavement hard.

My mind on him for a second, I fail to spot the pile of full bin bags piled up near a council waste bin and trip over the edge of them. Through some superhuman effort, I refuse to fall and bring my next foot forward and keep running.

There's a junction ahead and a pedestrian barrier to stop people just running straight into the road. Rather than slow to zig-zag to cross the road, I take the corner. I've lost track of what road this is.

I can start to feel the burn in my lungs.

A shape looms out of the dark. A tall man steps out in front of me. I give a wordless bark of shock and refusal. I twist to avoid him and look back.

Mac comes running along and the other man's arm swings round. With a sound that I can hear above the rain, that arm sweeps Mac from his feet as surely as if Mac had run straight into a tree branch. Mac goes down on his back. I don't know if his head hits the pavement. I hope it does. But he's got energy and momentum and is suddenly up again.

The other man has his hands out, warding Mac off.

Mac swings with his knife. The man holds back. In trying to avoid the knife, he doesn't see Mac's other hand and Mac plants a solid punch against the man's upper cheek. As they tumble and turn, I recognise this new man.

They circle.

Mac has for a moment forgotten me, and as he dances round, I grab his hoodie from behind and yank him back.

The taller guy comes in, quick. He grabs the hand and wrist holding the knife. Mac is caught between the two of us. The guy shakes the knife from Mac's grip and then with a quick authority, a skill even, he comes closer, puts a strong hand to Mac's elbow and bends his arm in a way no arm should bend.

I hear the crack of breaking bone.

Mac screams and staggers away, yanking his arm free. He casts about with wild eyes. Is he looking for his lost knife? Is he weighing up the options? Things don't look good. He screams like the wounded animal he is and runs away down the road, cradling his broken arm.

The man doesn't immediately turn to me. He's scanning the ground.

"You okay?" I say.

"Can't leave a knife lying around," he says and his soft Scottish accent confirms it's him.

It's Nick Ferguson, the firearms officer.

He sees the knife by the kerb and picks it up.

"You calling this in?" I say. "They could still catch him?"

"I'm suspended from duty." He shakes his head. "This is already too complicated."

Holding the knife in his hand, the flat of the blade tucked back against his arm, he turns to me. In reflected light, I can see there's a cut on his cheek.

"You're hurt," I say.

"I think we need to check that *you're* okay," he says and he starts to smile.

Of course I'm okay, I think, and then immediately follow that with the thought that of course I'm not okay. I'm really not.

"I was stupid," I say.

He tilts his head. "You run real fast."

"I'm still stupid."

"We're getting soaked," he says. "Let's get you a taxi."

"I'm at the Premier Inn by the station," I say, not sure if I'm telling him that's where I need to go or that I don't need a taxi to go that far. I look him in the eye, still coming down off this horrible adrenaline high of what's just happened. "This. This isn't a coincidence."

"You said you'd be at the nightclub," he says. "And then I saw you running."

"I thought you didn't want to talk to me."

"I was wrong. I want to talk. I need to understand."

Rain runs down his face, trickling into the cut on his face.

I nod. "You can come with me to the hotel. And then we can talk."

74

I'm drenched as we come from the rainy night into the lobby of the Premier Inn. My clothes cling to me in a manner that disgusts me. In the hotel light, I can see Nick's face properly now.

The cut on his cheek has stopped bleeding and the blood's been washed away by the rain, but there's a red line of a cut and the beginnings of a bruise around it.

"We'll get you sorted out," I say and swipe my card for the lift.

"I don't need to come up," he says.

"We need to talk. You want to talk."

He shrugs. He does.

"I've the tempting offers of either nearly-room-temperature white wine or a cup of instant coffee."

"Wow. That is tempting," he says.

We go up to the third floor and we go to my room. I'm very aware that I'm letting a strange man into my personal space. I haven't quite strewn all my belongings around the room, but I have to shove a suitcase off the bed to give us room to sit.

"I don't have a first aid kit," I say.

He takes off his sodden jacket and hangs it on the back of the door.

I go to the bathroom and get some cleansing wipes and several sheets of toilet roll.

He gestures to his cheek. "This is fine. Honest."

I approached and gently dab his cheek, to pat the rain and the trickles of blood from it.

"Rugby players get cuts all the time," he says.

"And patch 'em up with sticky tape and superglue," I suggest.

"Not quite," he smiles and takes the wipes from me.

I grab a fresh top and trousers and go into the bathroom to get changed. I'm soaked to the core. I feel like I might never be dry again. I throw wet clothes in the bath and come out feeling much better.

Nick is inspecting the bottle of off-licence wine he's found in the mini-fridge.

"I don't even know if that fridge works," I say.

"It works just enough to remind you what cold is meant to be like without actually cooling the bottle," he says. "If I open it, will you have some?"

"The night I've had, yes," I say. I fetch the tumblers from the bathroom sink and he pours for both of us.

Nick sighs. "I have to ask, why the hell did you want to come find me on Monday night?"

I shrug and sip my drink. It's not good wine but, on the other hand, it's wine. Whether Nick helps me or not, that bottle will be empty before I go to bed.

"I told you," I say. "I need answers. I'm running out of

options. That night ... the night Seamus Wollacott died ... I know what I saw."

"Yeah?"

"I saw a man with a gun. I saw a woman who I thought was in danger. I only came looking for you because I heard one of the other officers say your name. It could have been any of them I sought out. Because I want to know what you saw. I want to hear – even though I don't think it's possible – I want to hear that you saw a gun too."

"Ah," he says. He says it in a very heavy tone. He drinks half the glass in one go. "So, it wasn't me specifically you wanted to talk to."

I don't understand. "You were the one I was able to get hold of. I'm sorry that I came without warning. I didn't—"

"So you don't know," he says.

"Know what?"

He looks at me. His heavy brows give his gaze an intensity. I'm supposed to read something in that look but I'm not seeing it.

"It was me," he says eventually.

I open my mouth to ask what was him, then my brain catches up and stops me asking the stupid question. He shot Seamus Wollacott. It was him. That shot I heard fired that night came from his gun. He ended Seamus's life.

"Oh, God. I'm sorry," I say.

"I assumed you knew."

I look at him. His face hides a lot but I can see the pain. For much of the last week, I've carried the guilt for Seamus's death with me. It was my words that killed him. In my head, the police firearms officers were merely the mechanism by which that was enacted. But, no, Nick's been carrying his own guilt.

"You acted in good faith," I say. It's a bland statement.

"I reacted," he says.

He empties the glass and pours himself another. He tops up mine too.

"Can you tell me?" I say.

"Hmmm?"

"What did you see? What happened?"

We're sitting on the bed, twisted to face each other. We both have the need to search each other's face for clues.

"Why?" he says.

"I want answers. I need to know what really happened."

"Did you see a gun?" he asks. "I mean, really. Did you see a gun?"

"I did."

"Because the police can't fucking find one, Esther."

He's not angry. His tone if anything is one of desperation.

"I've been doubting myself and second-guessing myself ever since that night," I say. "But I saw one."

"And there was a woman?"

"There was. I saw her again tonight at the club."

"Really?"

"Yes, really. I wanted to speak to her but she ran."

He shakes his head in maybe disbelief and sits on the bed next to me. "Who is she?"

"I don't know. Not yet."

He's looking intently at me. "And did she see the gun? Can she back up your story?"

"I hope so. If I find her."

He takes this on board slowly.

"And you?" I say. "What did you see that night? Did he have a gun?"

He takes a very long moment before he answers. "I wish I

could tell you I saw something. It was dark, and everything happened so quickly."

"But you saw him well enough to take aim and fire. Sorry. I mean—"

"I know what you mean."

"What was he doing? How was he standing?"

"Esther." He knows my name. Everyone knows my name. "This is eating you up, I can tell."

"You're not my therapist. Answer the question."

"Yes. Right." He broods for a moment. "He'd positioned himself in a way that might have indicated he was concealing a weapon."

It sounds like a line he's fed into the official report.

"But what does that look like?" I say. "Show me."

He shakes his head and sighs. "Fine. He was like this." He gets up and then crouches down. "Pile of pallets here." With his hands he indicates of a pile of pallets that Wollacott's hiding behind. "He's peering round. We see him. We warn him. All he has to do is put his hands up, but he doesn't. I don't know whether he lost his balance, or thought he could run for it, or what, but he lunges forward. Tips forward. We had to end it."

75

Nick straightens and pulls a pained face before sitting on the bed again.

He ended it. He pulled the trigger and ended Seamus Wollacott's life. All of a sudden I feel as if I've intruded on this man's private grief. It is grief, coming to terms with the fact that you shot a man.

"I am so sorry," I say and place my hand on his back. He leans slightly into it.

"And now my life is on hold," he says. "Standard procedure. A shooting incident. We're all suspended from active duty and the IOPC, they—"

"I'm sorry, I don't know what that is."

"Independent Office of Police Conduct. Internal affairs. The ones who investigate the police. They're not even police officers, just pen pushers. But they're coming for me. That's all they do. That's their job. To go after police officers and get us fired. Or worse."

"Christ. Is that going to happen?"

He shrugs. I feel his muscles move under the palm of my hand.

"It doesn't matter if he was armed or not," he says.

"What?" I say, surprised.

"Legally," he explains. "When a police officer shoots someone, it doesn't matter if the person was armed or not. What matters – the only thing that matters, legally – is whether the officer reasonably believed the person was a threat to others."

"And you did?" It's a stupid question because there's only one answer he can give.

"I did," he says eventually.

He turns bodily to me. My hand drops to the space on the bed between us.

"This thing," he says. "Have you been feeling shitty and guilty about it ever since it happened?"

"I have."

"Is it terrible to be comforted by the fact that makes two of us?"

I laugh at the bleak thought. "I didn't want him to die," I say. "I would do anything to undo what happened."

"Yeah. That's not how it works though. I've shot people before. It's a split-second decision. Every time. You did what you thought was right and now you're being punished for it."

I'd never thought of it that way before, but he's right. That's the truth of the matter.

"That's what happens," he says. "Every time. You try to do what's right and you're punished for it."

"We need to forgive ourselves," I say, even though I don't really believe it.

He grunts in agreement. "I want answers. I want the truth. I want the world to see us vindicated. I want to help you find that woman. If you saw the gun, if she saw the gun, then I want to find her. That's what I need."

I put my hand back on him, this time on his arm. And I know what I'm doing. I've had my life threatened tonight. I've had my life torn apart for more than a week. I've had the man who I thought would stand by me through this betray me and try to turn the situation to his advantage. I've been screwed around by the whole world and here – in my bedroom with me now – is the one man who wants what I want.

And I know this is a reckless move, borne out of adrenaline and craziness and fear and half a glass of bad wine. But I'm thinking to myself right now that this man is possibly what inner me wants right now.

"I'm going to catch a cold if I don't get out of these clothes," says Nick.

I tug at the sleeve of his T-shirt.

"We need to recover." He laughs suddenly. "I've got a knife to dispose of."

He stands and my hand slides off his arm.

"You don't have to go," I say.

He nods like he knows this, acknowledges this, and wishes that he was going to stay.

"Give me your number," he says, taking out his phone.

I want him to stay, which means I don't want to be giving him my number. But this is, frustratingly, the right thing to do.

I tell him my number and he puts it into his phone and sends me a call so that his number comes up on my phone too.

He gets his jacket from the back of the door.

"I will see you again," he says.

"Good," I tell him.

He pauses and gives me the longest look, like he's trying to remember me for the future.

"I want to see you again," he says and leaves.

The door closes with a solid click. The silence of the room is suddenly engulfing. I look at the half-empty bottle of wine on the side and feel sensations in my core that refuse to subside even though he's gone.

I huff.

"Fuck."

76

DI Gill has asked to meet all of the Duncans at Whitwick Farm.

Walker didn't take the call, but from Rob's attitude as Rob drives the three of them over there, it seems that things are afoot.

This seems only confirmed when, at the end of the pitted driveway, Walker sees Neelam Gill and the Crime Scene Manager Sanjee Baksh standing in the yard.

"The gang's all here," says Gill as they get out.

"Sounds like you've got news, ma'am," says Walker.

She works her jaw and nods. "Would have done this over the phone, but Sanjee has got something to show us."

"Shall we talk about the gun first?" says Sanjee.

Rob gives him a questioning look and Gill nods.

"Ballistics report has come through," says Sanjee. He grins and rolls his eyes. "And in less than a week! What miracles have I worked for you?"

Walker nods appreciatively. That is fast. Someone must

have made it a priority. Low priority ballistics analysis can take weeks; often more than a month.

"There were factors in this investigation that warranted attention," says Gill. "The illegal firearm. Aaron's banking irregularities. And the blood spatter."

"Blood spatter?" says Josie.

"That's the next bit," says Sanjee, doing a little mime of pointing fingers crossing over each other. "That gun matches details on the National Ballistics Database."

"Interesting," says Walker.

"Oh, you'll like it," says Gill. "The gun was used in the armed robbery shooting of Remi Jankauskas in twenty-fifteen."

"Jankauskas," says Walker, ironing out Gill's hesitant pronunciation.

"I said you'd find it interesting."

Walker can feel Josie's gaze turn to him.

"Lithuanian drug dealer who fell foul of other Lithuanian criminals," Walker explains. "At least that was what we tried and failed to prove. I was part of the investigation."

"We both were," says Gill.

"This is the Degutis gang?" says Rob.

Walker nods and makes eye contact with Josie. "The Degutis gang—"

"Yeah, yeah," she says. "I do actually read our files. They come up in connection with Operation Chainlink. Moving stolen cars and equipment."

"She does read," Rob says to Walker with a smile.

Walker takes a moment to mentally put all the pieces in place. His brain is not as agile as it once was. A gun used by criminals with connections to rural crime has been used in the apparent suicide of this reclusive ex-Army soldier.

"This is all a pretty mess," he says.

"Let's talk about the blood spatter now," says Sanjee.

Gill moves the police tape that's across the farmhouse front door and takes out a set of keys to unlock it.

The house is even colder and darker than when Walker first came here. Misery clings like damp to the walls.

Gill leads the way to the kitchen with Sanjee eagerly trying to get past her.

The chair where Aaron Bashford died is still there. Nothing has been cleaned up since Aaron's death.

"Here, here," says the crime scene manager.

Sanjee steers them towards the end of the table, positioning them carefully. Walker is pressed up against a crowded little noticeboard where receipts and faded birthday cards are pinned. There is a flyer for something called 'AFVBC' above a picture of a fried breakfast.

"We've got some lovely photographs of this," Sanjee is saying. "Delightful, in fact. But I want to show you in person, because it's such a striking example."

Walker wonders what can be delightful about a bloody crime scene.

"Now, take a look down the table. Concentrate on the blood, and where it's landed."

Sanjee makes this sound like a fun party game. Walker wants to point out that this was the victim's blood. His actual blood.

The four police detectives stand together and look where they're told.

"We always look for voids," says Sanjee. "We've got more science up our sleeves to make sense of what we see here, but ... ta-da!"

"Fuck!" whispers Josie.

Walker realises they can all see it from this angle. Blood splashed out from where Aaron supposedly shot himself. Except there's a gap in the blood spatter.

A person-sized gap.

"Someone else was here when Aaron Bashford was shot," says Rob.

DI Gill gives a slow "Yep."

"So it was murder," says Josie.

"Yep."

Josie waves her hand to the world beyond these walls. "There's a CCTV camera on the driveway coming in. That would pick up anyone coming here."

Sanjee's normally smiling faces pulls a deep frown. "Mr Bashford's CCTV is working, but the cloud-based storage account is closed. Seems his subscription lapsed. No records."

"Shame," says Gill. "That would have made things easy."

77

Friday morning, I'm back in Hannah's office.

She messaged me, saying it's imperative that we meet.

I'm here partly because of that message, and also because this office feels like a safe oasis in a world that is extremely hostile towards me. What else can I do? Hang around my hotel room, maybe thinking about the man I made a half-arsed pass at last night?

The sense of comfort in Hannah's office vanishes almost instantly once Hannah has poured the tea and offered me a biscuit.

"There's someone I want you to meet, Esther."

She goes out of the door and returns a moment later with a woman.

"Oh."

It's the small blonde woman I saw in Grotto.

"I think the two of you might have met already. Esther, this is Karolina. Karolina, Esther."

I'm on the back foot, so I do the only thing that feels

decisive. I stand up and shake Karolina's hand. She nods curtly.

"Hello," says Karolina in that carefully stressed European accent I heard in the club.

We all sit down, and I have a chance to look properly at Karolina. If Mattel made an action-commando Barbie, they could take her outfit as a blueprint. She's wearing a dark polo neck and camouflage combat trousers, but she makes it look fashion-forward on her dinky frame.

"I told you that I have someone who does some detective work for me," says Hannah, waving a hand at Karolina.

"Like following me?" I ask.

Karolina rolls her eyes at me. "Don't be a princess, Mrs Butler. It's the job." Her accent shaves the edges off the blunt language, but not by much.

Part of me wants to jump up and yell in her face, tell her she's out of order. The other part wants to laugh.

I give in and laugh.

Hannah beams at the two of us. "And as you can see, Karolina brings a refreshing attitude to all that she does."

I purse my lips, wondering how come short stuff didn't come to my assistance while Mac was busy trying to abduct and murder me.

"I'd like to talk through the events at Grotto," says Hannah. "Partly to exchange information, and partly because it was very much against the agreement we had that you'd lay low, Esther."

Am I being told off? I think I am.

"Yes. Well. What can I say? I got a bit stir crazy. I wanted to do something."

"You need to work with me, Esther."

She's doing that thing where she's disappointed rather

than angry. I'm buying into it, too. I can feel myself squirming under her scrutiny.

"Sorry," I say.

Karolina reaches for a biscuit, rolling her eyes again, amused.

"You saw the mystery woman from the night of the shooting?" Hannah asks me.

"I did. She spotted me, though. Recognised me too. She ran off."

"Whereupon you were accosted by some thug."

"Yes." She is remarkably well-informed about my evening. "Mac Wollacott."

I turn my gaze onto Karolina. If she saw all of that, why didn't she lend a hand?

"What?" She meets my stare unashamed. "He was not going to stab you on a city centre street." She shrugs. "I had some business to take care of before I was gonna swoop in and save your ass. Turns out that your knight in shining armour got there ahead of me."

She smirks.

For a horrible moment I imagine she could somehow see inside the walls of the Premier Inn. That she witnessed my tragic desperation for human contact.

"What business to take care of?"

Karolina spreads her hands. "Making sure I find your mystery woman."

This knocks the air out of me. "What? You found her? You know where she is?"

Hannah leans forward, before Karolina can answer. "Karolina is very skilled at what she does."

Karolina shrugs.

"Now, it is essential that we handle this next part well," says Hannah.

"Right?" I ask.

"There's a good version and a bad version of making contact with this woman. I want to be sure we agree on what the good version looks like, and that we stick to the plan. Does that sound like something we can work on together?"

"Yes." Even I can hear the lack of conviction in my voice. I want to get out there and grab that woman by the scruff of the neck. She's caused me so much grief by not coming forward already.

"Let's talk through the good version then," says Hannah. "This begins with us pooling what information we have about her."

"Information?" I shrug. "Mine's easy. All I know is that she likes nineties nostalgia and she has a Juicy Couture hat."

"And we can surmise that she doesn't want to speak to you," said Hannah. "What can you tell me about her expression when she saw you?"

"Hm." I try to summon the scene. See if I can isolate and name her reaction. "Not fear. Pretty sure she wasn't scared to see me. It's more like she was annoyed."

"Interesting." Hannah bites down on a biscuit and waggles the stump at Karolina. "What do we make of that?"

Karolina gives an eloquent shrug. "Could be the classic British avoidance of getting involved." She mimes the air quotes.

"But you don't think so?" Hannah prompts.

"No." Karolina is unafraid of leaving large gaps in the conversation. She knows we are both waiting for her to speak. She takes a long, deep breath. "She is a business owner.

Works at a launderette on Maynard Road. I think she wants to avoid being drawn into this shitstorm."

There's a gesture towards me when Karolina says "shitstorm" that I don't appreciate. She's not wrong, but I don't like the way she thinks it's my own personal shitstorm.

"I suspect you're right," says Hannah. "Which tells us how we should proceed, I think."

"It does?"

"Absolutely. You need to find a way to get the police to go and see her. Let them deal with her directly. Keep her out of your own personal ... orbit."

I crack a smile at how Hannah chooses her words carefully. I wonder how on earth these two women ended up working together. They could not be more different.

78

Aaron Bashford's death is being treated as murder and DI Gill has commandeered an additional space in Mansfield House as an incident room. There are spare rooms to be found in many police stations across the county, reflective of the fact that the number of coppers on the force has gone down over the years.

Gill has put herself and a couple of her regular detectives in there. An Ordnance Survey map of the area around Whitwick Farm and a plan of the farm site itself have been pinned to a display board, along with the beginnings of a simple timeline.

The Duncans haven't been allocated to the investigation. Technically, they are there for any insights or links to Operation Chainlink, but the three of them loiter at the desks to the rear of the room as Neelam Gill does her briefing. Josie finds her manner direct. She speaks and commands in a no-frills manner, professional to the point of curtness. Josie finds herself wondering how Gill's direct and confident manner gets her promoted to DI while Josie's similar manner just seems to rub people up the wrong way.

"We've had the post-mortem on Aaron Bashford," Gill tells the room. "Instantaneous death by gunshot wound. No surprises there. Pathologist puts death at maybe eight or nine days ago. Rough estimate. That's last Tuesday or Wednesday. Two or three days before our friends in Operation Chainlink found him."

"There's an ANPR camera in Copt Oak at the end of the lane that the farm is on," says Rob, next to Josie.

"Already ahead of you, DS Joseph," says Gill. "I've made a request for every number plate picked up by the camera in that window."

"That's going to be a lot of vehicles," says Celeste Banks, one of Gill's DCs.

"Hundreds," the DI agrees grimly. "Celeste, you and Satnam are to go through those and prioritise. I think we can assume our murderer didn't turn up in a tractor or a freight lorry."

There's a couple of low chuckles at this.

"Bashford is not going to give us much in the way of leads. Only calls on his phone are to utility companies. He doesn't have a home computer. By all accounts, he was a hermit. We have to look more broadly for leads. Local surveillance and the weapon that was used to kill him are perhaps our strongest lines of enquiry."

"Actually, Walker's got an interesting idea for us to follow up," says Josie.

"Does he?" says Gill.

Walker clears his throat. "I saw a flyer for a thing called AFVBC in Bashford's kitchen."

"And what's that when it's at home?"

"I had to look it up. Armed Forces Veterans Breakfast Club. It does what it says on the tin. It's a support group slash social club."

"So, there's a breakfast club for ex-armed forces people?"

"They're all over the country, but there's one that meets up in the city centre."

"Was Bashford a regular?"

"Don't know," says Walker.

Josie pulls a confused face. "Everyone we spoke to said he wasn't a people person. Did he really go to social events or did he just, like, sign up for the newsletter?"

"No idea," says Walker. "But the Leicester one is meeting tomorrow."

"Volunteering to go?" Gill asks.

Josie puts her hand up. "I'll go too."

"Knock yourself out," says Gill. "Might be a great source of intel."

Josie's phone is ringing in her hand. She looks at it. Caller ID reads *Esther Butler*.

"Sorry, ma'am. Gotta take this."

"I think we're wrapped up here," says Gill. "We've all got work to do. Walker and Kaminski, if you can check out the breakfast club tomorrow, that would be great."

As the meeting breaks, Josie shows Rob the caller ID before answering the call and stepping into the corridor.

"Esther?"

"Detective Kaminski?"

"What can I do for you?"

Rob stands in the corridor, waiting.

"*I found the woman*," says Esther.

"You found the woman?"

She puts it onto speaker so Rob can hear.

"The one who was outside the casino that night."

Josie pulls an appraising face. "Blimey. So you've got some information to pass to us?"

"I do. The woman I saw that night works at a launderette on the Maynard Road. You need to go and see her."

"You have a name for her?"

"No."

"It won't be me who goes. It will be one of the detectives assigned to that investigation. Someone like Detective Sergeant Beaches who you spoke to before."

Rob nods approvingly at that.

"But thank you for passing on the information," says Josie. "How did you find her?"

There's a beat. *"I saw her in a nightclub."*

Something about the way that she offers it as a fragment makes Josie think that it's not the entire truth. She wonders what Esther's been up to.

After the call ends, she looks across to Rob. "What do you make of that?"

Rob makes a thoughtful sound. "It's interesting for a number of reasons. Not least of which is Esther's personal motivation."

"You think she went looking for this woman?"

"Oh yes. I do."

Josie is certain of it too. "You think she knows she might be facing charges?"

Rob shrugs. "She's got other pressures too. Tell Beaches. It's for him to deal with."

Josie goes round to the larger CID office to tell Dean Beaches about the phone call.

"How come she keeps calling you, not me?" he asks. He sounds a little peevish.

"I guess she likes the sound of my voice." Josie knows this isn't true. The truth is that she's probably a less terrible option than Beaches from Esther's point of view, but he won't want to hear that.

"So I need to go and talk to this woman. See if she was there that night."

Beaches isn't really asking her opinion, so Josie keeps her mouth shut. He seems to be trying out some ideas by saying them out loud. It's a habit Josie associates with stupid people. Although, depending on her mood, Josie thinks most people are stupid.

"Sure thing," says Josie and walks back to her own desk.

79

I expected more enthusiasm from the police over the information about the mystery woman. DC Kaminski's matter-of-fact attitude is a bit deflating. I text Jeety and we agree to meet for a run.

We're a few streets away from home. Far enough to avoid Kieran, near enough that we know our way round.

"That hair's a bold new look for you," she says.

"I keep forgetting. Then I look in a mirror and startle myself."

She grins. "You've been off-grid for days. Are you alright?"

"A lot's happened." I try to run through what she does and doesn't know in my mind as we set off on our run.

"Have you left Kieran?" she asks.

"I have. I got sacked and he wasn't the slightest bit supportive."

"Fuck."

I sigh. "Fact is, if I had some sort of stress-o-meter—"

"Stress-o-meter?"

"Yeah. If I was on a game show and there was a big

indicator that scored how stressy each thing in my life was, the Kieran thing isn't even a factor. Barely gets a ripple."

"Wow. Okay. What else is going on?"

"Where to start."

"You gave yourself a makeover, for one."

"I wanted to keep my head down. I was being attacked in public."

"What? Fuck, Esther. What are the police doing in all of this?" Jeety demands.

"I'm not sure the police are really on my side."

She shakes her head. It seems so wrong to her. She looks as if she's thinking of going down there and giving them a good talking-to.

"I found the policeman who shot Sean Woollacott. I think he's as messed-up by this thing as I am."

"Christ. Let me catch up with this. On the one hand, the police haven't got your back. On the other hand, you're feeling sorry for the one who put a bullet in that sleazeball?"

I laugh. "When you put it like that, it does seem a bit ridiculous. But yeah."

She rolls her eyes. "Ten out of ten for your sleuthing skills though."

"Oh, you'll love the next part then. I found the woman."

"What? Juicy Couture bitch? No way!"

"Yep." We jog for a few moments while I think about how to describe the weirdness of that evening. "Didn't get to speak to her. She ran off. Then Seamus Wollacott's brother showed up and tried to drag me off. Lucky for me, the police shooter guy was there and he clobbered him."

"Whoa. How come all of those people were there? Where we talking about?"

"Grotto."

"Right. So you've gone along to a fairly obscure place and all of these people turn up?"

I shrug. "Mac Wollacott must have been following me. I think."

She narrows her eyes at this.

"And Nick was there because I'd told him I was going there to try and find the woman."

"Nick?" She's in my face. Big questions and challenges are in her expression. "First name terms with the shooter?"

"It's like – it's like we're both casualties of the same horrible event."

She shakes her head at me. Then she brings out a waggy finger to make it clear that she means business. "Do not get involved with this man, Esther. I guarantee it won't end well."

I want to argue. Why shouldn't it end well? We're both just people. "No, course not," I mumble.

She relaxes and we get back into our stride, running down the pavements. "Is that everything?" she asks.

"No. I've been talking to this woman, Hannah. She does reputation management."

"Right...?"

"She called me. Said she'd do some work for free."

"Nobody does work for free. What's her game?"

I try to remember Hannah's words. "She calls it strategic altruism. I think the idea is that if she can sort out a mess like mine, then people will know how good she is."

"Huh. And can she?"

"I'm beginning to think that maybe she can. She's got this detective woman working for her."

"Why did you hold your hand out like that?" Jeety asks.

I look at my hand, see what it's doing. Seems that I'm sketching a subconscious caricature. "There's a crazy height differential between them. Hannah's one of the tallest women I've ever known. Elegant. Moves like she's doing ballet. Her detective is small and mean. Talks with no filters."

"She's pissed you off," laughs Jeety.

"Her work is good, but her attitude sucks. She found where the mystery woman works. I've told the police."

"Hoo! You should have led with that," says Jeety. "Fantastic news. This could turn the tide for you."

"I hope so."

I'm glad that Jeety is feeling optimistic.

80

All afternoon, I yo-yo between optimism that my information about the mystery woman is going to lead to some action and a growing pessimism that nothing is ever going to change.

Going for a run with Jeety always buoys my mood for a bit, but after going back to the hotel and showering off, that starts to fade. Ahead of me, I have nothing but the long slide into evening and keeping my head down, as instructed by Hannah.

As I come out of the bathroom with a towel round me, I see that my phone is ringing.

It's Nick Ferguson. I pick it up quicky.

"Hey," I say.

"Hey, Esther," he says. I can hear he's outside somewhere. *"Thought I'd give you a call and see how you are."*

Checking up on me, checking I'm all right – this shouldn't really mean anything, but I feel suddenly cocooned in his protective concern. It's embarrassing, really.

"Yeah. Yeah, I'm fine," I say. "What about you? You were the one who got walloped."

He chuckles. *"I've received far worse in a regular rugby game."*

"Trying to be the big strong man there, Nick?"

"I don't need to put on a front for you," he says. *"Anyway, they're calling me in for further interviews today. You got any more big ideas about finding out who the woman with Seamus Wollacott might have been?"*

"Actually, there's been news there," I say.

"Oh?"

"I know where she works. Some laundrette on Maynard Road."

"How'd you find that out?" he says. There's a note of excitement in his voice.

"It's a long story."

My phone is buzzing. Another call is coming through.

Detective Sergeant Dean Beaches, he of the shifty face and ugly moustache.

"I've got another call. It's the police. The investigating detectives, I mean. Gotta go."

"I hope it's good news," he says. *"Thinking of you."*

He hangs up. I switch to the incoming call.

"Esther?" says Beaches.

"Detective."

"Calling with an update on your case. I went to see the woman that you reported as being present on the night of the shooting."

"You did?"

"The woman you described who works at the laundrette on Maynard Road."

"Yes."

I'm gripping the phone tightly, as if I can squeeze the information out of it more quickly.

"She doesn't know what you're talking about."

"What?"

"On Sunday the seventh, she says she wasn't the woman hanging around the casino."

"But it's her."

"She's denied being in the area at all. Says she was home all evening."

This isn't correct. I'm not having this. "Right? And you're checking that out, right?"

"Due process is being followed." He sounds pompous, as if he's annoyed at me telling him how to do his job.

"Due process? I don't understand what that means. What's her name anyway?"

"I'm not able to share that with you, Mrs Butler. I'm sure you understand the reason we need to keep details like that confidential."

"What's next?" I ask. This can't be the end of it.

There's the sound of him sucking his teeth. *"Good question that."*

"Right?"

"See, the thing is Esther, we've not been able to corroborate several important things you've told us regarding your account of events."

"You have been unable to do that, yes." I want to change the emphasis. Surely it's about their inability, not what I told them?

He doesn't react to my tone. *"We need to start thinking about why you might have said Mr Wollacott had a gun. You had reason to wish harm to him."*

I swallow down my fear, and hope that he can't hear that

over the phone. "I can assure you that the two of us never met."

"Because," he continues as if I haven't spoken, "the police might seek charges against you. Perverting the course of justice can bring serious penalties."

I'm speechless. Literally, I cannot form a sentence. Partly, it's the gravity of what he's just said. Partly, it's fear that he might uncover the connection that very definitely does exist. I'm especially fearful that Baz might drop some ill-timed hint.

I'm obliged to respond, so I summon every ounce of control inside me. "I've never lied to you. Why would I lie to you?"

"I don't know, Esther," he says. *"Why would you lie to us?"*

He leaves the question hanging.

81

On Saturday morning, Walker meets up with Josie in the city centre. "Morning," he says.

"Mmm," she murmurs from within the fluffy hood of her coat. "Not sure I like being up for work on a Saturday morning."

He laughs. "We're going to fix you right up with a bacon roll and a cuppa. Come on."

"We told this veterans breakfast club we're coming?"

Walker nods. "We're looking for someone called Mog."

"And is Mog a man or a woman?"

"No idea."

The veterans breakfast club meets in a Wetherspoons and is very informal, according to the email exchange that Walker had with the admin yesterday.

Walker and Josie walk together.

"Do you reckon we're going to find a link between Aaron Bashford's murder-suicide-whatever and the Degutis family?" she asks.

Walker sniffs reflectively. "The Degutises have had their

fingers in lots of pies for years. The two brothers, Arturas and Darius, have been quietly running all manner of shady enterprises for twenty-plus years. The Remi Jankauskas murder the pistol is linked to had all the hallmarks of Lukas Degutis, Darius's son. Violent. Careless. That's sort of after my time."

"After your time."

Walker grunts. "Twenty years ago, I spent months – months – working undercover in drugs squad. Operation Kilkenny. I met a lot of people involved in the drugs scene in Leicestershire. Arturas and Darius were always a presence on the edge of things. But they were wise and patient crooks. That's how they've stayed in the game so long. But guns... Shooting people in robberies or tit-for-tat attacks, like the shooting of Remi Jankauskas. That's some young hot-head thing."

Up ahead, the Corn Exchange Pub sits right by Leicester Market in a grand old building. On sunny days, the white walls and the pedestrianised road outside make a little sun trap for outdoor drinkers. Today is not one of those days. It's a grey morning. Early drinkers are staying indoors.

"I don't know where Bashford's death will lead us," says Walker. "Quite possibly nowhere."

Inside, the two of them stand at the bar for a moment to see if they can spot the enigmatic Mog.

It's Mog who finds them.

"Saw you two at the bar and thought: 'they look like rozzers'," she says as she approaches.

"Mog?" says Walker, extending a hand.

She smiles broadly. "Hello and welcome."

Once Josie has put in breakfast orders, Mog leads them to the upstairs area in the split-level pub. A row of long tables is filled with people, eating, drinking and chatting. Walker had expected that it would be heavily male-dominated, but there are a good number of women here. Mog pauses to speak to people here and there before moving on and steering Walker and Josie to a smaller table, away from the rest of the group.

Walker gets the immediate impression that Mog is very much a social lynchpin for the group. She's around sixty, but looks extremely fit. Walker suspects she thrives on social things like the breakfast club.

Breakfast arrives a few moments later.

"Now, how can I help?" Mog asks.

"Aaron Bashford," says Walker. "He used to come here."

"He did."

"We need to understand him a little bit better," says Walker.

She makes an expansive gesture, like there's both everything and nothing to tell.

"Tell us a bit about this club," said Josie. "I didn't even know there were such things."

"Hmmm." Mog lifts her eyebrows. "The AFVBC. It's not joking to say that it can be a lifeline to some people."

"I can imagine," says Walker.

"And I thought it was doing that job for Aaron. I was sorry to hear of his death."

"It was a tragedy."

Josie sips at her tea and gasps at its heat. "He would come here ... how often?"

"Every month. He'd always be here. The routine can be very comforting if you're ex-military. Gave him a reason to get cleaned up and shaved, you know?"

"There's something I don't understand. The people that live in his village said he was quiet and surly. Never talked to anyone. What made him come here, when the whole point of this thing is to talk to people? I don't get it."

Mog nods. "It's a pattern we see very often here. You've got a cocktail of things going on with our members. Not all of them have complex personal trauma from their military experience, but a great many do. Aaron did."

"He had therapy, though?" said Walker.

Mog smiles. "Therapy is a very small word, isn't?"

"But surely the services make sure that people get therapy?" Josie asks.

"You might be surprised at how badly things have panned out for a lot of veterans. Would Aaron have been offered counselling after certain incidents? Perhaps. A lot didn't take it up at the time. Fear of stigma; fear of being excluded from future opportunities."

Walker can still see the confusion on Josie's face. Mog spots it too.

"Let me explain it a different way. Military life is its own special thing. Before you're deployed to a combat zone, they will make sure that you have a Will. It's seen as a practical necessity, yeah?"

"Right. Makes sense."

"But there's no equivalent when it comes to mental health. Any kind of therapy remains voluntary."

"Wow," says Josie. She inhales deeply. "Respect to you for doing this." She waves an arm across the other tables. "Sounds like it's needed."

Mog nods her thanks but says, "It's not about me."

Walker checks his notes. "Aaron was with the Black Watch until twenty fifteen. He was deployed to Afghanistan. Did he share stories about that when he came here?"

"Sharing stories probably isn't the thing you think it is,"

says Mog. "We don't get people telling tales of heroic derring-do like in those old war films. It's just not like that. Not here; not anywhere you get people who've seen action. Most of them would sooner put it behind them. Stories they share will be the small stuff. The silly stuff." She inclines her head. "We've just been hearing about how Turner adopted a wild goat as a pet."

"Who would Aaron tend to sit with?" Walker asks.

Mog leans back. "Turner's a good shout, actually."

She beckons to a man in his forties with close-cropped hair and an open, smiley face.

"Ay up?" he asks as he plonks down.

82

Rob is in his car when DI Neelam Gill phones.

"Sorry to call you on your Saturday off," she says.

"I'm not doing anything," he says, which is a bit of a lie. He's on his way to an artisanal café where he'd intended to spend the morning drinking coffee and reading a book on politics by that Rory Stewart guy. Drinking expensive coffee and reading improving books is one of the many habits he picked up when he was going out with Veronica. Veronica's long gone, but some of the habits remain.

"Good. Do you fancy a drive over to Braunston? I've got a riddle."

"Riddle."

"Late last night, Mac Wollacott was killed in a drive-by shooting."

Rob has no words. It's like he's waiting for a punchline.

"Mac Wollacott," he says.

"Mac Wollacott. Brother of Seamus, the guy shot in the firearms incident two weeks ago."

"Yeah, I remember. Where?"

She gives him an address in Braunston.

"And how do I help with this riddle?" he says. He doesn't want to say, *"I'm merely the detective in charge of missing farm equipment."*

"I'll fill you in," she says.

He doesn't quite race over there – a dead man isn't getting any deader – but he drives with a purpose and eagerness that takes minutes off the travel time. The whole street is closed with police tape, and a white tent has been set up halfway down. Local residents stand at the foot of their driveways to watch.

Rob shows his ID at the cordon and is noted in the crime scene log. As he walks down, he sees CSIs by a pair of houses, taking photos of bullet holes in the brickwork. There's one shattered window. An actual honest-to-God drive-by.

A gaggle of detectives stand outside the tent. Detective Inspectors Gill and Scabbard appear to be in the middle of a terse conversation.

"What are you doing here?" says Dean Beaches without an ounce of politeness in his tone.

"DI Gill asked me to attend," Rob says, then adds in a moment of sheer honesty, "I've no idea why I'm here either."

Dean tries on a sneer but doesn't have the conviction to carry it off.

Scabbard glances at Rob and then Neelam Gill sees him too.

"Ah," she says, striding over. "You were quick."

"You asked, I came." He gestures to the tent.

"Mac Wollacott. IDed at the scene." She glances at the sky as though reading the time by the position of the sun. "Local residents were woken shortly after midnight by the sound of gunfire. Some said they thought they saw a car, but there's no details. Several called the police, but it wasn't until five minutes later that some brave souls came out to check on him."

Rob looks up and down the road, trying to picture where a car might have come from or gone to. It's a residential street, very suburban. There are unlikely to be any businesses with CCTV in the immediate area.

"But," says Gill heavily, "Mac was alive when a neighbour first got to him."

"Conscious?"

She nods. "And before he died he managed to say a name. The neighbour thought it was 'Luke', or 'Lukas'."

Rob's mind races. "Lukas?" he says.

She raises her eyebrows and pulls a meaningful face.

Lukas Degutis. Rob tries to put the pieces together. Two weeks ago, Seamus Wollacott was shot by the police. A few days later, farmer and former soldier, Aaron Bashford, was found at home, shot with a gun previously connected to a crime that the police suspected was the work of the Degutis gang. Seamus and Aaron, two incidents that had no reason to be linked.

And now, Seamus's brother has been gunned down, gangland style, and might have named his killer with his final breath.

"How does any of that make sense?" says Rob.

"Oh, I've no idea," says Gill. "I'm hoping that since you and Walker and your new recruit have been keeping an eye on the Degutis family's activities, you might be able to help me work it out."

83

In the Corn Exchange pub, Mog makes the introductions between the police officers and army veteran, Turner.

Turner doesn't seem surprised to be talking to cops. Walker realises Mog must have briefed the group ahead of their visit.

"What would you and Aaron speak about, typically?" Walker asks.

Turner grins. "Boots. We chatted about boots more than once. Socks too."

"Small stuff, as I said," says Mog, getting up and leaving them to talk. She pats Turner on the shoulder as she resumes her role of bobbing in and out of everyone's chat along the tables.

"Boots," says Walker, prompting Turner.

Turner shrugs. "You have this love/hate relationship with boots in the military. What can I say? You break them in and they're your best friend. See you through thick and thin. You come out and everyone's wearing trainers. Bloody weird. And socks that wear straight through! Should be banned. You know what both of us found shocking?"

"No."

"You can't get shirts with insect repellent on the high street. It's not a thing. Who the hell decided that, eh?"

He beams widely, while Walker and Josie process the idea and nod politely.

"And did you and he ever cross paths while you were deployed?" Josie asks.

"No. Some of the same places, different times."

"Afghanistan?"

Turner nods. "By twenty-twelve, Bash and I were both in Afghanistan. Operation Herrick. My lot, the Royal Anglian Regiment, were based up in Sangin Valley. IED clearance." He taps his left ear. "I still have hearing in this one," he grins. "Bash was with the Black Watch in Helmand Province. They were training the Afghan forces who were due to replace them after withdrawal. That was a shitshow."

"The training?" says Josie.

"All of it. They had some brave lads – but imagine thinking that us and the rest of the NATO crowd could pull out and some local lads with basic training could hold off the Taliban." He makes a disgusted noise. "And of course, Bash had to deal with the green-on-blue incident at Nad-e-Ali."

"Green-on-blue?"

Turner wrinkles his nose distastefully. "Green-on-blue. That's when the Afghans – the ones we trained up, the ones who were supposed to be on our side – when they turned on us. Biggest cause of NATO deaths by the end of it."

"I had no idea," says Walker.

Turner shakes his head like it doesn't matter, shouldn't matter. "Isolated incidents mostly. Some Afghani policeman turns Taliban or something. That sort of thing. Bash... His lot were on mentoring patrol with the Afghan National Army – er, twenty-twelve – and they were approaching a checkpoint when the checkpoint guys opened fire. Next thing, the bloody Afghans with Bash's patrol join in. That's twenty-plus Afghans against ten of our boys." He shakes his head. "Nah. Bash should be the one telling this story. It's his story."

He stares for a moment, as though he's only just remembering that Aaron Bashford is now dead.

"I need a cup of tea," he says.

"I'll get you one," says Josie and stands.

Turner is silent for a while and then asks, "Did he kill himself?"

"We don't know," says Walker, which is a lie but the right answer in the circumstances.

Turner's nod is very slow. "We were gonna go on a lad's weekend to Skeg in the summer," he says. "Even Bash."

When Josie returns with a tea from the bar, Walker passes Turner a contact card. "Thank you for your help."

"Any time."

As they go outside, Walker sees a message on his phone from Rob. He calls him straight back and listens while Rob details the reasons why he's also working on a Saturday morning.

Walker finds it hard to believe what he's just heard.

84

It's Saturday morning and I'm on a solo run.

I almost succeed in kidding myself that it's just a run with no destination in mind, but then my feet insist on taking me over to Maynard Road. It's not that far from the Premier Inn. My promises to Hannah Douglas-Jones to lie low have not lasted long.

AUTOMATIC *WASHETERIA* says the sign above the door.

I slow as I get near, taking in the sort of place that it is. It's not as rough-looking as some launderettes I've seen. It's clean, well-lit and there are chairs where you can sit and wait for your washing.

I go inside and take a seat.

One thing about these places is that you can easily go an hour without seeing another person. It's not like a shop where someone is on hand to serve you. This is all self-service.

Sitting in running clothes when you've cooled right down is a bit ick. And quite cold.

I briefly consider looking at the news, or social media, to

see what the latest round of nonsense looks like. I quickly talk myself out of that. I can't think of a single time when that's ended well for me since this happened. The on-line world hates.

I have enough time, sitting there on my own, to wonder if this was a terrible idea. I've probably used up all my free passes with Hannah now. She made it crystal clear that I shouldn't do this – but here I am.

It was the call from Beaches that did it. The idea that I might be charged with a crime relating to the shooting is horrific beyond belief.

The nagging guilt prompts me to bring Hannah up to date with things. I call her.

"Esther! Hi."

"Hi. Couple of developments I should tell you about."

"Right. What's happened?"

I half expected that Karolina would be on my tail, and that Hannah would already know everything.

"I got a call from DS Beaches. He visited the launderette. The woman said she had no idea what he was talking about. She was nowhere near the casino or the shooting."

I'm speaking loudly, just in case the woman is somewhere where she can hear me.

"Well that's most unfortunate," says Hannah.

"It's not all he said. Apparently the police are now thinking about charging me. Me! With perverting the course of justice."

Hannah makes a thoughtful noise. *"Honestly Esther, I suspect that's just sabre-rattling. It would be very difficult for them to—"*

"I'm at the launderette. I want to see the woman for myself. Look her in the eye."

"Oh no, Esther. Please don't do that."

"It's too late, I'm doing it."

She heaves a loud sigh. *"Is this the sound of you saying that you do not want or need my help any longer?"*

It's a question that throws me off-guard slightly. Do I mean that? Have I given Hannah and Karolina a proper chance? I probably haven't. Not really.

I'm about to reply when the woman emerges from an internal door. I look at her face, the long brown hair. It's her.

It's really her!

"Got to go," I say to Hannah, and end the call.

I stand up and look at the woman properly.

She's just looking at me.

"Well," she says.

She doesn't look surprised. She's probably been watching me on CCTV.

I stand up and look at her. "Nice to meet you. I'm Esther." I hold out my hand.

She gives a small smile, like she's resigned to this, and shakes my hand. "Vicky."

She's got an edge to her in the cold light of day. Nothing I can put my finger on, but she seems less vulnerable than the woman I remember outside the casino.

"We should talk," I say.

"I don't think I have anything to say to you," she says.

"You do know who I am though, don't you?"

She hesitates and then nods. "I've seen your face on social media. You are ... famous."

"Yeah, but before that. You know who I am. Cos I know who you are. You were outside the Meridian Casino that night. You were with Seamus Wollacott."

She stares levelly at me.

I can't stand it.

"Please," I say. "I don't know what your situation is, but I need to know it was you. I need someone who might just believe my version of events."

And still she stares.

"You're right," she says. "You have no idea what my situation is. You have no idea what kind of a man Seamus Wollacott was."

"I do."

I remember Lisa McNally. I remember the fear in her eyes, in her voice. I remember the bruises that sometimes appeared on her face. I might never have met Seamus Wollacott until the night he died, but I have a very strong idea of what kind of a man he was.

"I know that Seamus Wollacott was a dangerous man," I say.

"No. You have no idea what kind of people he was involved with."

She's not admitted it. She's skirting round it and isn't denying it, but she won't admit she was there that night. She's perhaps the only person who can prove I didn't lie about the gun.

She sighs and I assume she's going to chuck me out.

"I'll put a brew on," she says. "And then we'll talk."

85

"Mac Wollacott is dead," Walker explains to Josie and then continues to speak to Rob on the phone. "You want us to come over?"

Walker nods and ends the call.

"Drive-by shooting, would you believe," he says to Josie.

They walk slowly through the city. The clock tower in the Haymarket is a grim sentinel on this grey spring day.

"Make it make sense," says Josie. "The Wollacotts are stupid thugs, by all accounts. One of them gets killed by our lot, and then the brother's whacked less than a fortnight later. I don't see the pattern."

"You might not be wrong about him being whacked," says Walker. "It sounds like a gang hit. Drive-by shooting. No witnesses. No CCTV. His dying words might have been 'Lukas' but I don't put much faith in dying words."

"Even if it is the Degutis gang, how are they involved with Seamus's death?" Josie asks. "Unless Esther works for them."

Walker scrunches up his face. "I don't see that. Pretty hit-

and-miss way of carrying out a killing, isn't it? Call the police and hope they shoot the person dead?"

"This feels like a mess of dead ends."

Walker laughs. "That's gangs. A mess. If you expect them to be run like a well-oiled machine, you'll be disappointed. They're made up of humans. They mess up. We're probably looking for patterns or causality where they don't exist."

He can see that Josie doesn't believe him or doesn't want to believe him. She walks as she verbally lays out the map of criminal activity that just won't makes sense.

"Sunday night, Monday morning, Esther Butler sees Seamus Wollacott and some mystery woman outside the casino where she works. She thinks there's something odd, claims that she sees a gun on Seamus, so she follows them. Esther calls the police and, in the meantime, the woman vanishes. Our boys corner Seamus in the building site next to the old station and – well, yeah, that's it for Seamus."

"Correct," says Walker.

"Meanwhile, someone has visited noted recluse Aaron Bashford and killed him and tried to make it look like suicide. The gun used, whether it was Bashford's or the killer's, is one that was definitely used in the murder of Remi something in twenty-fifteen."

"Remi Jankauskas."

"Thank you. Which either means that Bashford had links to them or the killer had links to them."

"Or the killer is one step ahead of us and wants to pin it on the Degutis lot."

"True," she concedes. "Meanwhile, Esther Butler, who might be telling the truth or spinning the most elaborate bullshit ever, claims to have seen her mystery woman again and given us a location. Did you hear Beaches on the phone to Esther yesterday?"

"Caught snippets," Walker says, with a shake of his head.

"He's been and spoken to the woman that Esther found, and surprise surprise, that woman says she wasn't there on the night."

"He only spoke to Esther Butler on the phone?"

"Right?" Josie's shaking her head. "You put a thing like that to a key witness, you want to be able to see her reaction at the very least."

"Lazy," says Walker.

"At least he went to speak to the woman at the laundrette in person."

"What laundrette?"

She shrugs. "Some laundrette. Um – Maynard Road."

Walker stops in his tracks. It takes Josie a moment or two to realise she's left him behind. She turns to face him. "What?"

"Laundrette. Maynard Road."

"That's what I said."

Some days, occasionally, Walker feels like old age is catching up on him. Creaking joints. Hair thinning a little. The sense that the cogs in his brain are turning a little slower at times. But then, out of nowhere, mental lightning strikes and a nugget of knowledge can be plucked from a career's worth of memories.

"The Degutis family own – or at least owned – a laundrette on Maynard Road."

"Really?" says Josie.

He nods. "Justina Degutis, daughter of Darius, so brother to Lukas, owns a number of businesses and she definitely owned a laundrette on Maynard Road."

"That's a hell of coincidence," she says, but he's already got his phone out to call Rob.

86

I watch Vicky carefully as she goes into the back room of the laundrette, in case she's about to leg it again. But that would be a bit crazy, unless she plans to stay away from her place of work.

She returns five minutes later with two mugs and sits beside me.

"What do you want to know?" she asks.

I give a wide shrug. "Everything. Let's start with why you ran away from me before."

She sighs and shakes her head.

"And why you told the police you weren't there on the night of the shooting."

"You want answers. Who can blame you, eh sweets?"

I sip my tea and wait for her to continue.

"What you need to understand is that Seamus Wollacott could be unpredictable at the best of times."

A woman enters the launderette with a bin bag full of washing. She dumps it by a machine and goes back outside.

"Yes?" I don't want Vicky to stop talking now she's started.

"Yes ... Seamus." She rolls her eyes. "He was all mouth and no trousers that man. He talked the talk and thought he was God's gift, he really did."

"So, you knew him well."

Vicky shakes her head. "I'd known him a few weeks by the time we went out that evening. I was... I was starting to get an inkling of what kind of man he could be. By the time you saw us, I'd had enough of him. I wanted to go home."

"You walked off and he followed."

She shrugs. "I didn't look back. I was done with him."

I take another sip of tea. It's very warming.

"But you didn't come forward," I say. "You didn't tell the police. You lied to them."

"I was protecting myself," says Vicky. "Seamus was known to the police. He's got a record. Can't a woman protect her privacy? Her reputation."

I want to tell Vicky that this is what I've been trying to do for what seems like forever now. Trying and failing. My character and reputation have been dragged through the gutter so long that I'm mentally exhausted.

I want to tell her all of that – in fact I want to shout it in her face – but then the customer returns with another bin bag. She empties each bag into a machine and then brings out her phone.

It's at that point I realise that these machines are operated using an app. It's been a while since I visited a launderette. Of course they'd keep pace with technology.

She puts each machine on, and I watch, fascinated. A slice of life I wasn't aware of: washing machines with apps.

At this point, I notice that Vicky's talking, and I haven't been listening. This is very unlike me.

"So sorry, Vicky. What were you just saying?"

Except the words that come out of my mouth are slurred and nearly incoherent. A wave of tiredness has come over me. Like four double vodkas hitting my bloodstream all at once.

The customer is looking at me with concern.

"Oh darling!" Vicky says loudly, catching me as I slip over sideways. "What have I told you about bottomless prosecco brunches, eh? You'll be the death of me, you will."

The customer says something but I'm losing consciousness and can't hear it. Vicky says something back to her.

"Let me call your brothers," Vicky says to me as I start to slide off the seat. "Help us get you to bed, eh?"

I catch a whiff of Vicky's perfume as my eyes close. Poison.

87

By mid-afternoon, Gill's incident room at Mansfield House police station has been expanded to include the investigations into the deaths of the Wollacott brothers as well as Aaron Bashford. Intelligence data is being collated and, though any links between the Wollacott deaths and Bashford's faked suicide have yet to be conclusively drawn, detective inspectors Scabbard and Gill have been required to pool their resources to bring their respective investigations together under the supervision of a detective chief inspector.

Josie sits at a terminal, looking over the ANPR camera data from near Whitwick Farm. Every vehicle that has passed by during the possible window for Bashford's death has been automatically logged and photographed. There are hundreds of them.

It would be nice if any of them had been flagged in relation to the Degutis family, but there's no such immediate luck. It would be equally nice if any of them matched the vague descriptions given for the car used in the drive-by shooting of Mac Wollacott. The ANPR data for cameras near where Mac was shot hasn't come through yet. Cross-comparison might yield a lucky result.

Behind her, Walker is filling Rob in on the visit to the Armed Forces Veterans Breakfast Club. Getting to understand the character and social life of Aaron Bashford seems rather secondary, now that the police have a fresh murder – and such a public one – on their hands. Walker's partway through explaining the details of the 'green-on-blue' attack Bashford and his Black Watch comrades experienced in Afghanistan when Scabbard calls for everyone's attention.

"Right boys. I've just had the go-ahead from on high that we can door-knock key properties in relation to the Degutis family. That includes the home addresses of Darius, Arturas and Lukas Degutis. We're also going to check some known bolt-holes and the laundrette on Maynard Road that Esther Butler, the 'witness' in the Seamus Wollacott shooting reported to us."

He says this without any glances towards the Duncans who raised that link in the first place.

Gill steps up beside him. "Everyone here is allocated to a team. No warrants. We're just shaking the trees and seeing what falls out."

"Ma'am," says Rob, "Arturas has a property just off the Narborough Road. Paul Mulholland, who handles stolen goods for him, operates out of there."

"We have limited people," says Gill, indicating the properties listed on the nearby whiteboard. "These are our key targets."

"And we're solving murders, not chasing after stolen

combine harvesters," says Dean Beaches, raising some chuckles from others.

"You have your teams," says Gill with a stern look at Beaches. "Let's see what we can find."

88

I wake up, shivering.

It takes me what feels like an age to make any sense of where I am.

I'm on a thin yoga mat. I feel like puking and I'm not sure if that's the after-effects of whatever drugs I was given, or the fact that my face is pressed against a pitted rubber surface that stinks of feet.

I can feel a slick of drool below my face. I recoil and my head bangs in protest with the movement.

I try to push myself up, and that's when I discover my hands are tied in some way, so I roll over to get some leverage. That makes my head pound even more violently, so I have to pause before I can get my upper half off the floor.

"Fuck."

My breathing is ragged – I wonder how long I've been out. I'm in something that looks like a cellar. It's a gloomy space with tiled walls and a rough concrete floor. There are windows towards the ceiling, letting in some daylight, so I can see that this room has been used as a dumping ground for broken furniture, building waste and other crap over a long period of time. There is a foul stench in here.

I realise that I'm handcuffed to a length of chain that's attached to a heating pipe.

"What the hell...?"

Panic starts to rise through me.

It turns to chilly dread when I see the commode chair and a water bottle.

They've been put within reach of me as though I'm expected to be here long enough to use a toilet and need a drink.

The last thing I remember was Vicky at the laundrette. I remember feeling unwell. I remember the cup of tea she gave me. She Rohypnoled me. It's insane.

And then I think about the yoga mattress, the commode, the handcuffs. This is a setup that has not been cobbled together because I came along and made a nuisance of myself. It's been used before.

The insanity of this is enough to make me want to scream. I only visited Vicky because I needed someone to back up my story. I needed to not be alone. When I saw Vicky with Seamus that night, I saw the tension between them, I could sense the danger just rolling off the man. I wanted her to be safe. I wanted to find her so that neither of us were alone.

I didn't want trouble. I wanted to help.

That it should come to this, is madness.

The panic and fear has been building in me ever since I woke and I can't hold it in any longer.

I yell.

"Help! Help! Down here! Help! I'm in the cellar!"

I pause a second to listen for a response, then I shout some more.

The cellar door opens at speed and Vicky comes down the steps.

"What the hell do you think you're doing?" she hisses and, as soon as she's at the bottom step, her hand swings to slap me.

I duck back. She doesn't like that so she grabs the chain where it meets my wrists, violently yanks me forward and then has a second go at a slap. That one connects hard. My foot tangles with the edge of the yoga mat and I sit down hard.

"You do not make a noise like that in this house!" she says.

She's hissing the words as though the commotion we're making might wake a sleeping baby.

"I ... I don't understand," I say.

"No, of course you fucking don't," she spits back. "You don't know anything, but you still came blundering in. None of this was ever meant to go like this."

"This. I don't even know what this is."

There's a shout from upstairs, a man's voice. "Hey, honey?"

"What?" Vicky calls back.

"Fucking pigs are here. Keep her quiet."

Fear clouds Vicky's face for a moment. "On the mat. On your front," she instructs.

"What?"

She grabs me roughly and pushes me down, flat on my front before I know what's happening. Once she has me down, she kneels on the small of my back. I hear a metallic click and something cold is pressed to my neck.

"One move and I'll kill you," says Vicky. "Right between your vertebrae. Lights out."

"Please," I whisper. "I don't understand."

89

It turns out that the Degutis family live in some of the nicest houses in the Stoneygate area of the city.

Josie looks up at the three-story Victorian villa and wonders how much this place would sell for. Most of the others in the road have been split up into multiple flats, but not the one they're visiting.

This is the house of Lukas Degutis, son of one of the founder fathers of the gang.

"Do well for themselves, don't they?" she says.

"Hmmm?" says Rob, who's looking at something on his phone.

Most of the parking along here is on the street, but there's a decent driveway to this house. A car is pulled onto the drive and there's a low brick-built garage behind it. Josie walks over to see whether she can find any gaps to see inside, but it's secure.

"Black Watch, you say?" says Rob. "The Scottish regiment."

It takes her a good long moment to work out what on earth he's talking about.

"Er, yes."

"And this incident. Twenty-twelve?"

"The fight with the soldiers who turned on them? Yeah?"

Gill is approaching the front door. Josie and Rob follow. Gill climbs the step to ring the doorbell and then steps back.

Gill's about to ring the bell again when the door opens.

Josie has seen Lukas Degutis's picture before. He's a tall man, but not especially muscular. If Josie passed him on the street, she'd take him for a university lecturer or a librarian. It's disturbing how harmless he appears.

He finishes wiping his hands on the tea towel he is holding and gives them all a genial and slightly bemused smile.

"Hello, officers. It is the weekend. Is this a social call?"

He wasn't born in the UK but this Lithuanian national speaks English like a native and without an accent.

"Lukas," says Gill, showing him her ID, "we've come to talk to you about a very serious matter. Can we come inside?"

"No," he says, simply and unconfrontationally. "What serious matter?"

"A man was killed, late last night. Shot."

Lukas's expression doesn't change. "And?"

90

Vicky's knee is grinding into my spine. It's beyond uncomfortable. It's sickening.

I try to angle my body to just put that knee somewhere else.

Above me, she thumps me in the shoulder.

"Keep still!" she hisses.

The sharp point of whatever she has held against my neck digs in sharply. I want to yelp and pull away, but there's literally nowhere for me to go. Instead, I cough with the pain.

Even though I can't see a damned thing, I can feel a tenseness in Vicky's body on top of me.

I picture her with her head angled up, trying to hear the conversation that's going on above.

I can't really hear much. There's my own breathing. There's the wet movement of my mouth as it's pressed against the yoga mat. Above me there are the general and non-specific sounds of a house: the light creak of wood, running water somewhere, muffled sounds that could be voices or music, or maybe some kitchen appliance.

If the police are here, I could probably yell out, but someone's sitting on my lungs and I can't move my mouth to a clear position. I dread to think what pathetic sound would come out if I tried to shout now. And it would be the last sound I make.

"Why are you doing this?" I whisper to Vicky.

"Shut up," she says and the sharp point pokes me again. I buck against her but I'm totally within her control.

91

The wind carries a noise to Rob's ears and he looks around to locate its source but it's gone and he's not even sure what it was.

DI Gill is getting nowhere with Lukas.

Rob's had no dealing with Lukas Degutis before, but it's clear he's been educated by his dad or his uncle in the ways of dealing with the police. He's polite. He doesn't say any more than he needs to. And, at every turn, it's a polite refusal. No, you can't come in. No, I won't come down to the station to answer some questions. No, I'm not going to look at any pictures for you or explain my movements. He stays utterly within the law and, if the police want to have a look around or ask him further questions then they'll need to come back with a warrant or arrest him.

The hope is that the police visit here or elsewhere might spook someone. If Lukas is behind the hit on Mac Wollacott and thinks he's insulated from accusations then this visit has blown that out of the water. Over the coming hours, there might be recriminations.

Gill runs out of imprecations after ten minutes and the detectives back off.

"We continue door-to-door inquiries close to the shooting and put feelers out in the community," she says as they walk back to the road.

"Someone somewhere will decide that bullets being sprayed at family homes goes beyond whatever code this lot think they hold to," says Rob.

"Maybe CCTV will throw something up, ma'am," Josie offers.

Gill nods like she's already thought of this. "Let's hope they were stupid and didn't think of that before going out to kill Mac, yeah?"

Gill heads to her own car. Rob pauses by his, ready to show Josie something on his phone.

"That incident in Afghanistan."

"You think it's important?"

He reads from his phone. "UK soldiers investigated over Helmand deaths."

"What's that?"

"A news story. Old one. Just googled it."

He offers her his phone and she reads. "*Four members of the Royal Regiment of Scotland's third battalion (Black Watch) have been arrested in connection with deaths that occurred while on patrol near Nad-e-Ali last October.*" She scans further down. "*...accuse UK troops of opening fire without provocation while questioning two Afghani men at a security check-point.*" She looks up at Rob with a surprised expression. "This is it. This is the incident. But Turner said it was the Afghans who opened fire. He said that a bunch of the men they were training just attacked them for no reason."

Rob takes his phone back and thinks. "Whatever happened, someone was telling porky pies."

Josie shrugs. "You think this has anything to do with anything?"

Rob gives a shrug. "If Bashford and his fellow soldiers are trigger-happy killers then that certainly paints him morally in a certain way. If he was innocent and let down by the military, that might explain a certain bitter and insular personality."

Josie's head jiggles display a general agreement. She gestures to her own car.

"You all right if I go check something out before going back to the station?"

"What?" says Rob.

"Something the DI said. Said that the killers, if they were at all clever, would avoid appearing on CCTV."

"And?"

"I want to go take a look at Whitwick Farm again."

"But the CCTV there doesn't work."

"Exactly," she says.

92

Eventually, Vicky gets off my back and I groan as I'm permitted to move again.

"You need to be more fucking compliant if you want us to treat you right," she says.

I roll over and sit up. I wipe my face where it's been pushed into the mat.

"Please, why are you doing this to me?" I say.

She sighs with disgust. "You keep asking that, sweets. You need to stop asking questions you're not gonna get answers to and think about getting into our good books."

I see now that the thing she had pressed to the back of my neck was a retractable craft knife. She slides it back with her thumb and the razor-sharp blade disappears. I try to reach the spot on my neck where she cut me twice, but it's hard to reach round with my hands cuffed together.

The cellar door opens and a man comes down the stairs. He's tall, fair-haired and in that shirt and those glasses, looks like he's just come home from a day at the office.

"Everything okay here?" he says.

"Perfectly fine," says Vicky. "We've just got settled in. A few house rules. What happened with the fuzz?"

"Grasping at straws. They're trying to pin the drive-by shooting on us."

"What makes them think it's anything to do with us?"

"Dunno," says the man. "I'll have a chat with Bixby later. I don't think it's a problem."

"What drive-by?" I say without thinking.

The man takes two steps towards me and thrusts a pointing finger in my face. "You need to shut the fuck up or things will go badly for you."

"I don't know why you're doing this," I say. I'm close to sobbing as I say it but I rein it sharply in. I'm not going to show that kind of vulnerability to these people. "I'm no one. I'm not important. You don't need me."

This causes both Vicky and the man to smile.

"We need you very much," he says.

"We still doing it tomorrow then?" says Vicky.

"Absolutely," he says, slipping an arm round her waist.

93

Clouds roll in and daytime is fading towards an early evening by the time Josie reaches Whitwick Farm. She drives up the track to the farm and mentally notes the CCTV camera on the post near to where the track opens out into the farmyard.

She steps out of her car and looks about.

The farmhouse – dark windows, flaking woodwork – seems to skulk in the dim light. Josie feels she should make some noise to counter the silence hanging over the place.

She only has half an idea of why she's here and needs to think her way through it.

She takes out her phone and starts to record video so, if something comes of it, she can show Rob or Walker later.

"Okay, so this is the area around Whitwick Farm," she narrates for the benefit of future viewers. "And there's the CCTV camera down there."

She's already picturing Rob's response.

"Yes, the CCTV camera doesn't work, or at least doesn't record, but if the person who came here and killed Aaron

Bashford didn't know that, then they'd avoid coming up this way." She hums to herself. "That's assuming they spotted there was CCTV here at all."

A killer who came just once, to kill Bashford and depart again, might not have known there was CCTV; might not even have noticed it. Which currently made them the luckiest assassin on earth.

"Okay," she says, "I'm working on the assumption that the killer had half a brain. Let's say they'd either been here before or had at least scouted out the place. If they knew there was CCTV but didn't know Aaron Bashford's account had been closed then they'd avoid coming this way. That's my theory, okay? So the question is: what's the easiest way to get here?"

She stops filming and orientates herself. She's seen the local area on a map. Ulverscroft is that way. The village of Copt Oak is that way. She walks round the farmhouse building. This is straightforward up to a point, although there is a pile of building rubble and a small mountain of pallets and rotten joinery wood to navigate around. The rear of the property looks over sloping fields and a small wood off to the left.

"Right," she says and takes a path through a gate that seems to lead at an angle across the fields.

Five minutes later, she resorts to her phone's satnav app to confirm her location among the scant landmarks. She's generally making for the woods, but even as she walks, the route becomes less certain. Mud clings to her shoes but she refuses to tut or comment at that.

A further five minutes later, she wonders what will happen if it gets dark before she finds her way back to her car again. She can already see herself wandering aimlessly, getting lost in the trees and facing the embarrassment of having to call out fellow police officers to come find her.

She slips in the mud, nearly goes down on her backside but just about manages to avoid it.

"This is a stupid idea," she says to no one and almost instantly, as though the words were part of a magic spell, finds that she has come to a path. It's only a track through a field, but there are muddy grooves which have been worn into it by a number of vehicles.

She crouches to inspect the track and finds what looks like recent tyre marks. Using the flash in the fading light she takes some photos. There's no knowing if these are recent, but given the width of the track, this vehicle was one of the very last to come down here.

She switches to video and starts recording again.

"There is a track that runs maybe quarter of a mile behind Whitwick Farm. Vehicles can access it. If the killer wanted to approach the house without being seen on the CCTV, this would be a good spot. I'm going to follow it this way."

She can see lights down the track, just visible through the trees. If her mental geography is as good as she thinks it is, then that's Copt Oak. Now the going underfoot is more certain, it's only a ten minute walk, along a track that becomes more defined and solid the further she goes, until she's walking alongside a fence which soon becomes the back fence of the car park to the Copt Oak pub.

She films where she's at for good measure, then passes through a gate in the fence. White security cameras sit at two corners under the eaves of the pub, viewing the same car park from different directions.

Josie struggles to contain her energy and she strides into

the pub with such force the door bounces back on the wall. People tucking into pub dinners look round. The woman at the bar looks at Josie sharply.

Josie pulls out her ID, seeing as she does so that her shoes and the bottoms of her trousers are coated in mud.

"Please tell me your CCTV outside works."

The woman – it's the same one from their visit on Monday – peers at the ID and then looks at Josie.

"What do you want?"

"I want to look at the CCTV footage from the sixth and seventh of March."

The woman nods. "You'll have to ask Brandon."

"Brandon?"

"The manager. He's the one who knows how to log into the system."

"Sure. Where is he?"

The woman's brow creases as she thinks. "Kettering, I think."

"Kettering?"

"His mum's birthday. She's just had a replacement hip. Not for her birthday, obviously."

"What? And he's the only one who can access the CCTV?"

She nods and turns to another customer who is holding one of the cardboard food menus. The man starts to give his order.

Josie waves at the woman across the bar. "Excuse me. Excuse me."

The woman's expression is not a pleased one. "It's Saturday night. We're busy."

"You got a number for Brandon?" Josie asks.

94

I sit on the yoga mat with my back against the cellar wall. I try and fail to comprehend what the hell has happened to me.

Vicky and her man are upstairs. I can hear them moving around occasionally. I get the impression that they're the only ones in the house. I've got no way of being certain.

On the floor, not far from my mat, is a plastic tray with a packet of crisps, a penguin bar and a ham sandwich. It's been sitting there for an hour now since Vicky put it there. I'm refusing to touch it, just like I'm refusing to use the toilet they've put in here with me. To use them is to accept them, and I'm still doing my best to refuse the notion that this is happening to me.

But I'm hungry and tired and I need to pee. I don't really know who I'm fighting against by refusing.

They took my phone when I was unconscious and my mind circles unhelpfully around thoughts of who exactly is going to be missing me at this moment in time, who might have called me. Has Jeety messaged me? Probably. Does she expect an answer? I don't know. Hannah Douglas-Jones the PR woman has probably phoned and rolled her eyes as she's required to leave another voicemail. I've been ignoring Kieran's messages anyway. If I don't respond to his next text about where item 'X' might be in the house – like I'm somehow keeping tabs on where everything is after I've walked out on him – I don't think he's going to imagine something's amiss.

My room at the Premier Inn will be entirely ignored until morning and, even then, the staff aren't going to give a damn about where I might be until my booking comes to an end.

No one knows I'm here. There's a strong chance that not a single soul is worried about where I am.

I exhale. My breath comes as a miserable, ragged sigh. How did my life take such a massive nosedive?

I shake myself and blink away any possibility of having a self-pitying cry. This is not helping.

"You've got to get out of here," I tell myself softly. "Yeah."

I am handcuffed. I've never seen a pair of real-life handcuffs before, let alone had them put on me. I can't tell if they're real. I mean they're obviously real and they are cold metal, but I don't know if they're proper police-style handcuffs. Maybe they're just toy cuffs or from a sex shop. There's a keyhole in each cuff but I wonder how complex the lock is.

If I had something I could use to pick at them, I might be able to get myself free. Or at least mentally distract myself from this nightmare with the attempt.

I need a pin or a nail or a piece of stiff wire. I've got nothing in my pockets. My keys were taken along with my phone.

The area immediately around the mat is dusty but bare.

There's nothing that can be stripped off the heating pipe I'm chained to. I walk on my knees to the commode. It's metal framed and held together with bolts. I reckon those bolts are going to be way too thick to use as lockpicks, even if I could loosen them.

I have no lockpicking skills. I have no reason to think I could open the cuffs even if I found the perfect lockpick. But first things first...

There are two broken chairs, old fashioned dining chairs with arms, by the other wall of the cellar. They look like the type that might be held together with long thin nails. But my chain won't allow me to get with five feet of them.

There's some old paint cans and dust sheets by a long pile of rubbish wrapped up in blue plastic sheeting. Nothing visually leaps out at me as useful, but at least it's in range. The extent of the chain won't let me reach them directly, but if I sit on the floor, with my hands above my head, I can reach out and grab the edge of the wrapped rubbish with my feet.

I snag the edge of the bin bag and then try to get a better grip. There's something solid inside. Hard. Maybe wood. That feels good. At this point, I'm thinking that if I can pick the locks, having something heavy to hit Vicky or her man with would at least give me a sense of control, however slight.

I grip my feet, bend my knees and pull. The wrapped rubbish barely shifts. That thing is heavy. I'm not deterred. I adjust my feet grip, find an indent in the unknown mass to hook my feet under, and pull.

It scrapes along the floor and a paint can falls over. I glance up, fearing that I'm making too much noise. I wait a full minute. I can feel my heart pounding. I can hear the sound of blood in my own ears.

The cellar door doesn't open. No one comes in. No one shouts.

I wait another minute and then pull again. The wrapped bundle shifts. I don't know what might be in it, but if it's the remnants of DIY projects then hooks, spikes, wooden pegs, wire... The options feel endless.

With crooked knees I pull more. It's slipped free of the paint-spattered dust sheets now. The plastic bundle, long and thin and heavy, is nearly close enough. I pull it back with my feet until I've got enough free chain to bring my hands round and use them.

My activity has stirred the air and the bad smell in the cellar is much worse. Maybe there's something damp and mouldy inside the sheeting. I pull it even closer to the yoga mat to give me space to tear the sheeting open. The plastic is heavy duty, but it's easier to tear than unwrap. I dig my fingers in like claws and pull.

Come on. Some wire would be best. Nice heavy-duty wire I can bend into a picking tool. That would be—

I stop.

The light is fading in the cellar and, in truth, I don't know if I saw or felt the contents of the bundle first.

I think I felt it first. The softness, the fibres. I think that for the tiniest fraction of a second, I thought it was something like loft insulation roll, a mass of tangled fibres.

It isn't insulation fibres. It's hair.

The hair is a lustrous orange colour. Even in this light it shines, like fire, like copper wire. I know this hair. And the shape of what I'm holding becomes sickeningly, mockingly obvious.

The long bundle of wrapped rubbish is a body. The rotten stink pours out of the hole I've ripped in the plastic.

I'm holding the head of a woman I thought – hoped – was safe and many miles away from the man who'd abused her.

It's Seamus Wollacott's old girlfriend.

It's Lisa McNally.

95

Rob enters the CID office on Sunday morning with a takeout coffee in one hand and a pastry in a paper bag in the other.

He does not expect to find Josie Kaminski already there, head supported by one hand while she clicks her mouse with the other.

"Don't tell me you've been here all night," he says.

"Not exactly," she says without taking her eyes off the screen.

"Uh-huh? Cos you look like you've been here all night." He recognises the T-shirt she's wearing under her jacket. "Same clothes."

"I slept in my car for a couple of hours."

"Trouble at home?" he says and realises he knows next to nothing about Josie's personal life. There's been no mention of a boyfriend or girlfriend, no discussion of family.

"I've been looking at the CCTV."

"Whitwick Farm?"

"Copt Oak pub."

He comes round the desk to look. She's got several computer windows open, including an ANPR list in a spreadsheet and poor quality footage from a car park CCTV.

"Okay," he says. "And what's this?"

She stretches and leans back. "So, working theory is that Aaron Bashford was shot by someone or, maybe, outside chance, shot himself while someone was stood next to him."

"Correct."

"And let's assume for a moment, bit of a leap here, that the shooter was clever enough to note that Bashford had CCTV but didn't know it wasn't saving the recordings anywhere."

"Okay."

"There is a track that runs pretty close to the back of the farmhouse." She draws a line across the CCTV image of the car park. "This lane here. Our shooter might have driven or walked up that lane so they could approach the farmhouse without being spotted."

"I like your thinking here," he says.

"Thanks, Sarge. So, I'm now currently on hour eighteen of forty-eight hours of footage at, five times normal speed, looking for sign of anyone or anything going up that road."

"You're not going to get a number plate at that angle."

"So, if there's anything then we can compare make and model to the frankly thousands of vehicles picked up by ANPR in the area."

Rob spots the timestamp on the ANPR data. "This is a fresh request."

"I expanded the search. We don't know how long beforehand our shooter might have cased the joint."

"You requested ANPR access on Gill's case?"

The automatic number plate recognition system is a

powerful data and surveillance tool and, as such, access is granted on a case by case basis and needs to be justified. The country isn't a police surveillance state – not quite yet.

"I told them it would be fine."

"Fine?" says Rob and bites his tongue. "You better get results or hope no one finds out. Preferably both."

She makes a disinterested noise and keeps watching the sped-up replay.

"Seriously, been here all night?" says Rob.

"Yep."

"Had breakfast?"

"Nope."

He puts the coffee and pastry on her desk.

She glances at them. "But these are yours."

"Duncans look out for each other," he says. "I can get more. Now I need to find Walker."

"Yeah?"

"He's gone to see a man about a dog."

She doesn't even acknowledge him but just tears into the pastry and watches the video.

96

There's no way I can sleep. I press myself hard against the wall, knees to my chest, arms around my legs, locked into a tight ball. I stare in horror as the darkness descends.

A night in the cellar with the corpse of former Meridian casino cleaner, Lisa McNally.

I stare into the darkness and try to think of anything. I try to think of nothing.

I don't sleep. I can't sleep.

And yet I'm suddenly jolted awake by hands grabbing me.

"What the fuck?" Vicky spits. "Lukas!"

I grunt. My brain is fogged up. The lights are on but no one is at home.

Before I can move my limbs or find my words, the man is down here too. They talk at speed and shout at me.

The padlock connecting the chain to the handcuffs is undone and I'm hauled upright. My legs ache and for a moment refuse to hold me upright. The man drags me to the stairs.

I look back and see the body wrapped in plastic and tufty strands of red hair and then I'm dragged upstairs into the house.

It's a big house, a nice house, thoughtfully decorated and furnished throughout. It's a big posh house and they keep women locked up in the cellar.

"What's happening?" I manage to say.

The man – Lukas, Vicky called him – takes me to a lounge.

"Stand there," he says.

I sway.

"Stand there!"

I stand.

He lets go of me, gets a fur effect throw from a low cupboard and puts it over a chair before pushing me into it. He doesn't want the dirty cellar woman staining his cream-coloured upholstery.

I sit and I look at him.

"Coffee?" he says.

I just look at him.

"Do you drink coffee?" he demands.

"I drink coffee."

He turns his head. "Coffee, honey. She'll take it black."

"On it," Vicky calls back.

This is fucking weird. And, in this situation, weird means terrifying. I don't understand anything and I'm a person who likes things to make sense, who likes to have some control.

Vicky comes in with a tray holding three cups of coffee. Two are in little white Italian cups on saucers. One is in a mug with a faded shop logo on it. That one will be mine. I see how this situation is going.

She puts the tray down and then puts the mug in my hand, not letting go until she's sure I've got it.

"We'll have to get her cleaned up," she says to the man: Lukas. "Do something about that hair."

"Does it matter?" he says.

"People will notice. We need to glide through, unnoticed."

He nods, accepting. He looks at the smartwatch on his wrist. "Mike and the boys will be here with the van at half nine."

"We can do that," says Vicky.

Lukas looks at me with disdain.

"You want to put her in some of your clothes?" he asks.

"I'm not going to give her any of my clothes."

He tilts his head. "Okay," he says and walks out.

Vicky sits on a seventies-style wicker chair opposite me and looks at me like she's studying something in a zoo.

"Drink your coffee," she says.

I realise that the mug in my hands is starting to burn. I take it by the handle and sip. It washes over my furred mouth and teeth.

"I suspect you have a lot of very stupid questions you want to ask," she says.

I take another sip.

"We are going to need you to do something for us very soon," she continues. "You are working for us. I need you focused. I need you on board. You are going to do exactly as we tell you and then you get to go back to your old boring life. That's a promise."

Nothing makes sense. There's a bloody dead body in their basement.

"Did you kill Lisa?" I say.

"Me personally? No. Seamus helped bring her here.

Didn't take long to find her in Coventry. She hurt herself in the cellar. We tried to look after her. She got a fever and one night she just died." She sips her own coffee. "If it helps, I'm really sorry that happened."

"Seamus ... works for you?"

She gives a momentary twitch of disgust. "*Worked* for us. Briefly. He owed us. You know he's only come out of prison recently? After he got out, he went to find Lisa and then came to us with a proposition." She shakes her head. "The man was an idiot. He deserved to die."

"He had a gun that night," I say. This really shouldn't be the most important question in my mind, but it's been burning inside me for days now and I can't help but ask.

"He did," she sighs. "Like I say, an idiot. I literally couldn't believe he had it on him that night. You saw us arguing, right?"

I remember the two of them, across the road from the casino doors, the body language between them. He was hyper. She was pissed off, both angry and afraid.

"You were arguing because he had a gun on him," I say.

"He'd watched too many movies. He was a liability. I couldn't get out of there fast enough."

"He had a gun on him but the police said he didn't have one."

"They're cops. They fuck up all the time. He had a pistol one of Lukas' boys gave to him for some stupid reason. If the police couldn't find it after they shot him then that's their problem. You know, you should have just kept your nose out of other people's business, Esther. You should have let this all happen and then you wouldn't have had to spend a night in our cellar with Lisa."

"I thought you were in trouble. That night."

"More fool you then," she says. "Just keep remembering that if you hadn't followed us – and if you hadn't somehow found me at that bloody nightclub—" She grinds her teeth. "If it wasn't for you, stupid Mac Wollacott would still be alive."

I shake myself. "He's dead?"

"You brought all the crazies out of the woodwork. I don't know what Seamus told Mac, or how much that runt had worked out for himself, but the moment he realised Seamus had been working for us, he somehow got it into his head that we owed him." She smiles, like she's telling a story about her busy week. "The day after you rudely sought me out at Grotto, he comes to us and asks for his cut. Not cap in hand, but demanding. 'I know stuff and I'll go to the cops if you don't pay me off.' Literally signing his own death warrant with every word."

"And he's dead?"

Vicky breathes in deeply. "It's a mess, but it is what it is. After we're done today, we can straighten things out." She drinks the last from her cup. "Seriously, three hours from now, it will all be over for you."

"What will? What's happening?"

The little cup chinks against its little saucer. "Esther, you're going to help us rob the Meridian Casino."

97

Rob going downstairs meets Walker coming up.

"Just looking for you."

Walker nods in greeting, but there's a dark look on his usually upbeat face. "We need to talk."

"What?"

Walker turns without a word and leads him downstairs again. Towards the rear of the building are the rooms that the uniformed patrol officers use. The general office where uniform hotdesk to complete their paperwork is badly laid out and is cramped when full. At ten o'clock on this Sunday morning, it's empty but for one officer.

Sergeant Sandy Bellows is an older officer with surely only a couple of years to retirement and a waistline that suggests he's not planning on moving much once he has. He's a nice chap in Rob's opinion, although he comes across as someone who treats the job as merely a source of income. Sandy is ex-military, which is why Walker had come to see him this morning.

"Sandy, you know Rob?" says Walker.

"I do," says Sandy. His tone is as dour as Walker's.

"Has something happened?" says Rob.

"I think we're just processing," says Walker.

"Processing what?"

Sandy leans back in his chair which creaks alarmingly.

"You wanted to know about the incident in Afghanistan with that Bashford character you're investigating. I know you can put a request into the army Special Investigation Branch, but I also know that if it's a case that didn't end in conviction, they would never give out the names of those involved. So, I had a word with a former colleague of mine who will forever remain nameless." He points a warning finger at the pair of them. "And this conversation never happened, right?"

Rob shrugs. "Did you find anything?"

"It seems the incident at the checkpoint in Helmand was not as described by our friend at the breakfast club," says Walker. "Some of the UK guys were involved in something with the locals. Selling off supplies. Making a bit of money on the side."

"That bit is unclear," says Sandy. "But it seems things went sour. Words were said. Threats were made. Shots were fired."

"By the British troops?" says Rob.

"Apparently."

"So, like murder."

Sandy twitches. "Things are different in active combat. I'm not saying what they did wasn't wrong but—"

"Sandy's got names," said Walker. "Names of the British soldiers, the four who were arrested. It didn't go to court martial or whatever as no one present was willing to give evidence."

"Okay," says Rob.

Sandy looks sick as he tells Rob the names.

~

TEN MINUTES LATER, Rob and Walker go back upstairs to CID. It's hard to know what to do with the information they now have.

As soon as they enter the main office, Josie stands and waves them over.

"I've got news," she says with a mixture of excitement and urgency.

"Yeah, us too," says Rob.

"I saw the car."

She's pointing at the CCTV. A slightly blurry image of a car can be seen on the track.

"Middle of the day. I've not seen any others go up that track."

"Right, yeah," says Rob. "Thing is—"

"And that's a Suzuki Jimny. I asked a couple of people and they agree."

"Okay, but—"

She flaps her hand at him, unwilling to be interrupted. "And there is one Suzuki Jimny out of the thousands of cars caught on the ANPR camera nearby. Passed through twice in the past two months."

"Yeah?"

She pulls a weird face and beckons Walker and Rob to come even closer. "I looked at the registration," she says, lowering her voice. "You'll never guess whose car that is."

Rob and Walker look at each other.

Walker clears his throat.

"Is it Authorised Firearms Officers PC Nick Ferguson?" he suggests in a whisper.

Her eyes widen.

"Is it?" says Rob.

"It is," she says. "How the fuck did you...?"

"He served in Afghanistan with Aaron Bashford. Both were under suspicion of committing war crimes but were never prosecuted."

The three of them stare at each other.

"What the hell?" Josie says again.

98

Vicky puts a pack of cleansing wipes, an oval mirror, and a hairbrush on the table in front of me and tells me to sort myself out.

I resist at first but what's the point? I angle the mirror and take out a wipe.

"You know," she says from her seat opposite, "at first I didn't believe it."

She pauses and waits for me to ask "Believe what?", but I'm not her puppet.

"Lisa told Seamus that not only was there cash and drugs in the strong room at the Meridian, but that you planted some of them in Seamus's car to get him arrested."

I glance at her a second.

"I say she told him," says Vicky. "I'm imagining that when he first found her in Coventry that he had to ... apply some pressure to get that information out of her. But a story like that is almost too crazy for someone to make up. A safe, full of cocaine and cash. All belonging to the KL group. You know them?"

I shake my head.

"You should do," she says. "They own your casino. They owned you while you worked there. Your boss, Gabe Savage, was their little proxy. One of the biggest, if not *the* biggest, providers of cocaine, crack cocaine and meth in the East Midlands."

"I know nothing about that," I say.

"Of course you don't," she simpers, sarcastically. "Seamus was looking to get back into the game and sold that information to my man." She looks towards the door as though Lukas is standing there, but he's not. "My man has ambition. I have ambition. Running a laundrette for Lukas' sister is not my idea of a career plan."

I wipe the sides of my nose and across my brow. It's going to take more than wipes to erase the sense of filth and contamination I got in that cellar. I'll never be able to wipe away the sight of Lisa's body, and I don't want to. The thought of her lying there, unmourned and forgotten, burns at me.

"Once we had Lisa here we had her tell us everything backwards and forwards. She drew plans of the building." Vicky laughs soundlessly. "She drew like a five-year-old, but we got the idea. You don't really use the strong room as such – for the casino I mean?"

"The world is cashless," I say.

"Drug dealers still like cash. You know the combination for the safe."

I consider lying and saying I don't, but I get the impression she knows I know. Maybe she already knows it herself.

"There's a staff area behind reception," she goes on. "And a corridor that leads right past the strong room to a fire escape at the back. You open that door and there's only like two metres from the external door to the strong room."

I want to tell her it's not that simple, but actually it is.

"You open that fire door and the alarm goes off," I say.

This doesn't seem to bother her. "Fire alarms create panic. All we need is two minutes to get into the strong room, open the safe, and take the contents."

If the casino had its own piles of cash to worry about, any prospective robbers would need to worry about the double key system we used to have, but things have become lax as the cash take dropped. On paper, Meridian probably handles less cash that the tiniest corner shop. Not worth the effort. The thing that stops people robbing the stuff hidden in the safe is a) the fact no one knows it's there and b) the fact that they'd be robbing from what I assume are some of the most dangerous people in the city.

"If you steal that cash, those drugs, this KL group will want it back. They'll be mad," I say.

"Absolutely incandescent," says Vicky, unconcerned. "We're not just taking their money – we're taking their business." She holds up two fingers. "Two birds one stone. The KL group's going to implode. My Lukas can deal with those who kick up a fuss as it does."

I drop a scrunched wipe on the table and pick up the hairbrush.

"You want me to tell you the safe code," I say.

"More than that," says Vicky. "Our one problem – our one real problem – is getting into the staff corridor to open that rear fire exit. I could send someone in, but they don't just let members of the public in."

Cold realisation washes over me. "You want me to go in with you?"

"Arm in arm," she says.

"I was fired."

"Only last week. Given the disgusting spectacle you made of yourself in the press, Gabe Savage probably had no choice."

She opens a handbag and takes out a phone. My phone.

"Look," she says, and before I know what I'm looking at she's used my face to unlock the phone.

She clicks and swipes and hums to herself.

"I – that is 'you' – will message Gabe right now to tell him that you'll be in later today to pick up some personal things you left behind, and to say hello. Who'll be on reception today?"

I'm about to say I don't know but I do. "Georgette. Until two."

She scrolls. "Georgette Meridian in your contacts here? Right. I'll let her know as well. You and I will walk in together. We breeze by."

"They won't let me," I say. "It won't work."

"Then you'd better make it work, sweets, otherwise your story gets a very sad end indeed." She finishes texting and smiles. "A couple of missed calls. Who is Nick Ferguson?"

"He called?"

She picks up on the involuntary hopefulness in my tone. "Oh, is he a sweetheart?"

"He's a cop," I say. "He knows about you."

"Oh. Interesting," she says. "You've tangled everyone up in your web, haven't you?"

She really doesn't seem to care that there are people who might know she's linked to this situation. Whatever happens, someone must start knocking on doors and asking questions.

"Brush your hair, Esther," she says. "You look a mess and we need you to make a good impression."

99

Rob has a choice of detective inspectors to take this new information to and opts for Neelam Gill.

"A word, ma'am, please?" he says to her and when she nods takes her into a side office.

Walker and Josie follow them in before closing the door.

"You three always travel together?" asks Gill.

"Dead End Duncans stick together," says Josie.

"It's sort of a team effort this," says Rob.

"Whatever," she says. "You have something?"

Rob nods grimly. There's no good or easy way of saying this.

"Nick Ferguson killed Aaron Bashford."

Gill's eyes bulge. "What?"

"PC Nick Ferguson, part of the AFO team that shot Seamus Wollacott. He likely killed Aaron Bashford."

To an increasingly stunned DI Gill, Rob leads the explanation for their suspicions. The fact that Nick and Aaron served together and were both implicated in a war crimes incident in Afghanistan. The fact that Nick's car was seen accessing a track that ran behind Aaron's farm around the time of his death.

"But why?"

"I've got a theory," says Josie. Gill looks at her plainly. "Whitwick Farm was dying. Bashford was not living in any kind of luxury. But he was receiving regular payments of a thousand pounds. Cash deposits. What if Bashford was blackmailing Ferguson?"

"With what?"

"With the details of what happened in Afghanistan, for example. No one had turned witness over that event. Could Bashford have threatened to go to the military police if Ferguson didn't pay up."

"Speculation," says Gill.

"But it's a good narrative," says Rob.

"But this all ties in with the Wollacotts and the Degutis family somehow," says Gill.

"No. I don't think it does," says Walker.

Gill's gesture suggests that the simple existence of the incident room beyond these walls suggests otherwise.

"I have another theory," says Walker. "It's about bodycams."

"What?"

He steps back to give himself some floor space and crouches. "We might need to check with the footage from the event, but police bodycams have a wide angle lens that covers everything from here upwards." He makes a line from his chest down to the ground at an angle. "What if...?"

Rob can see where he's going with this and it sends a literal shiver down his spine.

"Ferguson shot Wollacott," says Walker. "He was first into that confined building space. It was dark, lots of debris, little space to move. What if – and this relies on Ferguson taking a big risk – what if as he approached Wollacott's body, he saw, maybe out of the corner of his eye, the gun Wollacott had been holding. Maybe he'd been holding it when Ferguson fired, maybe he'd put it down, maybe he'd even tried to hide it."

"You are not seriously suggesting the Wollacott gun is the same weapon that was used to kill Bashford?" says Gill.

Walker is still crouched on the ground, taking on the role of Ferguson. "It's mad. It's impulsive. But it's a split second decision. Ferguson, we think, was being squeezed by Bashford, and if Bashford snitched on him then that's a life sentence for murdering innocent Afghans, plus the end of a promising police career. Prison v pension."

Walker pretends to feel around on the floor, keeping his head up so his imaginary helmet cam is angled elsewhere. He mimes picking up the gun and then flicks aside the tails of his jacket to put the pretend gun away.

"He might even shine his own head torch into the bodycams of anyone facing his way, to obscure the view. We saw some of that on the footage."

He gives Gill a pleased look, his little pantomime done.

"Crazy," says Josie.

As Walker straightens up, Rob strokes his chin in thought. "So there is no link between Bashford's death and the Degutis family. But there's a strong suggestion that Seamus Wollacott was working for the Degutis family, either now, or back when that gun was used to kill Remi Jankauskas."

Gill's hands are pressed to her temples. She's been given all the answers but she's not best pleased.

"Who else have you shared these 'theories' with?"

"No one," says Rob.

"We were passed certain intel that brought everything together," adds Walker. "Anonymous military source."

"Hell's teeth," Gill seethes. "Right. I need to do this in the right order. First, this gets escalated to superintendent level at least. We will need Professional Standards involved and the IOPC will need to be immediately informed." She closes her eyes. "An outside force will need to handle all the interviews."

She descends into a string of mutters as the task ahead of her grows. She shakes her head.

"You've told no one?" she says again.

"No, ma'am," says Rob.

"And you tell no one. None of our colleagues out there need to know any of this, not until they need to be involved."

"Understood."

She gives a bitter huff. "Of course, if this all turns out to be correct then it means that Esther Butler was telling the truth all along."

"It does," says Rob.

100

There is a commotion in the kitchen of Lukas and Vicky's grand house. I hear other voices, men's voices. I sit on the armchair in the lounge, tidied up for what's to come but still handcuffed. Dazed, frightened, bewildered. None of this feels real.

Abruptly the door opens and Lukas enters with another man: broad and bearded.

"We're going," says Lukas.

The man hooks his hand under my armpit and drags me from the seat. My legs have to almost run to keep up with the rest of my body. Out the lounge, along the hallway and outside to where a blue van is parked on the driveway, its back doors open.

The bearded brute doesn't bother to lift me as I'm pulled inside; my knees bang against the rear bumper and then drag along the floor. I gasp. Still ignored, I'm pulled up and dumped on a side seat. Vicky climbs in and sits opposite. There's a couple of men up front.

The doors are slammed shut, the engine coughs into life and we set off.

"We're going to the casino?" I ask.

"You shut up," says the bearded brute. He's got an interesting accent. Not British.

"We're swapping vehicles first," says Vicky. "Then yes. The casino." She looks to the grimy rear window of the van. "Sunday morning. As quiet as the casino gets."

"There will be people there," I say, pointlessly.

"Unavoidable, darling," says Vicky. "But you and I are just going in like regular visitors. You're going into the back to collect some things and I'm..."

I wait for her to continue, but she doesn't. She makes circling motions with her hand for me to speak. I see the hand is holding the retractable craft knife.

"You're my cousin who's come into town for the day," I say.

"Good. Good. Maybe we're going for lunch later. That'd be nice."

She seems very confident that I'm simply going to get her through the staff doors round the corner from reception. I mean, I can see it happening. I can see it's a possibility. But her confidence that this will happen is nauseating. I wonder what will happen if I fail? I wonder what will happen if I disappoint her?

And I am suddenly faced with a question that I've been deliberately ignoring for some time now. Even if everything goes to plan will they let me live?

"You know the casino has CCTV, right?" I say. "You'll be seen on the cameras."

Vicky laughs. The bearded brute chuckles dutifully.

"The owners of the casino will know it's us," she says. "We want them to know it's us."

"But the police—"

"The police? Do you think Gabe Savage is going to call the police and tell them that some nasty people came in and stole all his cocaine? You think that's what's going to happen? For a woman who has spent her career among hustlers, gamblers and crooks, you really don't seem to understand how things work."

We drive on for a further fifteen minutes. When we stop and the doors are opened, we're in a concrete yard in an industrial estate I don't recognise. The ground is wet but the sky is clear, bright even. There's a cool breeze. The world has been cleansed.

For reasons I can't explain it really does feel like the kind of day on which I might die.

The bearded brute leads me to a second van, this one white.

101

Walker is sitting with Rob and Josie at their desks, ostensibly working through the material they've been assigned, but in truth, loitering; waiting for DI Gill to come back with directions.

"Where the hell is Kaminski?" bellows Greg Scabbard, striding into the incident room.

Scabbard's shout is enough to make Walker momentarily jump.

Josie stands. "Here, sir."

"You want to tell me why the fuck I'm hearing from Force Intelligence that you've made ANPR access requests under my name?" says Scabbard.

"Er..."

"'Er'?" he shouts. "'Er'? I ask you a question and you give me fucking 'Er'?! My office!"

He storms towards his office.

"You told Force Intelligence *he* authorised those ANPR searches?" says Walker.

"I needed sergeant or inspector sign-off," she says.

"I'm your bloody DS, Josie," Rob says.

"You weren't around in the middle of the night." Regret and other unhappy emotions tug at her face. "Choices were made, okay?"

She walks off, following Scabbard.

"Loose cannon, right?" says Rob as she leaves.

"She's actually growing on me," says Walker.

Ten seconds after Josie has left, DI Gill walks in. She silently eyes Rob and Walker and gestures them over. They approach her.

"Where's Kaminski?" she asks.

"Being bollocked by Scabbard," says Rob.

She gives this only a moment's thought. "You two will do. We're going to arrest the target now."

"We? Us?" says Rob.

She leads them down the stairs. "I have spoiled the morning of three superintendents so far. It has been decided that, given the sensitive and very public nature of the Wollacott murders, we need to act now. The individual is to be brought in for questioning."

Walker notices that she's not mentioning Nick Ferguson by name. Even though there appears to be no one around as they walk, she's not bandying names around.

"The Professional Standards Department's Integrity Unit will make the actual arrest. Four officers will meet us near the target's address. We three are back up."

This makes sense to Walker. The Integrity Unit is the force's anti-corruption team. If a serving police officer has committed a major crime then it becomes their investigation.

She's leading them to the back exit and the car park.

"We make the arrest quietly," she says. "No fuss. No attention drawn. Patrol units are being posted close to the area but not being told why. Ferguson is a trained soldier but command has agreed that a quiet arrest with plain clothes officers is both feasible and…" She screws up her face. "Chief Super Ayres used the words 'media optics'. Basically, we're not going to make a public song and dance about this."

"Understood," says Rob.

102

"I mean, Jesus H Christ, are you going to give me any sort of answer?" snaps Scabbard from behind his desk.

Josie can sense his energy for this conversation waning but he's still going.

"I had a thought about the Bashford killing," she says. "CCTV at a nearby pub picked up a vehicle taking a track towards the rear of Whitwick Farm. And I thought that—"

"You thought that a middle of the night fucking Road to Damascus revelation like that meant you could use my authorisation to look at ANPR records?"

"It was a credible lead in catching an armed killer."

"What is the procedure for getting ANPR data?"

"Well, it's—"

"You put in a proper request to Force Intel, with the VRM, dates, and a solid reason tied to an active investigation. It gets logged, authorised – *by me!* We don't go fishing. It's there to catch suspects, not to see where someone's been out of curiosity. You could have fucking phoned me! You have my number!"

Something snaps inside her. It's a bad thing. It's a thing that should not snap. When it snaps, Bad Josie comes out and does things she regrets. But it's snapped now. Too late.

"Oh, I definitely have your number, Greg," she say.

"You address me as—"

"I've got more than your number, Greg, sir. Ever since what happened that Sunday night when— No, scrub that. For longer than I can remember you've had it in for me. My opinion, my good calls, my frankly sodding amazing insights – all of them you ignore or belittle until you can scoop them up and claim them for yourself."

"You're treading on thin ice, Kaminski—"

"Walking on frigging egg-shells, more like, sir. You don't like me, do you?"

She gives him a second to reply. His mouth hangs open. "I..."

"You don't. You don't like me and, before you even think to say it, yeah I'm sure there's lots of other people who don't like me. But you're my guv and you have a duty of fucking care to me."

"Right. That's enough."

"No, it's not."

"You're clearly acting out. You've got a lot going on in your—"

She scowls in fury. "Don't try to do basic human decency at this point, sir. It really doesn't suit you. Yes, I made an ANPR request and was over-zealous with—"

"You broke protocol!"

"I did. Put me on a disciplinary. Let's take this to HR if you like. Do you want to do that?"

Scabbard is hesitant now. He can hear the edge in her voice. It's not even an edge – it's a blood-drenched sawblade. Give him five minutes to recover and he'll realise that her snogging him in a hotel lift while off-duty is hardly personnel dynamite, but right now he's thinking about how loud and inconvenient her shouting might be for him.

With lips pressed tight, he gestures to the seat opposite him. "Will you sit down?"

"No."

"Sit the fuck down, Kaminski," he says and, despite the swearing, his tone has softened.

She sits.

He breathes hard and stares at her.

"I don't need to go over the problems between us."

She shrugs and shakes her head at the same time. "I'm strident and loud. I stick my nose in where it's not wanted. I rub people up the wrong way. I overstep the mark."

He tries to wave it away. "You're right," he says. "I don't like you. I wish you were somewhere else."

She's tempted to mention her intention to apply for a transfer to New Zealand. While that might feel good for a moment, it would only be ammo for him.

"This ANPR thing is not okay," he says. "There's acting out and then there's breaking data regulations. You can't fucking do this."

She sits on any fiery comeback. The storm is nearly over. "Sir."

"I moved you to Chainlink for a reason."

"Yeah?"

"Because I want you as far away from real police work as possible until you've calmed your tits and learned to play ball."

"Because you don't like me."

"I don't like you," he agrees. "No one likes you. And lots of people don't like me. Don't think we've got anything special going on." He flicks his hand at his computer screen. "I will ignore this ANPR breach. This once. But you need to..." He sighs and leans forward across his desk. "You really need to fuck off and stay out of my eyeline every day between now and the end of time, Kaminski. It's like a massive game of hide and seek. You hide and I don't want to have to seek you. Do you understand?"

"Nothing would make me happier," she says.

"Good." He waves his hand. "You can start by fucking off right now."

She stands and leaves and has no idea who came out of that conversation on top.

She walks through the incident room. There's no sign of Rob or Walker anywhere.

"Where's Rob Joseph?" she asks the room at large.

"Gill took them off somewhere," says Beaches. "Ten minutes ago."

"Where?"

"I don't bloody know," says Beaches.

They've gone off without her. Damn.

She sends a questioning text to her two fellow Duncans and snarls to herself when she doesn't get an immediate reply. She grabs her jacket and heads for the door.

"I'm off out," she says.

"No one cares," Beaches calls after her.

103

The van stops.

It's not just pausing at traffic lights. It's properly stopped.

Lukas at the front turns round. "This is you, honey."

There are seven of us in the van. Me, Vicky, Lukas and four other men whose names I never want to know. At least three of them are carrying firearms. I suspect they all are. An unshaven guy in a three-quarter length coat has a sawn-off shotgun under there. I'm so awash with fear that this doesn't even strike me as extraordinary.

Vicky moves across to me. There's a key in her hands. She undoes the cuffs.

"Arm in arm. Happy friendly ... cousins, is it?"

"Cousins," I say weakly.

One of the men opens the side door. I recognise where we are, by St Nicholas Place. We're less than a hundred metres from the casino.

"Parked round the back," says Lukas from the front, then

the door is closed and the van with the five men in it drives on.

Vicky holds me close. She's wearing a thick and loose woollen cardigan, and in the dangling folds of her sleeve she holds the retractable knife sheathed against my side.

"And we walk," she says cheerily. "First sign of trouble and you lose a kidney."

"My kidneys aren't there," I find myself saying.

"Liver. Fucking whatever," she says.

And we walk.

The city centre is quiet. Most of the shops aren't even open yet. Cafes and pubs are open for breakfast but it's still early.

We walk together.

"What do I say?" I ask.

"Whatever it takes to get us through the door."

A thought hits me and I feel guilty that I've not thought it until now. I've been so focused on myself.

"You're not going to hurt anyone," I say.

"Is anyone going to give us trouble?"

"No one's going to give us trouble," I say. It's more a hope than a prediction.

And here it is. Meridian Casino. The white stone archway of whatever grand business originally occupied this spot. The glass doors are propped open and we go inside.

It's been nearly a week since I was last in here, since I was fired. I can't express how I feel about being here under these circumstances. It's like I'm returning in a dream, a nightmare.

To the side, Mrs Wan and her friends are starting to set up for Mahjong. They've only just arrived. A silent husband has been dispatched to the coffee station beyond the fruit machines to sort them out with hot drinks. Georgette is at reception.

"Hey, Esther," she says. "This was unexpected."

"I know," I say, putting on a sigh and trying to sound casual. "I realised I needed to come in."

"I like the hair."

"Oh, this?" I touch my dyed curls with my free hand. "I needed a change."

The more we talk, the more this seems natural. I'm playing a role. I'm playing the role of Esther-is-perfectly-normal-and-not-freaking-losing-her-mind. With each second the role gets easier and I don't want it to.

Georgette's eyes are flicking to Vicky who is pressed up against me, holding tight.

"My cousin. Jane. We're going to go out to eat once I've, you know..."

"I love Leicester," says Vicky, while simultaneously applying pressure to steer me on, towards the back of the building and the staff areas.

"Anyway, we'd best get on with it," I say and we move on.

"Catch you later," says Georgette. *Catch you later*, like that's it, that's the only trial we're going to face on our way in. It shouldn't be this easy. I'm in the grip of a psycho, an armed robber and – what? – we're just going to waltz in? How is no one stopping us? I don't want them to but this is too simple. It's like I'm rolling down a hill through soft gentle grass but there's a cliff edge at the bottom. The path to my own death is smooth and simple.

Baz, on security, is lumbering down the spiral stairs from the gaming floor above. I step swiftly towards the rear, moving past the point at which I would have to encounter him.

We pass by the bar and food counter. There's only the sports betting area, currently unoccupied, between us and the door marked *Staff Only*. It's a punch and twist code combination door. I am ninety-five percent certain Gabe won't have changed it since he fired me.

I reach out for the code panel and then a voice behind says, "Stop, right there."

I turn.

104

Josie walks with angry energy, not even sure if she's actually angry.

She doesn't know what she is. There's so much about herself and her situation she simply doesn't understand.

At work she's like a pinball, bounced from one thing to another. A cog that doesn't fit in regular CID, and now she's snugly in place with the Duncans – which is just another cog that doesn't fit.

And her work life makes more sense and has more solidity than her personal life. Her personal life is a big fat 'meh' – a routine of bills and bad meal choices and half-started dreams and hobbies. The only true positive in her personal life is turning off her social media accounts so she doesn't keep comparing herself to old school and college friends and their curated perfect existences with boyfriends, husbands and entitled little brats.

Josie doesn't know what she is, but dwelling on such things does not help.

She's left the nick and her feet are automatically taking her towards the halal sandwich shop of Belgrave Gate. Another coffee and another calorific snack seems tempting but, really, she's just walking. She just needs to walk.

There's no reply from Walker and Rob. Have they gone with Gill to arrest Nick Ferguson now? Or has Gill just moved them out of the way to get the details of the investigation written up?

If their hypothesis – which is both concocted out of thin air and compellingly sound – proves true then it draws together a very interesting web.

If the Bashford weapon is the same gun Seamus Wollacott had, then Seamus was carrying a gun that was used in a robbery, one in which rival criminal Remi Jankaukas was killed. Police intelligence linked both the gun and the robbery to the Degutis gang. And the woman seen with Seamus by Esther Butler, Vicky Nolan, had her own link to the Degutis gang – even if it was only that she worked at the laundrette owned by the family.

Seamus, Vicky, the gun, the Degutis family, murder, robbery.

And Mac Wollacott was gunned down in the street. The Degutis family implicated again. A shooting in the street implies a level of recklessness. Desperation?

Was Mac a threat? An embarrassment? Was he working for someone else? Threatening to snitch?

What did Mac know?

What was it that Seamus and Vicky were up to that night? Were they just out socially? A date?

But Seamus had a gun on him, like he'd gone armed for something.

Esther saw them from the casino entrance. Josie tried to

remember the details of her statement. The two of them had been standing there long enough for Esther to point them out to a colleague, to talk about them.

They'd been standing, still, opposite the casino.

Were they there deliberately? Were they going to the casino?

Two people, one a criminal, one with links to a crime family. Standing outside a casino. One with a gun. Two people arguing, disagreeing. She remembers Esther's words – "*He was up. He was raring. He was cocky.*" An armed man ready for action.

Sandwich shop forgotten, her feet take her onward down the high street towards the Meridian Casino.

105

Orla Hawkes stands there in the casino, hands on hips, a stern look on her face.

Vicky holds me close. Something hard but not yet sharp presses into my ribs.

"Oh, hi Orla," I say.

"Don't you 'Hi Orla' me, girl," she says. "Why'd you not tell me you were quitting?"

"Well, actually I didn't quit. Gabe fired me."

Her face loses none of its fire, but the quality of it shifts.

"I knew it! I knew it!" She gives a fierce hum of annoyance. "That bastard."

"Oh," I say, shaking my head, trying to wrap things up. "He had no choice. It wasn't his fault."

Orla scoffs.

"Anyway, I've got to pick some things up."

I can see Baz approaching. He's not really picked up on the fact that it's me. For a security guy, his perception and general people-sense is turned down real low. But I realise that he's actually seen Vicky before. He was with me that night on the door. It would be a disaster right now if Baz Obi were to see her, recognise her and start asking questions.

"I'll catch you later," I say to Orla and turn straight back to the door.

I reach for the code combo.

"Don't be a stranger!" says Orla.

I nod without turning, punch in the code – C457XZ – and twist. It still works.

106

Josie walks towards the Meridian Casino. She doesn't have a plan in her head. She's walking through an idea: the idea that maybe, possibly, Seamus Wollacott and the woman with Degutis gang links, were there for a reason. Maybe they had designs on the casino.

It's a half-formed idea, but it's a distraction from the fact that she's had another run-in with Scabbard and that Rob and Walker are off doing grown-up things somewhere with DI Gill.

As she passes by the little service road that goes round the back of the casino, she sees the back of a white transit van poking round the edge of the rear wall. There's nothing unusual in that, just as there's nothing specifically unusual about the glimpse of coat and leather gloves she sees of the man disappearing out of view round the back of the building. And there's nothing specifically unusual about the sound of several voices, talking indistinctly in low, terse tones.

But a police officer's curiosity pulls her down the side of the building. She approaches the corner and, still hearing the voices, looks round. In a glance she sees the short concrete steps leading up to a solid door, and four men bunched together on the steps. All four have their heads covered. She only catches a glimpse of the gun in the hands of one.

She backs away immediately, holding in any exclamation.

She's not got her police radio on her.

Shit.

She backs away to the road, pulling out her phone, and calls 999.

107

Rob is driving to Nick Ferguson's address in Evington when Neelam Gill next to him comes off her radio.

"Change of location," she says. "Neighbours say Ferguson is at the Oadby Town Rugby Club. He does practice sessions there."

"I know it," says Rob and takes a right turn to make towards Oadby proper. Concerns gather in his mind and he sees no reason not to voice them. "Rugby practice. That means people."

"We're just going to approach him, social-like," says Gill.

In the back, Walker grunts. Rob can't tell if it's a good grunt or a bad grunt.

They pass a marked police unit on Brabazon Road. "Is that part of our operation?" asks Rob.

Gill nods, but it seems like a nod of assumption rather than confirmation.

The rugby club car park is half full. A lot of the people

hanging around are giving Rob parent vibes. The pitch itself is behind the clubhouse.

They park and get out.

"Where's Professional Standards?" says Walker.

"They were driving over too," says Gill. "Two cars."

It's a cliché that coppers, even plains clothes ones, stick out in a crowd, but Rob can't see anyone about who looks like they might be detectives from Professional Standards. Gill stands close to the car and gets on the radio again.

"We'll see if Ferguson is here," he tells her.

"But do not approach," Gill says.

"Not our collar," he confirms.

Rob gives Walker a 'shall we?' incline of his head and the two of them walk up the path round the clubhouse towards the pitch.

"You much of a rugby man?" Walker asked Rob.

"To watch or play?"

"Either."

Rob considers it. "No. I'm more of a lone wolf when it comes to sports."

"Athletics?"

"I used to do quite a bit of karate."

"Ah."

"Good for the mental focus, actually. I should get back into it."

"Nothing stopping you."

"Only time." He taps Walker's arm and points.

They've rounded the building and now look out across the green playing fields. The adult coaches are easy to spot among the sea of kids in rugby shirts.

"There he is."

"Nick Ferguson," agrees Walker, also clocking the man.

He begins to report it on his radio and though Nick is well out of earshot, it's as though he hears them and at that moment chooses to look over.

A particular look crosses Ferguson's face.

Leicestershire Police has over two thousand sworn officers. The number of civilian support and admin staff plus PCSOs more than doubles that number. It's a workplace where an employee can't possibly know everyone else. But in the course of the job, you see a lot of faces. Rob is sure he's seen Ferguson in passing before, not known him, but known of him.

Ferguson looks at him with that slight frown, the thought that he should recognise these two men. He's possibly trying to work out where from.

Next, he'll see their clothing. Walker is wearing a suit jacket. Rob is wearing a tie. They're not dads come to drop off their little darlings. Ferguson sees them and knows they're cops.

And the half-frown turns into a half-smile of greeting but freezes partway because he's now wondering why two colleagues have come down to the rugby.

Nick Ferguson is some distance off but, in that moment, Rob can read that expression perfectly. PC Nick Ferguson knows why they're there. He knows exactly why they're there.

Rob takes a step forward.

108

We go through the door and into the staff corridor at the back of the casino. Vicky propels me ahead of her. The door swings shut behind me and clicks. I feel a weird relief at that. Whatever horrors are about to happen, the people out front are excluded.

The red-painted walls stretch down the corridor past the break room, the toilets, the strong room and towards the fire exit at the far end. Vicky is propelling me faster now, almost wanting to squeeze past me.

“Go ... go...”

We reached the end and I try to hold back, but she’s having none of it.

She puts her hand on the emergency exit bar and pushes.

Before the fire alarm even starts to sound, a gloved hand grabs the opening door from the outside. It’s Lukas. He’s wearing a balaclava, but it’s him. There’s a pistol in his right hand. Behind him, the three other men, similarly dressed and armed, crowd in behind him.

109

Josie sees two women walking down the road in the direction of the casino. They're chatting.

With her phone to her ear, Josie waves at them in a vigorous motion.

"Get back!" she hisses. "Police! Get back!"

They stare at her. The call to 999 line connects.

"This is DC Kaminski out of Mansfield House. I'm off-radio. Four armed men in balaclavas seen at Meridian Casino by Highcross. Suspected armed robbery in progress. Immediate armed response required."

The women are still staring at her. One of them is smiling. The other looks at Josie like she's a nutter.

Josie tries to find her ID badge while the operator asks her questions.

"White transit van," says Josie. "Didn't see the VRM. No further description on suspects."

She waves the ID badge at the women. "Off the street. Quickly!" She looks round. "Likely exit for suspects Highcross Street down to Vaughn Way."

"Keep the line open," says the operator. *"Units en route. Seek appropriate cover."*

"Appropriate cover?" she mutters to herself. Armed men are at the back doors of the casino. There will be people inside.

She debates the right course of action, then makes for the front of the casino. She's at the door when she hears an alarm go off inside.

110

The armed men rush past me like a tide.

Vicky has hold of me and drags me along with her.

The high piercing sound of the fire alarm fills the air.

Into the unlocked strong room. Cash is locked away in the secure boxes beneath the counter. Vicky's robbers are not here for this. Lukas leads onto the inner room.

He violently kicks aside the yellow carrier bag of grocery shopping that's been left in the doorway. I find myself momentarily and absurdly annoyed at the cashier who left it there. Using the strong room as temporary storage is an ongoing battle, like the struggles with the pizza oven in the kitchen.

"Code!" barks Lukas, shouting to be heard over the alarm.

Vicky shoves me forward.

It's been seconds since we arrived, but time is like treacle right now. It already feels like the alarm has been ringing forever.

I raise my hand to the code pad. My fingers are shaking. My mind is floating in terror. The distance between my brain and my fingers seems like miles.

"Put in the code!" Lukas demands.

I mash my trembling index finger into the pad. Five digits. That's all it is.

Beep, beep, beep, beep, beep.

A green light. Lukas turns the handle and opens the door and I'm dragged out of the way.

"Bags!"

One of the thugs flicks open a gym bag and they start emptying the shelves.

I know nothing about the drugs business. Honestly. I was wilfully blind to Gabe's arrangement with the owners over the years. But it's nothing to do with me – that's what I tell myself.

I can't even begin to put a genuine price on those plastic wrapped bricks of white powder. Thousands. Tens of thousands. More. They slip into the bags along with rolls of banknotes.

Lukas and two bag men are in the inner room. The other guy is in the outer room with me and Vicky.

When the strong room door opens, the man swings round with his stubby shotgun.

Baz doesn't even get to utter a word before he sees the gun.

"Down! Fucking down!" yells the gunman.

Baz raises his big meaty hands and then makes the decision to run. He's out of view behind the open door when the first barrel is fired.

I scream. It doesn't come from anywhere real, any sense

of emotion or thought. It comes straight out of the unbearable tension inside me. The gun bangs and I scream.

The gunman steps out and I can just see that he's angling the down the corridor now. Did he miss? Did Baz escape?

He fires again.

111

Staff and customers are running out of the front of the casino.

Josie waves them across the road towards the Highcross shopping precinct.

"Do not stop! Go to the shops! Get inside!"

They do not need any encouragement. It's possible that they've not even heard each other.

The two gunshots from within the casino have propelled them out, some silent, some hollering.

A member of staff supports an older Chinese woman as they cross the road. The sagging husband follows obediently behind, ridiculously carrying a disposable cup of coffee.

"Get to cover!" Josie shouts.

She has let the phone slip from her ear.

"I repeat, two shots fired from inside Meridian Casino. No visual confirmation."

"Units are less than two minutes away," says control.

112

I'm still screaming.

Vicky punches me on the side of the mouth, a hard rabbit punch, that seems to surprise her as much as it does me. It knocks the scream from me.

"Time!" yells Lukas.

The last brick of cocaine is thrust into a bag. One guy zips his up. The other is struggling and swears as he half-zips his.

They move en masse to the door. There's a bottleneck as we enter the corridor. The first man hits the fire exit before Vicky and I are out of the strong room.

Barely audible above the alarm, I hear approaching sirens.

113

Nick Ferguson walks slowly towards Walker and Rob.

Walker tries to make a judgement from Nick's walk, his manner. How much has he inferred from the arrival of two detectives? Is he ready to run? To fight? To bluff?

Rob turns away a second to speak on his radio.

"Suspect has seen us and is approaching." A pause. "He's approaching, ma'am. I can't not engage. Where's Integrity?"

Walker touches Rob's arm to shush him and raises his chin in greeting to Ferguson.

"Nick," he says.

Ferguson's eyebrow twitches in curiosity. "Didn't know you two were rugby fans?"

"My Oscar was into it for about eight months," Walker says casually.

"Uh-huh. What's he into now?"

"*Call of Duty*. I think."

Ferguson looks from one to the other.

"You know I'm not supposed to talk to anyone, apart from

my superior and IOPC right now? I'm suspended. This is about the Wollacott thing, right?"

"Not exactly," says Walker.

"Professional Standards officers are on their way," says Rob. "They want to talk—" He grimaces. "They want to talk about Aaron Bashford."

Walker's watching and ready. It doesn't matter what he's ready for. Ferguson is nearly twenty years younger and three inches taller than Walker. If Ferguson decides to do something stupid, Walker is unlikely to make a difference.

But he's watching and he sees the micro-expressions ripple across Ferguson's face. It's like how the light can suddenly change on a cloudy day, even though nothing physical seems to have altered.

"Bashford," Ferguson says numbly.

"Professional Standards want to talk about your time together in Afghanistan," says Rob. "The money you've been paying him, and the last time you visited him at the farm."

Nothing Walker sees on Ferguson's face suggests they've missed their mark at any point.

Ferguson starts to nod and then holds himself still.

"How much…?" He smacks his lips as though they are suddenly dry. "I don't know what you're talking about."

"That's fine, Nick," says Walker. "We're just here to assist." He jerks a thumb over his shoulder. "Shall we take a walk round front? Do this quietly?"

Ferguson nods fully this time. He turns back to the training session. "Lindsey! Lindsey! I just need to deal with this!" he calls and, getting a signal back, gestures for Rob and Walker to lead on.

Walker trails behind Ferguson. Ferguson says something that Walker doesn't catch.

"What's that?"

"I need to tell Esther that I'm sorry," he says. "I sort of put her in this situation."

"It's okay. I'm sure you'll get chance to tell her," says Walker.

114

The gang rush to the door and I'm about to be pulled along with them but then there's a sudden confusion.

Outside in the small rear car park, the driver for the gang is out of the van. His confused face is looking our way. The sound of sirens is rising.

"*Sėsk į sušiktą furgoną!*" Lukas yells at him.

The group suddenly isn't moving as one. The early arrival of the police has fractured them. As two men run to the van, the driver decides he's not hanging around. He runs to the commercial waste dumpsters by the back wall of the car park and climbs up with the intention of jumping over onto the pavement of the dual carriageway.

One of the bag men throws his bag towards Vicky and me so he can use both hands to ready the automatic pistol in his hand. The bag lands pretty squarely in my hands. I don't mean to grab it, but the weight of it is a strange comfort in this surreal moment.

Vicky moves up and grabs Lukas.

Between the fire alarm and the sirens, I don't hear what she says.

He puts a gun in her hand and I hear him. "Stay down. Keep safe."

He's looking out the rear door.

I'm going to die if I stay here.

These men are going out prepared to open fire on the police. They've moved beyond everything I'd consider normal or rational. My life is meaningless to them in this moment.

And no eyes are on me.

They're deciding which way to run or whether to risk taking the van. I'm literally at the back and, for the time being, totally forgotten.

I back away, clutching the bag. It feels like it takes no energy, no bravery, to back away footstep by footstep. But it takes an effort of will to turn around, grab the locking knob of the door to reception and twist it.

"Hey!" shouts Vicky behind me.

I fling the door open and run.

115

Two police cars speed down Highcross Street and stop twenty metres up from the casino.

Josie, crouched behind a car parked across the road, looks down towards Vaughn Way at the other end of the short street. There's regular traffic moving along the dual carriageway but no sign of the police.

"We need to block off the exit to the dual carriageway," she says into the phone.

She can't hear the reply.

There's shouting as a masked man emerges from the side street and looks over to the police cars. An officer shouts at him. These guys are only armed with harsh words and maybe tasers.

"Where's the armed response?" Josie says into the phone. She knows it's redundant. They're on their way. Her badgering isn't going to make them appear any quicker.

Daylight flashes on the front doors of the casino as they open again and, across the bonnet of the car, Josie sees Esther Butler run out.

Her hair is a different colour from the last time Josie saw her but it's definitely Esther Butler. She has a black canvas bag clutched to her chest and is running towards Vaughn Way.

Two seconds later, another woman stumbles out. Josie doesn't know her but she sees the long brown hair and wonders if this could be...

"No..." she says.

The woman has something in her hand, a gun. She raises it to point at the fleeing Esther and fires.

116

I hear the bang of gunfire. I've no idea where it came from.

Vicky is shouting something behind me and I can hear her footsteps on the pavement.

I run.

Running is a thing I can do. I might not be a sprinter, but I can run and I just hope that I can outrun her.

I glance back and see the gun in her hand as she fires again. There's a flash and an ear-shattering crack. My insides turn to liquid. I don't even have time to see if I've been shot. No time to check if I'm already dead.

I run on. There's nothing else I can do. I run to the edge of the dual carriageway and look for a break in the traffic.

Just shy of two weeks ago, I followed this exact same route.

I followed Seamus Wollacott and Vicky Nolan in the darkness because I saw a gun in Seamus's hand. Across this road we went, down the cut-through to the building site where Seamus died.

And now it's all the same pieces, shuffled in a different order. Vicky and me. A gun. This road.

I take a chance and run between two cars driving at forty plus towards the Southgate Underpass tunnel. Horns blare. I reach the traffic island and press on unwisely. A motorbike swerves into the other lane to avoid me.

"Stop! Police!" shouts a woman behind us.

On the far pavement, I turn. Vicky, on the dividing kerb between the opposing traffic has whirled. Across the other side... It's Detective Constable Kaminski. No idea where she came from.

"Put the gun down!" says Kaminski. She's not armed. She's literally holding her hands out, fingers spread, like that will stop a bullet.

Vicky's arm straightens and she fires. Kaminski cowers on the spot, nowhere to hide.

I'm not taking this. I'm not allowing this. I can run for my own life but I'm not letting this policewoman put her life on the line for me.

I run back into the road, almost smearing myself against the side of a car passing in front of me. I reach the traffic island with the bag of stolen drugs and cash already swinging in my hands.

Vicky senses me too late. She turns and I pound her bodily with the bag. She twists and folds around it. Her gun arm swings round and she wraps her other arm around me. She grunts as we fight. I try to grab the gun. My fingers grip its cold barrel. She spins, she pulls. The gun fires again. It bucks from my grip.

As she pulls away, Vicky manages to bring a leg up and kick me, toe first, in the thigh. It's enough for her to break away from me. She steps back onto the road.

I drop painfully to one knee and look up at her.

"Always interfering—" she says.

It's the last words she says. A lorry – no horn, no squealing tyres – sweeps past, straight into her and she is gone.

Shocked, I watch it brake sharply this side of the tunnel and rock to a halt. Traffic is slowing all around. Kaminski, looking only slightly less dazed than I feel, picks herself up and runs to the lorry. There are voices, questions, a shout of anguish from a driver.

I sit on the ground. Sirens fill the air and somewhere the sound of a helicopter, but I don't raise my head to look for it. I hold the bag, like it's a toy dolly, something to cling to.

At some point, Kaminski comes over to me.

"Are you hurt?"

I look at her. She crouches beside me.

"Are you hurt, Esther? Are you okay?"

I know what's she's asking, but who can answer a question like that? It's been so long since I was okay that I don't know what okay even feels like.

"We'll get you some medical attention," she says and puts her arms under my elbows. "Can you stand? Can you walk?"

She holds me as we cross back to the pavement.

"We found the gun," she says.

It takes me a long moment to work out what she's talking about and, when I do, I'm glad she's still holding me.

117

Josie raises her coffee cup to Rob and Walker.

"This stuff isn't that bad at all," she admits.

"The Duncans' stash of coffee sachets is a thing of wonder," says Walker.

The three of them are in the lobby to the interview suite at Mansfield House station.

Lukas Degutis is currently in an interview room with Scabbard, Beaches and the Degutis solicitor, a middle-aged woman with a no-nonsense matronly air. Walker pointed her out as she came in – Cynthia Fellowes – always there when a Degutis is brought in.

"Esther really did see a gun," says Rob.

"Everything she said was accurate." Josie shakes her head. "But none of us truly believed her."

"She'd be a Duncan if she worked in our nick."

There's a brief pause in the conversation during which Josie judges nobody is prepared to say that unlike the Duncans, Esther might now be able to move on.

Josie knows that she'll need to explain her actions on the dual carriageway. A death during a police operation triggers certain processes, and her behaviour will come under scrutiny. Will she be commended for bravery or get bollocked for being reckless? Possibly both. She's already wondered several times today if she'd be alive if Esther hadn't tackled Vicky on that traffic island.

Rob takes a sip and glances over at Walker. "You come across Vicky Nolan before?"

Walker shakes his head. "Never met her, but I gather she was the driving force behind Lukas Degutis trying to spread his wings. A woman of ambition."

"His wings are gonna be properly clipped now," says Rob. He smacks his lips and inspects his coffee.

"Actually, I think we should invest in a pod coffee machine," says Rob.

Walker smiles and looks to Josie. "He's just giddy from the fact that he's got to arrest someone for the Bashford murder."

"Officially, it was the integrity unit," says Rob.

"But only officially." Walker sighs. "It's always a sad day when a colleague takes a fall."

"He's a murderer," says Josie. She can't make herself feel sorry for Nick Ferguson.

"Must have been feeling pretty desperate to pull a stunt like taking that gun from the Seamus Wollacott shooting."

"Nope. Fuck him."

Rob and Walker exchange glances. There's a deeply thoughtful look on Rob's face.

"You think Josie will learn the acceptance and forgiveness that is the trademark of the Dead End Duncans?" says Walker.

"Hmmm?" Rob shakes his head. "Our Josie is thinking of transferring to New Zealand?"

She grunts with laughter. "Thinking about. Just thinking about it."

"Right."

Walker's phone is buzzing. He looks at it. "Helen wants to know if I'll be home for dinner." He walks off to take the call.

Rob glances down the corridor. "They're going to be in that interview for a while yet. Time to head home?"

Josie shrugs. "Nowhere special to go." She wants to know what's going to happen. It seems certain Lukas will be charged with armed robbery offences, false imprisonment and, hopefully, the murder of Lisa McNally. But well-funded criminals with expensive solicitors can be slippery fish.

Rob takes Josie's empty cup from her. "I'll go make another."

She nods and sits on one of the stained soft seats in the lobby area. She wonders if Lukas knows that his girlfriend is dead. She wonders what that'd do to a man in custody.

She sits back and lets out a noisy, self-satisfied sigh.

She realises she could easily drift off to sleep if she allows herself to do so. The click of a door pulls her back from that. She has to tilt her head to the side to be able to see down the corridor.

Scabbard has stepped out of the interview room and is followed by the Degutis solicitor, Cynthia Fellowes. They stand close in discussion, his head bowed to come closer to hers. There's a familiarity there, Josie thinks. He's probably heard her try to make bargains on behalf of various Degutis gang members in the past. Lawyers always think there's a deal to be struck.

Josie starts to smile but then sees Fellowes dip into the

handbag over her shoulder and pull out a manila envelope. It's not large but it looks thick. She passes it to Scabbard and, quick as anything, it slips into his inside jacket pocket.

The action is so smooth, so practised, that it's over in a second. Blink and miss it.

Josie's mouth falls open in surprise.

She knows what that just looked like.

It *can't* be what it just looked like.

Was that a pay-off?

She sits bolt upright as the enormity of that thought hits her. There's a noise in the corridor. She risks another look. Greg Scabbard is striding straight towards her. The solicitor is hanging back by the interview door.

"What the fuck are you doing there, Kaminski?" says Scabbard.

"Er, nothing, sir."

His glare shifts, questioning. Josie swallows, a reflex action. She's keeping her mouth closed but her face is probably just telling him everything.

"I've... I've got work to do, sir," she says and stands, though he barely gives her the room to do so.

Awkwardly, she turns to leave. Suddenly his hand is on her elbow in a grip that's not merely tight but painful. He twists her round.

The last time he touched her was in a hotel lift, two weeks ago. This is so different. She recoils but he's not letting go.

He pulls her close to hiss in her ear.

"Whatever you thought you saw, you didn't, Kaminski. Got it?" She can feel his warm breath on her cheek.

"I didn't see anything," she says, voice cracking.

"Damn fucking right. You think putting you with the

Duncans is the worst I can do to you? You have no fucking idea."

She tries to pull away and, when he's slow to release her, she yanks her arm free from him.

She steps back, glances at his jacket, at where he'd put Fellowes' bribe, and then hurries out.

118

I'm in a hotel for a week while I sort myself out.

It's not the Premier Inn – it's a cool little fifth floor rental apartment with a kitchenette.

It's also got a tiny living room, where I'm hanging out with Jeety. She's dressed in running gear in eye-watering shades of pink, yellow and green. It's like a pinata has exploded against the sober furnishings.

"How is this place free?" Jeety looks deeply suspicious.

"It's free for a week," I tell her with a shrug. "Hannah, the PR woman, tells me that a local business wants to sponsor me. No strings."

"There's always fucking strings," Jeety says with a suspicious scowl, topping up our glasses.

"Just a discussion about some publicity work afterwards." I shrug. I do trust Hannah. She's had my back throughout this crap, at least to the extent that I've allowed her.

"I guess you're hot stuff now," Jeety says. "Kieran must be wetting his pants, wanting you to talk about his pisswater energy drinks."

I'm still ignoring Kieran's messages. I've got enough on my plate without his whining.

Jeety holds up fingers to count them off. "So, number one. You're physically fit. All signed off?"

"I am. A few scuffs and bruises from being, you know, held prisoner, but I'm fine."

"Hm." She looks at my face, sceptical. "Right. And mentally? You've had a shitty time of it."

"Yeah." I take a long slow breath and really think about how I want to answer that. "I thought I was completely losing it. Nobody believed me about what I saw."

I catch her eye and there's hurt and guilt in her expression.

"Nearly nobody," I say because I can't torture my friend for her reasonable doubts.

"The online stuff was hard, but there's been a whole load of U-turns there," I say.

I'm not talking about those shady, misogynistic bastards who will continue to talk me down in their own dark corners of the internet; but the mainstream has cooled off a little bit. Paul Peters-Mouldon, TV presenter and rabid misogynist, has suddenly gone magically quiet about the whole Esther Butler thing. In fact, I'm seeing a lot of positive things being said about me now. I'm some sort of poster child for victim-blaming, according to Hannah.

"Anyway," I say, heaving all thoughts of that aside. "Do you know what's a really good cure for being wrapped up in your own head and drowning in self-doubt?" I take a hefty sip of wine.

"Do tell."

"Looking death in the face."

Jeety laughs, and her eyes widen. "You recommend it then? As a grounding experience?"

"Totally." My face is deadpan.

"We could offer that as a service. Open up a wellness retreat where we threaten people with guns." She nods in appreciation as she stares into the middle distance, entertaining the thought for her own amusement.

"You're enjoying that idea a bit too much."

"Pfft. Got a bunch of people I want to try it out on." Her face sobers again as she comes back to the conversation and counts off the next finger. "Is there any comeback on you for the casino stuff?"

I grimace slightly. "I'm in the clear. Gabe ... less so. I don't think the police will come after me for that stuff, though. I was sacked, after all."

"What about the security guard guy?" she asks.

"Baz?"

"Him."

I smile. "I went to see him. I actually think he's very slightly pleased that he got shot."

"Shut up." Jeety looks at me. "Who the hell would be pleased to be shot?"

"Not exactly pleased – but I reckon it will be like a badge of honour for him, once he's recovered. His arm's in a sling in the meantime. He's lapping up all of the fuss he's getting down at his mum's restaurant."

She rolls her eyes. "We getting a drink then? Or ordering pizza in and slobbing on the sofa?"

Her husband Joel is taking the kids bowling tonight. Jeety is mine for the evening and I'm grateful for her.

"We can do both," I suggest.

She picks up her phone to see what pizza places will deliver here. I go to the kitchenette and take a bottle of cava out of the fridge. As I stand by the sink to open it, I look out the large side window that gives a view down onto the busy street far below.

Cars flow in both directions and there are pedestrians passing by.

My eyes latch onto a woman. Her cornrow plaited hair is drawn back into a ponytail. Her shoulders are hunched as her hands are stuffed into the pockets of her denim jacket. A man is walking in the same direction, twenty yards behind her on the pavement.

I watch the woman, wondering where she's going and what she's thinking.

Then she turns the corner. And she's gone.

ALSO BY BECK LEWIS

OPEN WOUND

Can saving someone be the biggest mistake of your life?

PR consultant Hannah Douglas-Jones makes her living managing other people's reputations. But she finds herself involved in a story like no other when she stops at the scene of a house fire and pulls a young woman from the flames.

Fire victim Natasha – calm, capable and self-assured – is now homeless. Hannah offers her a place to stay and a job. Natasha is exactly the person Hannah needs to rebuild her struggling business and help with a hectic home life. But as Hannah's fortunes rise, she starts to doubt who this woman really is – and what she wants.

DC 'Walker' Smith is part of the investigation into the fire. Six people died, locked in the cellar. As the investigation grows, Walker realises that this crime has links to shameful secrets in his own past – and that Natasha is the key to unlocking everything.

One fire. No accident. Everyone's playing with fire.

Open Wound

SAFE SPACE

When your memories are missing, how do you know you're not the one to blame?

A year after a carbon monoxide accident left five people dead, Cassie O'Donnell wakes from a coma to find her life erased. She's homeless, unemployed, and her mind is filled with shadowy memories she can't trust.

Desperate for answers, Cassie joins a support group run by the survivors - a safe space where they can grieve and heal together. But then one member of the group dies of an apparent drugs overdose...

An ex-girlfriend begs DS Rob Joseph to investigate this latest death and he secretly joins the support group. But he soon discovers that the survivors are all carrying secrets.

Both Cassie and Rob begin to suspect that someone inside the group knows what really happened in that house on the night of the accident - and is willing to kill to keep the truth buried.

One tragedy. Five survivors. No one is safe.

Safe Space

BV - #0116 - 130226 - C0 - 198/129/25 - PB - 9781068241857 - Matt Lamination